M000019227

ORDINARY MONSTERS

ORDINARY MONSTERS

A NOVEL BY

KAREN NOVAK

BLOOMSBURY

Copyright © 2002 by Karen Novak

All rights reserved. No part of this book may be used or reproduced in any manner whatsoever without written permission from the Publisher except in the case of brief quotations embodied in critical articles or reviews. For information address Bloomsbury, 175 Fifth Avenue, New York, NY 10010

Published by Bloomsbury, New York and London.
Distributed to the trade by Holtzbrinck Publishers

Library of Congress Cataloguing-in-Publication Data

Novak, Karen.
Ordinary Monsters: a novel / by Karen Novak
p. cm.
ISBN 1-58234-241-5
1. Automobile travel – Fiction. 2. Mothers and sons – Fiction. 3. Missing persons – Fiction. 4. California – Fiction. I. Title.

PS3564.O893 O73 2002
813'.6–dc21
2001056526

Author's note: Passages from *The Tempest* were taken from the Pelican Shakespeare edition, edited by Peter Holland (1999). Although most appear without any typographical distinction from the rest of the novel, I have little doubt that the reader will be able to distinguish my own 'rough magic' from 'the stuff that dreams are made on.'
P.S.: I made up the weather stuff.

SOUTHERN CROSS
Words and music by Michael Curtis, Richard Curtis and Stephen Stills
Copyrighted 1974 (Renewed) Three Wise Boys Music LLC (BMI) and Gold Hill Music, Inc. (ASCAP)
International Copyright Secured. All Rights Reserved.
Reprinted by Permission.

First U.S Edition 2002

10 9 8 7 6 5 4 3 2 1

Typeset by Palimpsest Book Production Limited,
Polmont, Stirlingshire
Printed and bound in the United States of America by
R. R. Donnelley & Sons Company, Crawfordsville, Indiana

With love beyond language to
Barry
and our daughters,
KC and Robyn.
You are the reasons why
of my entire life.

ACKNOWLEDGMENTS

Thank-yous and an abundance of blessings to the usual suspects: Karen Rinaldi and Elizabeth Sheinkman for the priceless gift of their faith; Alona Fryman and Andrea Lynch, emergency backup goddesses – you rock; Norm Mitchell, Nancy 'Black Bird' Hanner, and Shannon Hetz (put the book down and go finish your novel); Steve Heilman, book reshelver extraordinare; Deborah Morrison, who is reading this on horseback (Hi, Cody); Fred Busch for answering the phone in spite of caller ID; Matt Leone and everyone involved on any level with the annual weeklong miracle that is the Chenango Valley Writers' Conference. Profound appreciation to Lorraine Berry and Elisabeth Lindsay for their generosity and insight in explaining the realities of chronic pain – Lorraine, I owe you a book tour. A one-woman standing ovation for Barry, KC, and Robyn; yes, it's safe to come in the office now. Unending gratitude to my parents, Richard and Virginia Larson, for showing me the Mojave.

I love you all.

So we cheated and we lied and we tested,
And we never failed to fail,
It was the easiest thing to do.
    – Crosby, Stills & Nash, 'Southern Cross'

These are not natural events; they strengthen
From strange to stranger.
    – William Shakespeare, *The Tempest*

I. Inadequate Magic

One

Her skin prickled with feverish heat, her throat felt abraded; she had wanted no more than to sink down into her bed, back into sleep. Her bed, however, could no longer be considered hers, and so, what she wanted to do would have to be ignored in favor of what she needed to get done. She needed to get on the road by noon, before Paul would be able to return certain phone calls of solicitous curiosity from the bank. For that reason, at 12:02, still half weeping, she was negotiating the first curves of State Route 9 as it climbed out of Brattleboro into the Green Mountains. She had her big plastic shopping bag, now crammed with packets of twenty-, fifty-, and hundred-dollar bills, the whole of their savings, stuffed under the driver's seat of her paid-in-full-as-of-this-morning Saturn. She had a highway atlas open beside her. She also had a plan, what she was calling a plan, partially open in her mind. Both the map and the plan seemed more feasible, less flat-out insane, if glimpsed in quick, unfocused blinks during those seconds it seemed safe to take her eyes off the road.

The more she looked at it, the more the map seemed to mock her ambitions, what with its tangle of threads tightening into impossible knots around the very places she sensed he might be. Her navigation was founded on the magical thinking of maternal concern, the faith that she could predict his movement down to pinpoint coordinates by reading the intensity of her fear. The closer to outright terror a specific point on the map generated, the more likely that that was a place he'd choose. The problem was, the map was such a dense weave of those fearsome places that her vision blurred whenever she tried to single one out.

She'd set her priorities, therefore, in accordance with hints she'd gleaned from the statistics of grief: West, they went west – or south – with the reflexive surrender of night-flying insects caught in the gravity of light. They were impelled toward climates of reliable warmth, toward the cities of wealth implying endless resource and ready access. They followed the supply, which meant he might, at that moment, be on the move himself. If she found the right place, she might still miss him; she might stand in the very alley or beside the exact curb from which he had – just an instant before – disappeared. For that reason, she saw him everywhere and nowhere and trusted neither sighting. She suddenly realized she was twisting her thumb and forefinger around the rim of the steering wheel, unconsciously opening bottles. Chastened but not surprised by this gesture, she flexed her hand hard. 'No,' she said aloud. The sensation of her own voice gouged at her throat. All right, this was more than the aftermath of screaming; she was definitely coming down with something. Surely no one could fault her one small –

'If you think about it . . .' she said as yet another unfortunate winged thing collided with the windshield. 'It's better not to even think about it.' She wrapped her fingers back around the steering wheel in proper form, hands at ten and two. The needle of the speedometer had inched over seventy. Joyce eased her foot off the accelerator until she was back at a less provocative speed.

Outside Wilmington the traffic slowed to a sluggish lurch behind the tour buses and bus-sized recreational vehicles attempting to crawl up the mountain. Frustrated, Joyce banged the steering wheel with her fists. She had planned on making Albany by three o'clock but had not allowed for the glut of weekend leaf peepers, that annual end-of-September pilgrimage to witness nature's self-immolation. It took more than fifteen minutes to move two miles, inching past ski shops and bed-and-breakfasts, toward the traffic signal in the center of town. She watched the clock on the dashboard morph through successive numerals, her left foot tapping the floor mat faster than the seconds passed. As though a mirror to her mood, the sky grew steadily dimmer. The phalanx of snow clouds that had been slouching down the mountainside finally overtook the sun, and the colors of the natural world bled out in an instant, the wash of shadow serving to brighten electric signs of invitation: coffee shops, restaurants, bars. Joyce was alerted to the slip in her attention when the minivan behind her beeped its horn. She'd been considering the red neon of a beer sign rather than the red of the signal and had not noticed the latter turn to green. She waved an apology in the rearview mirror. The driver behind her gave her a thumbs-up and motioned her forward. She tapped the accelerator and just cleared the intersection as the light cycled back to yellow.

At this rate, she wouldn't make New York until after dark, and driving after dark was not part of the plan. She'd have to get a room for the night, and then, early tomorrow, before the streets filled up, she'd look for him. Wouldn't that be something? If he were there? In Albany, of all places? Even if he were not, the looking would be worthwhile; she wanted to refine her searching skills until once more she could set the car on autopilot and focus absolutely on the ultrasound of her intuition. She had to be able to detect the echo of soap bubbles bursting. That way, she'd be better this time, more careful, more competent, less apt to accost and frighten a young man of vague resemblance, begging him to come home because the heartbreak was cannibalizing what little was left of his father.

The hotel was not within her budget, but the drive had been long, more tiring than she'd anticipated, and the room included breakfast, and they had a restaurant on the premises, and she could have dinner without having to get back in the car. Besides, she was sick; her throat hurt, she told the hostess, an older woman whose head was a mass of poodle-tight white curls. She wore a beaded pink cardigan pinned with a name tag that read SHERRY.

'Poor dear,' said Sherry with the practiced concern of a grandmother-for-hire. She handed Joyce a menu. 'Can I get you something to drink?'

Who would blame her? 'No, thank you.'

'You sure? Not a nice hot toddy, warm rum for that raw throat?'

Her mind was seized by phantom sirens: the warmth of the mug in her hands, the slippery, buttered heat as it slid through her bloodstream, the gorgeous numbness a mere syllable of assent away. She swallowed; it hurt. Logic used the pain to tick off its talking points. It wasn't as if she were driving farther tonight. And she was sick. And her husband was gone. And her lost, junkie son might never be found. And it wasn't as if anyone cared. Who with an iota of basic compassion left in his being would blame her? She swallowed again. 'No,' she said, and touched her fingers to her lips. 'No, thank you. I'll have tea.' She opened the menu. 'Tea for right now.'

She opened her eyes, again, and blinked at the dark of the hotel room ceiling. The red light on the smoke alarm blinked back. Time to face the fact that sleep wasn't coming anywhere near anytime soon; she shouldn't have had that third cup of tea – let alone the fourth or fifth – but it had felt so soothing on her throat, and what was done was done. Joyce shoved herself up to a sitting position against the headboard and grabbed for the television remote on the nightstand.

An all-news channel came up, and she watched that until they started in on the coverage of the wildfires out west. The video clip of spreading flames and thick smoke brought unwanted memories of Paul's fury. She tried to fend them off by digging a trench of numb indifference between herself and the past, but as usual, her efforts were overwhelmed. She couldn't escape the illusion that it wasn't brush burning in a California canyon there on the screen; it was her maps and photographs, igniting instantly as Paul threw them onto the blazing fireplace. The televised sound of sirens became Paul's shouting *What the hell is wrong with you?* over and over. Her head began to fill with the watery ache of wanting to cry. She wasn't about to do any more of that today. She changed the channel.

She settled on an old-movie station showing a sci-fi fantasy, one she'd seen before although she couldn't recall its title. The sets were surreal and futuristic in a way that the future had yet to express itself. The special effects were 1950s primitive – including a particularly graceless robot – but the story was a pretty good one. Walter Pidgeon played an expert in languages who lived with his daughter, a nubile Anne Francis, and the silly robot, named Robbie, all alone on a deserted planet. Alone, that is, until a spaceship full of well-intentioned rescuers – in form-fitting polyester uniforms – landed and began trying to fulfill their mission. Walter Pidgeon, it seemed, did not wish to be rescued; he'd gained control over a mysterious alien power that provided everything he needed. Matters were cordial enough until Leslie Nielsen, the commander of the rescue party, fell in love with Anne Francis and tried to convince her to return to Earth with him – along with the artifacts of the alien power he intended to carry back to humanity. The combined losses proved a severe blow to Walter's need for perfect order, and as might be expected, that's when the monsters started to show up.

At an intermission-type break, the film's host, an actor whose career began with a bit part in the film, walked amid a display of posters and props as he explained the similarities between the plot of this film – *Forbidden Planet,* that was it – and Shakespeare's play *The Tempest.* The actor was forty-five years older now, and Joyce wasn't sure which was the more remarkable, that he had aged so much or that he had ever been so young. Joyce yawned and thought what a lovely thing it would be to stop the action like that, just take a break and have some future self explain what was happening right now, why it was happening, how matters would resolve themselves. This was her problem exactly, she said to the actor who was still pointing out the parallels. She never could find a moment when things stopped long enough so that she could adequately explain herself. And heaven knows, she'd tried.

The movie came back at the point when the monster inhabiting the planet began its assault on Leslie Nielsen's spaceship. Whatever it was, it remained invisible; all the camera showed was the steady press of footprints in the sandy surface, big footprints of a creature with a giant hooked claw. You saw it climbing the spaceship gangplank, or the effect of its climbing, as the metal stairs sagged under its weight. A few seconds later, there was the sound of a man screaming in terrible pain. It would have been much more frightening if Joyce had not seen it all before.

She slid down in the pillows and turned on her side, closing her eyes. The television played on softly; it was nice having other voices in the room. She was listening to the characters yelling *Something is coming! Something is coming!* as she let herself drift into the dimness of semisleep.

She put down the pen and pressed her palm to her cheek, imagining the silver line of mercury creeping up the length of a thermometer. She was tempted to lean against the cool glass of the window beside her. It was snowing big, slushy flakes that melted on contact with the retained warmth of the ground. She was sitting in the hotel lobby at one of the small round tables near the complimentary breakfast buffet, the map of Albany opened before her. She tore a chunk off her stale raisin bagel and dunked it in the equally stale coffee. The taste combined with the pain of swallowing forced a reflexive cringe that got a giggle from a plump young girl seated at the next table. The girl giggled once more before running her tongue over the icing left on the cellophane wrapper of a sweet roll.

Joyce smiled and opened a second paper packet of sweetener to stir into the steaming styrofoam cup. 'You're right; it needs sugar,' she said, her voice just scraping a smidgen of sound from her throat. The girl averted her eyes, pretending she'd been looking elsewhere. Joyce picked up the pencil this time – so that she could erase later – and wrote in small, careful letters, in the blank border around the map: DRUGSTORE. Then she took up the pen once more and used its permanent ink to trace a path from where she was on the outskirts of Albany, across the Hudson River, and into the grid of the streets of Albany.

Beneath the reminder to get medication, she developed a list of exit numbers and street names, noting one-way corridors with arrows drawn in the appropriate direction. Each addition brought an increasing familiarity, a confidence in her organization and efficiency. It was as though time had looped back on itself to return her to the exact moment before she had lost her way.

She looked up from the map. It was snowing still, the thin morning light stronger, a brighter sheen of gray. The lobby had emptied out and breakfast had been put away. All right, her skills weren't back in first-rate form, yet. Time was escaping her. She'd let herself sleep late, let herself linger here parsing the map longer than she would have normally permitted, but her health had to be taken into consideration. Besides, it was Sunday; the streets of downtown Albany were going to be vacant of anything but local traffic. An early start wasn't imperative. Joyce put the cap back on the pen and folded the map against its existing creases so that it was inside out with her notes facing up. She slipped the map into a beat-up accordion file, the one artifact of her search she had saved from the hearth, its charred brown paper pleats now stretched fat again with dozens of recently purchased maps still unfolded.

The Saturn idled, the defrost vents blasting cold. The windshield wipers cleared away the heavy clumps of snow that had accumulated while she'd been in the drugstore scrutinizing labels. Now, armed with a bag full of alcohol-free syrups and pills, Joyce huddled into the bulky cables of her sweater and sucked on a lozenge that tasted of chemical cherries. The anesthetic started to take effect, wearing down the serrated blade in her throat. Better.

She took the box out the glove compartment. Paul had made it for her, as a gift for their first anniversary. A simple rectangular box fashioned from some scraps of bird's-eye maple his father had given him. The project had taken him weeks. He'd done it all by hand, mortising out the dovetailed joints and the rabbets for the lid, carving his and her initials in it with a tiny chisel. He'd lacquered and polished the wood until the dark whorls of the bird's-eye seemed to bore down into the darkness inside the box. If, on that horrible night, he had known that the box on their dresser no longer held the jewelry for which it was designed but had become instead the repository for the talismans of her search, he would have, without a second thought, thrown the box and its contents onto the hearth with the burning maps.

She ran her fingers over the brass catch, almost expecting an interdiction, Paul's enraged shouting, all those awful words. Nothing sounded but the rush of slowly warming air from the vents. No one was going to stop her this time. She opened the box and was reunited with her former self.

It was all still there. She felt herself grow lighter and more awake, as though opening the box had allowed her to draw her first real breath since that night, as though these were the only possessions left to her that did not smell of smoke. She picked up a strip of photographs by its edges. In spite of her care with the cheap finish, it was suffering from age and handling. It was a set of five black-and-white shots from a picture booth at the mall. Though the strip was undated, she knew the photos must have been taken just hours before they vanished, more than two years ago. They were the only pictures she had of the two of them. Her son and Maddie.

Maddie was not the object of Joyce's search – she worried

what she might do if she ever saw the girl again – but he had left with Maddie, and they might still be together. It was worth pointing her out to others: Maddie's ravaged beauty, her mismatched eyes, her soot-colored mane stuck in the mind; people remembered seeing Maddie, and therefore, they might remember seeing him. Maddie realized she marked him, and that's why she had shorn her fairy-tale tresses to the sparse, uneven clumps in the photograph. Their pose was the same in all five: Maddie hanging on his shoulder, her head about the level of his jaw line. The only change was the smile emerging on her sharp little face, inch by inch, in time-lapse fashion, down the length of the five shots until in the final frame she was showing her teeth.

Maddie's presence in the pictures almost overwhelmed his. He stared straight into the lens, his eyes sleepy, his mouth soft. Joyce found it difficult to focus on the whole of his face and instead saw only parts, like a jigsaw puzzle that had been jostled apart. She could pick out remnants of Paul's once-muscular huskiness behind the shopworn delicacy in the jumble of features he'd inherited from her. He'd ended up with her long nose, her thin lips, and her long lashes; her tendency to close down and brood. In these photos, he was wearing his hair loose, touching his shoulders. When they were taken, it was the same length as she wore hers now, the same nondescript shade of brown that translated as lightless charcoal in the gray shades of the photograph. In the picture his hair hung limp, unclean, and tangled, serving to deepen the shadows in the hollows where his scaly addict's skin sank between his bones.

Joyce held the photographs to the edge of the map while she slid six paper clips onto the strip in correct order, one into the black space separating each shot, fitting each clip into the appropriate impression left by previous searches. The map was then secured to the sun visor with rubber bands. Next, she took a tarnished silver locket from the box and straightened the kinks in the necklace chain. She held the large oval charm to her ear, shook it. It rattled, the *clickity-click* of his first baby tooth muted by the bit of curl

11

she had kept from his first haircut. She slipped the chain over her head. The other items stayed in the box: the charred spoon and syringe he'd left with the photographs on the kitchen table, his sole gesture of good-bye. When Joyce became tired or lazy, when her faith began to question its sanity, she had only to glimpse these artifacts, and the urgency of purpose returned. If Paul had known she had these in her possession, it would have only confirmed the accusations he had shouted at her, over and over, his fingers deep in the flesh of her arms, shaking her, trying to keep her from diving into the fire to save her work. She was, Paul had bellowed, his tear-reddened eyes fixed on her own, no different than that damn kid.

She pressed the accelerator, gaining speed. Her head was clearing. The radio was on but quiet, a steady waltz beat tripping against a melody she knew well enough to hum. Snowflakes plopped against the windshield, but up ahead, farther than she was going, the sun had broken through the clouds in cathedral beams of pearl-colored light. It was about two miles to the junction of Route 5. This would put her on the main artery from which she wanted to work. Particular street names on the Albany map had caught her attention; the way they were grouped seemed significant, like the bird names: Lark, Dove, Swan, Hawk, Eagle. She'd listed these first, being drawn to the portent in the obvious hierarchy, the progression from songbird to raptor. He'd be drawn to that, too.

A sign over the highway told her the exit was three-quarters of a mile ahead, the next right. Her heart, already racing, upped another notch. She snapped down the visor to review the list of street names. Her hands tightened on the wheel. A cottony thirst wadded against the roof of her mouth and made her lick her lips. She leaned into the forward momentum, into the excitement of being this close to the possibility of a different outcome. It was almost enough to push aside the memory of Paul's disbelief, the slack shock that had altered his face when he at last understood

12

what she had been doing day after day. Immediately ahead, the exit ramp veered off to the right. She flipped on the turn signal. 'This time will be different; this time I will make it different.' She said this aloud to the photograph of her son. And then Maddie smiled at her. Because Maddie knew. This time was going to be like the last time and the time before that. It was never going to be different. Never. Joyce surrendered, falling before the inevitability of habit; she pressed her foot hard against the accelerator and sped, as she always did, right past the place she planned to begin.

Entr'acte: Joyce

I suppose none of this makes any sense. It's been a year since Paul found out, a year of nothing. Why did Paul choose today? Maybe it's because today, this last day of September, is our son's birthday, and Paul found me too much of a reminder. Who knows why people do what they do?

His birthday comes less than a week before mine. I used to tell him he was my birthday present. When he was very young, he thought it was kind of special, he and his mommy being so close on the calendar. I made only one birthday cake each year, an extra big one, and I'd save a quarter or so for my own. He enjoyed that, when he was little, seeing the icing letters from his name on my cake. Look at this photograph. He'd just turned three. See the cake? See how happy he is?

I don't have many pictures left. Paul saw to that last year when his grief overwhelmed mine, and he made it clear that 'this nonsense' was going to stop. These few weren't in the albums with the others. These I found tucked in drawers while I was packing.

This one. This one was taken when he was five. I was teaching him to ice-skate. The pediatrician said he seemed to have a weakness in his ankles and perhaps the stroking motions of skating would build up his strength. I was happy for the project; a couple weeks earlier, I had found out that there would be no more babies. My body apparently had weaknesses of its own. I took him out to Nickerson's Sports, and after lengthy discussions with the salesman on the virtues of hockey skates (speed) versus

15

figure skates (control), I bought two very good pairs of the figure skates. One for him. One for me.

We had plenty of rinks in our area, but those were always packed with speed-demon teenagers whizzing around the outer edge of the ice, and future Olympic medalists twirling leaps and spins in the center. In my mind, I kept seeing his little feet bend inward on those weak ankles as he strained to keep his balance; I'd see that balance fail him, see him tumble, see those big careless kids collide with my child, cutting him to ribbons with their recently sharpened blades.

I took him instead out to Miller's Pond, where the ice, although uneven and blemished, was ours alone. We'd wait for a particularly cold day in a particularly cold week when I was certain the ice was solid enough, and off we'd go with a thermos of hot cocoa and a box of graham crackers. We'd park next to the bare-branched elm on the edge of the frigid pond, and I'd leave the motor running for warmth while I laced up first his skates, then mine. I'd make him wait there, in the warm car, watching while I went out by myself to test the pond. Back and forth across the hazy surface, I'd skate, listening for a suspicious crack or pop – splintering ice comes with a specifically horrific noise. No matter how thorough my skating, I'd imagine the spot I failed to check splitting apart and swallowing him without so much as a splash. He'd watch me through the windshield. Sometimes he'd be crying because he thought the safety check took too long. Yes, it took a long time, but he was also an impatient child. I didn't expect him to understand the risks. None of them do.

At long last, the wait would be over. I'd knot up his scarf and make sure his hat was down tight over his ears. We'd skate, with me holding his hand, helping him not to fall, while he tried to figure out the way it worked. 'Stroke,' I'd say as we pushed through the steam clouds of our breath. 'Glide off the edge of the blade.' He'd get frustrated because it was hard and it hurt his ankles and it was cold when he fell. He'd want to go home, but no matter how he

16

insisted, no matter how dramatically he rubbed at his tears and runny nose, I'd make him stay out the hour. He was never going to get stronger if I let him quit. Now I can say that it made my heart ache to force him to keep going, but I put on the tough mom act for his benefit.

It worked. By the end of that winter, he was caroming all over the pond as I skated willy-nilly behind, pleading with him to slow down and be careful. I took this picture on what turned out to be the last day of safe ice that year. That's him, that bundled-up dot of a boy, waving from the other side of the pond.

This next one is from his sixth-grade graduation party, a barbecue we gave for his entire class. You almost can't see his face, the way they all piled together for this group photo. They had such a good time; look at those beautiful smiles. We had a professional photographer that day. I wanted it all to be so special. We rented one of those wooden dance floors for the backyard lawn and had a DJ come in to play music so they could dance, but they didn't. They preferred to play on his old swing set. I had to keep chasing them off; they were too big, and the way it bucked, pulling away from the ground as they swung, I was terrified it was going to topple over on them. Paul grilled hot dogs and hamburgers. He glowered at the children and mumbled about the cost of things, but you could tell he was having great fun, too. I made a ton of potato salad and coleslaw. We had a massive cake on which I'd had the bakery write *We are so proud of you!* followed by each of their names. One hundred forty-seven names in all. I had some games planned: a piñata, fortune-telling – nothing silly or babyish, no pin-the-tail on anything. None of them were interested in any of it. They wanted only to sit around and talk to one another, which they did, their faces serious and tight.

Every so often, a group of the bolder children, those independent, rebellious types, would try to sneak off into the woods behind us. I'd round them up, explaining that we, Paul and I, were responsible for their safety and, you know, there might be bears back in those trees. That got them laughing, and I glanced up to see my own child's face beaming with relief that I had not yet humiliated him too horribly. It was such a hectic afternoon that I never got a single bite of food. I kept my energy up with a few beers and on an empty stomach – well, it probably explains the later photos where I'm shimmying my shoulders, trying to get the kids out on the dance floor. I may have been a bit tipsy, maybe a bit more than tipsy, but no harm done. They laughed at me like they laughed at the idea of bears. If I was yelling at him that night, it was because I was tired and, yes, hurt, that so many of my efforts had fallen flat in his eyes.

I suppose it wasn't the complete disaster I felt he was accusing me of. Not if you go by this picture: all of them together, their arms entwined, leaning into and onto one another, fingers lifted in bunny ears behind one another's heads. Faces radiant with childlike joy. Except for his. He wasn't paying attention, so when the shutter snapped he was looking off to the side. 'At nothing,' he said when I asked what had he been staring at, why he had to go and ruin such a good picture. 'Just looking,' he said. It was a gracious response, I guess, considering that it was me making all the unfair accusations. Did I realize that then? Probably. I'm not blind to the implications of my behavior, but my sight does dim when I've been drinking, and I was drinking a lot.

Actually, I think I may have asked him what exactly he was looking at that was so goddamn important. I can't recall if he ever gave me a plausible answer. Now, from the distance of these years, I can't help imagining that it was Maddie he was looking at, or maybe looking for. She wasn't there that day; her family wouldn't move into town until later that summer, in August, right before school began. Still, I can't help interpreting his distraction as a premonition.

That eerie sense of omen follows to the yearbooks. What with Maddie's family name differing from ours by only the addition of the final *e* so that the two of them always ended up next to each other in the class photographs. See, here are the pages from the seventh-, eighth-, and ninth-grade annuals. See, how over the course of those years their posture changes so that by their tenth-grade pictures, their last school portraits, they are actually looking at each other. That has to mean something, I think, but you only tend to see a pattern after it's complete, when it's too late for the interpretation to do any good.

They became friends in seventh grade. Maddie was the new girl; he said that she was very smart, but shy, and the other kids were standoffish because they found her strange. She was exotic, almost otherworldly to our small-town sensibilities. Porcelain-doll complexion, those two unmatched eyes peeking out alternately, first the blue, next the gray, from beneath the masses of jet-dark spiraled curls. She carried a soft, prepuberty roundness when they first met; it gave her a docile appearance, unlike the aggressive edges emerging on the girls he'd grown up with. It was a feint, of course, the morsel of angel cake baiting the trap. He'd never had a girlfriend, or shown interest either, but it struck me, from the very beginning, that the interest was more complex than the inevitable ripening of hormonal buds. He said that she was sad a lot, and quiet. They spent hours on the phone together, voices low, conspiratorial laughter.

She gave him odd gifts. For his thirteenth birthday, she gave him page 419 ripped from *Webster's Ninth New Collegiate Dictionary*. In the lower margin she wrote *1987,* the year of publication, I would assume, and in yellow highlighter she'd illuminated the words *Episiotomy, Episode, Epistemic, Epitaph, Epithalamium, Epithelioma, Epithelium.* At the top of the page she'd printed in block letters, THIS IS LIFE. She'd framed it, and it wasn't until two years later, when I removed the thing from his bedroom wall while cleaning, that I saw the writing on the cardboard backing of the frame:

The Ninth New. The Ninth Old. Beethoven. Ode to Joy. Owed to joy. Odd. OD'd. I can hear people breathing. All of them. The whole world. I hear it. I watch their noses, the way the nostrils twitch and flare as the air rushes in and rushes out. I see the air, all full of God. I see what is happening. The cycle is synchronizing. Soon all will be inhaling and exhaling simultaneously and one day there will be too many inhaling and the air will disappear into our insides, we'll suck in the air, the earth, the sky and all the planets. And God. We will suck ourselves into nonexistence. The only way to prevent stop stop stop stop this disaster is for some of us to stay off cadence. Off the beat. Out of phase. To devote ourselves to a never-ending awareness of the in and out back and forth coming and going of God and to disrupt it, even if that means we are stared at, and asked meaningless questions concerning our health, our healthy thinking. Since we are the ones who hear it see it know it we are the ones who must stay both inside and outside the breathing.

Later, I asked him what it meant, and after he'd finished the predictable diatribe about his privacy, he said it meant nothing. It was a poem. He said she had problems at home. Poem or not, it was disturbing. I didn't give it back to him. I hadn't realized, until this morning, that I'd hidden it in the back of the file cabinet where I hid the key to the safe-deposit box. From where I sit now, Maddie's poem is clearly a statement of intent, bordering on prophecy. I read these odd words now, and I have to believe, from the very beginning, he was trying to save her.

A valiant undertaking – I'm sure that's how he saw it. It was as if he and Maddie had gone skating on Miller's Pond without considering the conditions. The ice had given way beneath his friend, and he was honor-bound to rescue her, even if it meant surrendering to the cold watery depths in which she was obviously drowning.

I found a syringe like this one in the den, on the coffee table in front of the TV. 'Maddie's diabetic, Mom. I told you that.'

'You never told me any such thing.' 'You just don't remember. You were drunk.' He lifted his head high as though anticipating the slap of my hand. The force of impact rocked his head back. A red palm-shaped wedge appeared on his cheek. He looked me in the eye and smirked. He'd finally seen that I couldn't hurt him as much as he could hurt me. He straightened the cuffs on his oversized, too-warm-for-the-weather rugby shirt. He turned around and walked away from me.

And yes, I went straight to the liquor cabinet and poured myself a glass of eighty-proof respite. I was not as deluded as he liked to think. His father wouldn't talk to me about anything but his work and my failings. The company I worked for was crumbling into ruin; I did not know from week to week if I still had a job. When I wasn't worrying myself into exhaustion over my marriage and my paycheck, I worried about my child. My mind labored continuously. The disconnection that followed a few glasses of whatever provided the loveliest blank spaces in time. I craved that blankness. Not the booze. You don't have to tell me. I didn't need any meetings or interventions. I knew it then. It was wrong. It was cowardly. It was selfish, but I wanted only what everyone wants, a life that I can, from day to day, recognize as mine. This thing that was my life was becoming alien and untenable to the one who had to live it. Everything was falling away. I needed a way to hold on to myself, to keep myself from slipping into the void. Drinking was self-preservation by means of self-destruction. It's what people do.

That same night, I woke with a spinning head in a spinning room. It was late, around three. I heard laughter from down the hall. Maddie. She was in his bedroom, which was absolutely forbidden. I got up carefully, so as not to disturb Paul, who always slept so deeply in such utter stillness, he was more like a statue of a man sleeping. I threw on my robe and charged down the hall, already rehearsing yet another version of the 'As long as you live in my house, young man' speech. The door to his room was half open. His desk lamp cast a pure white halogen beam onto an open textbook, across which was draped a spool of rubber tubing and a pair of my sewing shears. They were sitting on the bed, facing each other, naked, or mostly so, her arms and legs wrapped around him, her eyes closed, head thrown back, hair rolling in cascading waves as he thrust his pelvis into hers.

What is it children do? Make love? Have sex? Screw? Fuck? I stood there, not as shocked as you might expect. Maddie, body lurching with the rhythm of it, turned her head toward the door. Her eyes eased open. She smiled at me.

What I remember, what I want to remember is that I closed the door and went back to bed. I did just that, but not before doing something else. I had the pair of shears at some point, and I have vague memories of shouting, a lot of shouting. I remember saying it would wait until morning. I remember closing the door. Although I probably shouted the words and slammed the door. I don't remember much of it, I try hard not to. Whatever I did, it must have been awful, because by the next evening they were gone.

These pictures are from the photo booth at the mall. I have often thought these pictures were as much an accusation as a farewell. Maddie's evolving horror of a smile, her hair shorn to tufts. Her arms around my child. *See how far I'll go? See how far he'll have to follow?*

I did what parents do. I went immediately to the police and the public agencies. At desks and counters, on phones and by faxes, everywhere I was given kind words but little hope. The officer in Missing Children had told me, in all honesty because he was too weary of the work for anything else, my best chance was that my kid might wake up from his self-induced nightmare and come in on his own. I'd told him about Maddie, what few details I could bring myself to tell about the hours before they left. The officer checked some files for her name. He came back and said the best advice he could give was to grieve and get on with the business of living. What he didn't bother to explain was how, exactly, one managed to do that.

Unready, unwilling to just give up, I called people and posted fliers. This is one of the fliers I hung all over town and at highway rest areas and at bus stations. See, it has his picture both before, when he was all right, and later, after Maddie. When nothing came of that, I hired a private detective – that sounds so romantic – but that's what she was. She found lost kids. It was her specialty. She came highly recommended. I still carry her card in my wallet. Leslie Stone. See? A plain little card for such a complex business.

I went to see her at her office in the city; I figured it was time to admit he and Maddie had outrun the boundaries of Vermont. The detective's office had an entire wall crowded with photos from grateful, reunited families. Their joy only fueled my hope. The detective – Leslie, Ms Stone, I was never sure what to call her – wasn't what I expected. She had kids of her own – she volunteered that fact – but she didn't offer anything like comfort or even empathetic commiseration. She was attentive, however, one of those people who leans into your words as though, in getting closer to your voice, she could get closer to your meaning. While she listened, she started to bite at her nails and then shook her hand out hard as though she were angry. Old habits – I said I understood but I did not explain what or why. I talked a lot; she never interrupted. When I started to cry, she let me cry; she didn't point out the box of tissues on her desk or move them in my direction the way people do when they think they're being helpful but what they want is for you to stop crying. She asked only one question: Did I feel my son wanted to be found? I had only one honest answer: I wasn't sure what he wanted. She then gave me papers listing her fee schedule, as if any price were going to be too high. I waved those away and spent the next hour filling out forms with his birth date and Social Security number and doctor and dentist names, his teachers, his friends, cousins, uncles, aunts, pets, employers, clubs, known allergies, known infirmities, marketable skills, hobbies, favorite music, favorite movies, girlfriends, boyfriends, sexual history, drug history, legal history, history, history, his story – the more I offered, the more I realized how little I knew of this child who had drawn his first nourishment from my bloodstream. How was that possible? How had my single reason for living become a mystery to me? I handed over the forms, wrote the detective a check, and went back to my hotel.

Ms Stone called me the next morning. I had barely awakened from the first decent night's sleep I'd had in months. 'Already?' I said, only able to whisper into the phone. She asked me to come back to her office, please, as soon as I could. Her voice was different from the day before, softer, warmer. When I put down the phone, I realized I was terrified. I threw on my clothes and caught a cab to the address. I knew I was hurrying, but each minute rolled out slower than the one before it so that by the time I was sitting across from her at her desk again, time had stopped completely. The joy in the photographs on the wall had shifted, darkened somehow, and was now more like the greed-edged triumph of the winners on some hideous game show. I braced for horrible news.

It was worse than that. It was no news. Ms Stone pushed my check back across her desk and quite kindly said she couldn't take this case. 'Why? Is there a problem with the funds?' She shook her head and rested her chin on her interlaced fingers. I saw how badly bitten her nails were, gnawed right down to the cuticle. Bandages on two of them. She caught me looking, and for the first time she smiled at me, but it was a sad smile. She said she'd reviewed the information I'd provided and simply felt she couldn't take my money when the prospects were so . . . uncertain – that's how she put it. I took a guess. 'You talked to my husband, didn't you?' She said some cases were more complicated than she felt comfortable taking on. 'What is so complicated? My child is missing! I need to find him!' I think I must have shouted. I'm pretty sure I shouted. The detective stood abruptly, indicating the meeting was over. She extended her hand. When I didn't take it, she let it fall to her side.

24

I had been afraid she was going to dismiss me with a feeble wish of good luck. What she said, though – and I recall this as though she'd said it just a minute ago – what she said was 'You know, Joyce, sometimes life is just too fucking hard.' Exactly.

So I went back to Vermont, almost hopeless. Still, I was certain he'd call, just to let me know he was – well, *safe* wasn't the word. I sat and slept by the phone, day and night, promising myself, him, God, whomever would listen, that if he would call once, just once, it would be enough. He didn't have to come back. He didn't have to tell me where he was. Just call. Just be all right.

When the call did not come, I was certain he'd send a letter or a postcard. *Dear Mom, I'm all right.* Two lines of salvation postmarked from the place where being all right was still possible. The mail brought nothing. The last hope fell away quietly, like late autumn leaves, leaving me nothing but the stark, unrelieved probability that he and Maddie had gone to the street and were doing what they had to do to keep flesh and fix intact. The plea to *be all right* distilled itself down to a simple *be alive*. It was then I decided *I* had to find him. It was then I began to dread that I actually might succeed.

It took Paul a few weeks to catch on. I'd been laid off, at long last, from the shipping company, and he thought, from what I said, the way I said it, that I was out looking for work. I'd make sure to be home when he came in from work, which wasn't a challenge since he was managing his helplessness by working longer and longer days. Still, I had to be careful to get in ahead of him, get my maps hidden. I'd make us simple late suppers of canned soup, and salads from bagged greens and bottled dressing. He'd eat while I chattered in between sips and swallows, the tinkling ice cubes accompanying the frustrations of my day. I didn't lie: '. . . and I looked everywhere. Talked to people who would know if I had any chance of finding anything . . .' Paul would nod and advise me not to give up, not to settle for less than I wanted, and eventually I would nod off into a recurring nightmare.

It was a few days shy of the first birthday after his disappearance; I nodded off too early. I drank too much – tall icy glasses of gin and tonic – too fast and fell asleep at the table, my head down on the clutter of maps and notepads. I was awakened by the smell of smoke, the noisy crackle and pop of flame, and Paul's huffing sobs as he stabbed at the fire with the poker. I saw the last of my maps go in, and then baby albums and scrapbooks, and I was yelling, and he was yelling, *It's over, Joyce! He's gone! It's over!* as he fought, wrenching my arms as I flailed and kicked, to keep me from digging into the flames to save what was left of my child, what was left of myself.

I stopped looking. I stopped drinking. I stopped. I spent a year sitting on the couch, my hands in my lap. I was sitting there last night when Paul said he couldn't take any more and he was leaving. 'You were here?' I asked. He said he was sorry and walked out of the house. I just sat there, a long time, my hands in my lap, and then I started screaming. I screamed until my voice disappeared.

Today, September 30, is his seventeenth birthday. I've cleaned out the bank accounts, the safe-deposit box. I have cash and the title to my car. Everything I need. I'm going to find him or find the place where he can't find me. I am aware that sounds like nonsense, but sometimes life *is* too fucking hard, and nonsense is all a person has left. Nonsense and the knowledge that she's doing the best she can.

Two

The snow had given over to rain, a fine drizzle glimmering in the headlights. It was after eight. She was somewhere in western Pennsylvania, well south of Pittsburgh, on a two-lane stretch of state road that bumped and gullied through undulating terrain. Maple, pine, and birch trees crowded close to the pavement, wet leaves and trunks flashing ghost-white in the headlamps as she passed. It seemed hours since she'd seen another car. Sick as hell, she'd plowed through the entire bag of lozenges and was now sipping from the bottle of multisymptom syrup tucked in the cup holder. The resulting buzz was slight, a vague dizziness in her vision and a nervousness in her limbs. She needed to be in bed but didn't trust herself to stop the car just yet. She'd stopped once for gas around dusk, and now, with every imperfection in the road, she had to endure the merry clinking of beer bottles from the dark of the backseat. So much for plans.

'It's all right. You should have made allowances for how hard it was going to be.' Joyce was talking to herself, in part to block out the happy invitation of the bottles and in part to better believe her attempts at reassurance. 'You should have figured that you'd have to start where you left off. It was going to take time to get going again. And he wasn't going to be in Albany, anyway. You knew that.' She was so intent on her self-lecturing that she scarcely glimpsed the yellow signboard, its bent arrow warning of the sharp curve coming up. Fatigue and pharmaceuticals had dulled her responses so much that by the time she realized what she had seen and what it meant, she was in the arc of the hairpin turn and moving too fast. She jammed her foot against the brakes. The rain-slicked asphalt didn't provide enough friction to countermand the gravitational forces; the abrupt halt became a forward-skidding spin. Joyce fought the steering wheel. In the backseat, the beer bottles tumbled and clanked. The headlights sliced circles as the car spun round and round in the dark.

Then it was over. Joyce, shaking, gulping breath, clung to the wheel. The car was still on the road; it had come to a stop in the bowl of the curve straddling the double yellow dividing line and putting her in danger of being hit from either direction. The prospect of that was the only argument that could persuade her foot off the brake and back on the accelerator. The Saturn jumped at the first prod, as though it, too, had been made skittish by the near miss. She maneuvered the car back into the outer lane, but she wasn't sure from which direction she had entered the turn. 'Worry about it later,' she said, ordering herself to act. She nudged the gas until the car gained enough creeping momentum to get out of the curve and onto a straight stretch. The road sign on the other side of the road told her that at least she was moving in the right direction.

Disoriented and holding her speed at a timid twenty miles per hour, Joyce drove. She scanned the roadside for a sign or landmark to tell her if she was moving forward or merely backtracking; she recognized nothing. The farther she went, the more a queasy panic churned beneath her breastbone. She tried to focus on the driving, tried not to see the playback of potential disasters running soundlessly in infinite loops on the walls of her imagination. 'You aren't lost,' she said. 'You're all right, and you aren't lost.' She crested a slight rise in the road. Her headlights hit the red lenses on the tail end of another car. The glint was reflective, off to the side; the car was obviously parked and, given the surroundings, probably disabled. As she drew closer, she saw it was little more than a rattletrap wreck of a compact. Its green paint was mottled with rust, and the rear fender was being held in place with a twisted coat hanger. The plates were from California. Joyce gave the car a wide berth, slowing to allow herself a better look. Her lights caught the compact's front bumper, and as though she'd hit the trigger on a jack-in-the-box, a figure bounded up from the shadows, arms waving. He ran into the middle of the road, directly into the path of Joyce's lights. He held his palms up, indicating she should stop. He was shouting at her. For the second time in a few minutes, she slammed on the brakes in an unthinking response.

He didn't move; he just stood there, palms outstretched, his face as startled and full of pleading as Joyce felt hers must have been. She could see that his right hand was crudely bandaged with a white cloth stained with fresh-looking blood. He was wearing jeans and a white hooded sweatshirt. The hood was cinched tight against his face, which, if she survived whatever was coming, she would describe as pasty-pale. Details, remember details: wide-set eyes, a stump of a nose, an unkempt copper-wire beard that all but hid his mouth. He had not ventured from his spot on the road but was now pantomiming, pointing at the compact with an unsteady hand.

Joyce realized how young he was. She double-checked the power lock on the doors and then lowered her window about an inch. The drizzle blew against her skin.

'What do you want?' She had to shout it a second time to overcome her laryngitis.

'I'm sorry. I didn't mean to scare you,' he yelled, starting toward the car window.

Joyce leaned on the horn. 'Stay there.' He froze.

'Yeah. Sure. I didn't mean to scare you. It's just that – I ran out of gas.'

'You ran out of gas?'

'Yeah. Stupid. I know what you must be thinking, but I've been out here for over an hour. Yours is the first car to come by.'

'Ever hear of walking?'

'To where?'

True, she couldn't remember the last time she passed as much as a house. 'I'll send someone back to help you.'

'That would work.' He jogged in place a couple steps and looked down at the asphalt. 'It's getting cold.'

'I'll stop at the first place I come across. They'll be here in no time. I promise. Is your hand hurt?'

He looked at the bandage. 'Naw. Jabbed it on a tire iron when I was changing a flat yesterday.'

'Sounds like you've had an interesting trip.'

'Way too interesting. How are the gas station guys going to find me?'

How are they going to find me? She sighed; common sense fell away before the old prayerful hopes of what others might risk for her son. 'I should warn you,' she said as she used her foot to shove the shopping bag full of cash farther under the car seat, 'I don't have any money with me.'

'I can give you some,' he called back as he dug into the pocket of his jeans. 'I think I have fifteen, twenty bucks left, at least enough for a five-gallon –' He peered into the windshield, his expression going sad with comprehension. 'Oh. I getcha. Yeah. It's OK. No problem. You can't be too careful these days.'

'Get in,' she shouted, and unlocked the doors.

He pulled off the hood and ran his hands over his crew cut. His name was Jake, he said, and he was on his way home to Maine. He'd been on the road for four days straight, fueling himself on No Doz, black coffee, and chocolate bars. Joyce drove. Jake talked. And talked. And talked, as though his words were being chased. '. . . And so this guy at the truck stop says he has this foolproof shortcut that will save me three or four hours because there's no traffic and the cops don't patrol it much but I think I took a wrong turn back in Ohio. I was trying to find my way back to the interstate when my tank went dry, which was weird because the gauge isn't even on Empty; I'm just so freaking happy you came along when you did; I feel bad about jumping out like that; Jesus, that must have scared you . . .'

He clasped and unclasped his hands as fast as he spoke; he interlaced his fingers, working them like a jerky hinge; he took off the seat belt, shifted his torso, crossed and uncrossed his legs and put the seat belt back on. He was still talking. 'So, I'm trying to get home before my money runs out but at the same time I'm in no hurry, you know, because of the shit I'm going to get for flunking out of school –'

'In California?' Joyce interrupted him just so he'd be forced to take a breath.

'Yeah. In L.A. Man, you're sick, aren't you?' He backed against the door a bit. 'My old man was all "You don't need no fancy L.A. college; go to school in state; I'll teach you everything else you need to know." He always assumed I'd be taking over his business; it never occurred to him that I might want to start up on my own, do things the way I want to do them.'

'What do you want to do?'

'You mean what did I flunk out of? It's OK. You can ask, but you wouldn't have heard of it. It was magician school. It's OK; you can laugh if you want; a lot of people do. I couldn't cut it. I'm too clumsy and too slow.' He looked at his hands. 'They said I lacked dexterity, the "requisite adroitness." Clumsy and slow, that's what they meant.'

Joyce imagined him having to hand back his cape and top hat; her heart hurt for him. 'Perhaps things will work out with your family's business.'

'Doubt it. Dad's a magician. Merlino the Mysterious. He does dove and bunny tricks. He'll be doing dove and bunny tricks until the day he dies. I wasn't going to need a cheesy stage name. Jake Matthews, simply that. Elegant. I was going to levitate cities and pull elephants out of thimbles; now I'll go back to working the hardware store so Dad can get a discount for his next "saw the

31

chick in half" box. It sucks.' His voice thickened as though he were fighting back tears.

Joyce took her right hand off the wheel, her fingers dancing in hesitation against the impulse to touch his shoulder and say that everything would work out for the best. It was too late for such comforts; Jake had learned enough of the world to know she would be lying. She put her hand back on the wheel. 'You put anything on that cut?'

He held the bandage close to the windshield as though trying to get more light. 'I washed it out. The counter guy at a doughnut shop gave me some antiseptic gel stuff. The thing keeps bleeding. It freaking hurts.'

'When was your last tetanus shot?'

He laughed. 'You a doctor or something?'

She smiled, shook her head. 'I used to schedule drivers at a shipping firm. Somebody comes in bleeding, you ask about his shot record – and no matter what he tells you, you check his files to see if he's right, which he never is.'

'The school made us fill out health forms and shit like that. I'm sure if I needed it, they'd have made me get one.'

'Get one anyway. Soon as you can.'

'Sure. But I freaking hate needles.'

'Me too.' She said nothing more. Distracted, as though anxious over the idea of the shot, he fell silent and chewed on his thumbnail.

The road wound on and on until, finally, they reached the intersection of another, better-traveled state road. On the corner was a large service center shining green and white like the Emerald City. Joyce pulled beneath the brightly lit canopy and stopped beside one of the six pumps.

'I'll see if they'll lend me a gas can,' he said as he opened the door. The Saturn's interior light switched on. He leaned over toward Joyce, squinting at the posted prices. 'Christ. I'll never get home on –' His attention had shifted to the visor, his brow creased in deepening thought. 'I don't believe it.' He grabbed the strip of photos; the paper clips flew off in six different directions. Jake held them up close to the ceiling lamp. 'I know them. I mean, I met them, I talked to her – he didn't say much, but I did talk with her for little while a few days ago. The day I left L.A.'

Joyce was falling up. Out of the car, off the planet, into the void. 'Don't –'

But Jake kept going. 'It was at this roadhouse I ate lunch at on my way out of Los Angeles. Wait.' He dug in his pocket and pulled out a folded book of matches. 'This place, the Hoodoo Bar and Grill,' he said, reading the black printing off the white cardboard, 'Lágrimas, California. I don't even know why I took these. It's not like I smoke or anything.' He was grinning big, amazed by the coincidence, but on reading Joyce's expression, his smile faltered. 'They were OK. I mean, they looked OK. Her hair was a lot longer.'

From the outer ring of a distant world, she heard her own voice. 'Did he, did either of them say where they were headed?'

'Like I said, he didn't talk much, and she didn't say anything about traveling.'

'You're sure?'

'Yeah. In fact, I sort of got the impression they lived in the area.' Jake held the matchbook out in his bandaged palm. 'Do you want this?'

Joyce had to will herself to respond; she managed a bit of a nod. He closed his fist over the matchbook, waved it about wildly, and then reopened his hand. The matchbook was gone. Before she had a chance to protest, he reached over and appeared to pull the matchbook from behind her ear. He fumbled, almost letting it fall from his fingertips. He sighed.

'Dove and bunny tricks,' he said, placing the bloodied matchbook in Joyce's shaking hand.

Three

Lágrimas was the smallest of dots labeled in the mapmaker's most miniscule font on the southern edge of the Mojave National Preserve. She had been headed toward that dot for four days now, driving nearly five hundred miles a day, in a straight line. She gauged the distance she'd covered not by the names of cities she'd passed or by the geographical changes in her surroundings but rather by the cycling tides of daylight and dark. Plus her receding symptoms. The closer she got to Lágrimas, the longer the days became and the better she felt. That had to mean something, didn't it? She asked that question aloud a few times, talking to the clattering beer bottles bouncing around the backseat like bored children.

Each night, in the room of a roadside hotel, Joyce studied the map and calculated her progress. Satisfied, she slipped beneath the rough white sheets and imagined the reunion, his expression when he saw her, what she'd say to him, what he'd say back. She floated off to sleep on the buoyancy of these imaginings only to drift, rudderless, into the currents of old nightmares. On waking from the dreams, in the indifferent dark of the rented room, she'd lie unsleeping until dawn, warning herself to remember the difference between getting lost and leaving.

On the fifth day, a Friday, she was running behind schedule. She had stopped at a shopping center in a smallish city called Larkin and bought some clothes that were more appropriate for the warmer climate; some sleeveless shirts in white cotton, one which she wore now with a white cardigan over a new, red-print skirt, her feet comfy in new, white canvas mules. She wanted to look nice for him; he would see she was better now and not angry anymore. The salesclerk, who had clipped off the tags so that Joyce could wear her purchases out of the store, told Joyce that she'd be grateful she had the heavy sweaters and jackets. Desert nights were cold. She had returned to the highway feeling hopeful and refreshed.

It was nearing noon when she reached the exit off I-40 that would take her into Lágrimas. She saw the signboard, confirmed the number with her notes, and sped – again, again – right past into the dazed astonishment that always descended after her failure of nerve. 'I'm sorry,' she told the beer bottles. She was a coward, and she knew it. He was there. She was certain of it this time. She had proof – well, she had the word of one who had no reason to lie to her. The bottles clunked in sympathy; they understood. This was an arduous undertaking full of potential sorrows and distress. And yes, she was feeling stronger, but viruses can be insidious. For all she knew, her body may not yet have been up to the emotional demands of a reunion; perhaps she had done no more than acknowledge her fatigue. Besides, it was not just any day, damn it. 'I'm forty-four years old,' she said to the beer bottles. 'Happy birthday to me.'

She shifted in the seat, settling in for another long day's drive. Los Angeles was the next logical destination. The prospect of a new goal lightened her outlook in general. She noticed, for the first time, how clear and open the sky was, a bird's-egg blue that deepened as it dropped behind the hills that fortressed the horizon – although a dark, almost opaque haze clung to the ridges of the distant mountains directly in her path. This would be smoke from the forest fires she'd been hearing about on the car radio for the past few days. She worried for a bit that the roads she wanted might be blocked, but now, how could it matter? Might as well enjoy the drive. The desert was scruffier than she'd thought it would be, a dusty gray rockiness studded with clumps of surly-looking plant life. The flatness was broken only by the random stand of what she recognized from travel magazines as the 'spiky' yucca and 'grotesque' Joshua tree. She felt as though she were traversing an alien world, which of course meant she was the one who didn't belong there.

She was glad it was daylight, glad she wasn't alone on the road. The traffic was minimal, a few cars among the occasional packs of eighteen-wheelers, all of it seeming to be headed west. That couldn't be right. This was a major highway; someone ought to be going the other direction. She watched for oncoming vehicles across the divider. No one. She came over the brink of a long, sloping descent; she saw an array of red and blue lights strobing in the distance. It looked to be four or five Highway Patrol cars blocking both sides of the interstate. The traffic slowed as the officers directed them off the highway, across an expanse of scrub to what looked like an unpaved road that ran at an angle toward the hills. The road and the cars and trucks on it were obscured by the thickly billowing dust kicked up by the vehicles' wheels. This deviation struck Joyce as more than an inconvenience, and she attempted to steer the car, search the map, and hold the reins on her panic all at the same time. The map held no indication of what this unpaved road might be or where it went.

Her lane, the left, crept closer to the place she'd have to leave the pavement. It brought her alongside a refrigerated truck that sported a faded painting of a freckle-faced boy in a farmer's straw hat. 'Hmmm. That's fresh!' said the boy, his words caught in a cartoon balloon. The truck driver, a sharp-chinned woman with a shocking pink bandana tied around her head, was talking into the transmitter of a CB radio and making angry gestures with her other hand. The truck driver apparently felt herself watched and turned to look at Joyce. She shook her head and mouthed something in Joyce's direction. Joyce hit the button and lowered the window on the passenger side. The driver cranked down her own.

'There's a multi-car pileup couple miles further on,' shouted the driver. 'Forty or more vehicles involved. Road's going to be closed for hours. They're detouring us around. Problem is there ain't nothing to detour us onto but these old desert roads.'

'Can I follow you back to the highway?'

'Sure,' she said, laughing. 'Long as you understand I'm following the guy ahead of me, and I don't got a clue where he's headed.'

It was like driving through fog – dim, heavy, and gray. The words on the back of the truck – JAMESON'S PRODUCE – disappeared behind the swells of dust, which became so dense she could no longer make out the taillights. She let the truck put some distance between them, thinking that that might help alleviate the worst of the dust. It didn't. Even with the vents closed and windows tight, the finer particles managed to seep into the car; Joyce ran her finger across the dashboard, making a trough in the dust already accumulated. She could feel it settling in the corners of her eyes, in her nostrils, down her throat. It made her cough, which made it hard to see. The car pitched and shimmied, and she had to work at steering a straight line.

She hit a bump, the wheels grabbed, and she was suddenly gliding on a smooth, solid surface. Not far beyond her, patches of sky filtered through the thinning clouds of dust. And she was out of it, back in the sun, picking up speed down a two-lane road running through an endless flat of desert terrain. The produce truck was not ahead of her nor – she kept checking the rearview – was anyone behind. She had obviously veered off course from the detour because of the dust.

Easy to fix. She U-turned and started back in the other direction, assuming that she'd catch up with the flow of traffic fast enough. How far could she have deviated anyway? She passed the place where she had emerged from the dust and drove carefully through the mistlike plumes that had overtaken the road. She drove quite a ways, seven or eight miles, without seeing anyone and was starting to think that she'd turned around too soon when she spotted a T-intersection farther ahead where the road she was on ended. The red octagon of a stop sign was visible even from this distance, and beside it was a green board with a reflective white arrow that shone in the sun. Joyce could only hope it would point her back toward the interstate. It wasn't as though she had many options. Going left would take her straight back into the choking depths of dust. She'd had her fill of that; any more, and she'd be downing all six beers just to be able to breathe. She backed off the gas pedal, allowing the car to slow in approach to what seemed a wholly unnecessary stop sign. Habit made her flick on the blinker, signaling her right turn to no one. She came to a full stop at the sign and sat there, her foot firm on the brake pedal, reading the road sign. LÁGRIMAS – 21. Joyce considered the dust and her reticence about driving back through it. 'Don't be stupid,' she said as she smoothed over the finger trails on the dashboard. 'I'll run into another road in the next twenty-one miles.' Of course she would. It was a direction, not destiny, painted on the sign. She made the turn.

The road cut through a ridge of rocky hills that muscled up against one another to loom over the asphalt like a gang of toughs. Then, as though satisfied by the implication of a threat, the hills parted to reveal a broad valley lying naked to the noon sun. As yet, no other road had presented itself. Joyce watched the odometer rolling through the tenths of miles, and with each one she felt herself more disconnected from her will, as though her body had become robotic, a machine operated by forces as remote and mean as the retreating hills.

'You don't have to do anything,' she said, trying to regain her sense of control. 'You can drive straight through; no one will even know you were here.'

But what if he sees you? What if he happens to spot the Vermont plates and looks into the window as you drive past? What if he mistakes your cowardice for rejection? Like the last time.

Her inner debate was interrupted by a faded billboard on the left side of the road. Bright pink script on a black background proclaimed her welcome to LÁGRIMAS DRY LAKE: HOME OF WORLD FAMOUS FLOR DE LÁGRIMAS GOURMET SALT. Beyond the sign lay ash-colored earth, crazed with fissures that sparkled back sunshine with a weird coral-pink tint. The car rocked in a sudden gust of wind; seconds later, a loose cyclone of dust lifted from the lake and scurried off toward the hills.

The road banked in a long, gentle curve away from the dry lake. Soon after, she could make out, through the heat shimmering off the pavement, a meager skyline – a water tower overlooking a few squat buildings clustered on either side of the road. This could be only the town of Lágrimas. On the outskirts of the tiny town, almost defiant in its separation, was another building that she was coming up on fast. 'Turn around now,' she said to herself, to the car, to the whole idea, but it was as though she were on the track of a carnival ride – spinning the wheel in either direction would have no effect on her ultimate destination.

The building sat on the far side of an intersection of unnamed roads. It was a rough-finish stucco painted the same coral pink of the sparkling lake bed. The architecture echoed that of the mission buildings she'd seen in those travel magazines dedicated to Southern California, what with the ends of rough-hewn beams protruding from beneath the scalloped roof line. An empty arch, presumably meant for a bell, embellished the crowning curve of the façade. The only windows were the long, narrow panels of glass that made Joyce think of gun turrets. A sun-beaten board hung by the front door. The board was painted with uneven lettering: PROPERTY AND BUSINESS FOR SALE, INQUIRE INSIDE. The sign looked as though it had been hanging there for many years; the letters had been painted over at least three times, in three different colors. Joyce pulled into the nearly empty parking lot, her tires slipping a bit on the gravel surface. She steered her car into the space between a turquoise-blue Thunderbird and a dusty red pickup truck with a Harley Davidson motorcycle tethered upright in the cargo bed.

She sat there for a while, tapping the gas pedal, listening to the engine rev before she shut it down. Looking into the rearview mirror, she watched the front door; no one went in and no one left. She twisted around in her seat to gather up the scattered bottles of beer, shoving them back into the brown paper bag, shoving the bag under the passenger seat. Joyce opened the glove compartment and took out the box. She had decided to bring the photograph inside but hadn't yet decided if she was going to show it to anyone. She curled it into her palm and hit the button to unlock her door.

Stiff from sitting and tense with nerves, her legs wobbled her along, her feet sliding on the pea-sized gravel. She paused on the small concrete pad of a patio, thinking she might crack the door just an inch or two and get maybe a quick peek inside, but as she grabbed hold of the black iron pull, someone on the inside pushed to exit. The door swung wide. Joyce leapt back. An elderly man with a bushy shag of silver hair and ice-blue eyes mimicked her surprised leap and grinned at her with broken, yellow-stained teeth. He wore faded dungarees and a shirt of threadbare russet flannel.

'Didn't mean to spook you, darlin',' he said, tipping the brim of an imaginary hat. He sidestepped out of her way and held the door. 'You coming in?' His breath smelled of tuna fish and cigarettes.

'Is this the Hoodoo Bar and Grill?'

'The one and, thank-you-Jesus, only. Lunch is on for a few more minutes, if you want to wander round out here and wait until the kitchen closes up – make it safer to go inside.'

'Thank you, but I'm –'

'But you're hungry. Well then, best of luck to you.' He tipped his imaginary hat once more. 'Freezer's been out for a couple of days, so I'd steer clear of them cut-price specials.'

'I appreciate the advice.' She tried to offer him a smile, and the muscles in her face complained. Her palm was damp against the photograph. *This is a nice man; I'll ask him; he'll say no; and I won't even have to step inside and –*

41

'Pardon me, darlin',' he said, studying her face with narrowed eyes, 'I certainly ain't the one to pry, but I stole a glance at them plates and have to ask what would bring a Vermont gal way here out on the Mojave?'

'That's kind of complicated.'

'You looking for someone?'

'No.'

'Family, maybe?'

'I don't think so.' She barely heard her voice above the bellowing approach of the dream-locomotive in her head. The photographs crumpled within her tightening fist.

'Never mind – I certainly didn't mean to be harassing you. It's an old wager me and a couple of the boys got going. We got us a lost kid been hanging round more than a year, and I have a ten spot saying that sooner or later a friend or relative will come a-tracking –'

'How old is he?'

'Ain't sure. We figure around seventeen. But you just said you weren't in search of –'

'What's his name? What did he say his name was?'

'He didn't. We've been calling him Danny, and he doesn't seem to mind – Darlin', you look to be needing a sit-down.' He reached out and took her elbow, steadying her. 'Why don't you come inside?'

'Where is he now?'

'Inside.' He guided her forward, pulling when she resisted. 'Danny's right in here.'

She stepped inside the Hoodoo, her vision shutting down in the abrupt shift between full sun and the interior shadow. Her equilibrium shut down as well; it was as though she'd lost her gravity and pieces of her were falling out of orbit and away into the infinite dark. Her eyes began to adjust, and she could now discern the expressions of curiosity on the faces of the few patrons in the place.

A young woman standing near the bar that ran along the back wall lifted her chin and said something in Spanish. The patrons chuckled. She called across the room. 'You picking up the innocent *turista* chicks again, Charlie?' Her voice held only the slightest accent and much humor. She had pretty, agile features and quick dark eyes that she widened meaningfully at the three men who were settled on the tall stools at the end of the bar. She wore the flounced skirt and apron of a cocktail hostess from fifty years earlier. For some reason, she'd dyed her hair an unnatural near-fluorescent shade of orange. 'You ought to be ashamed of yourself, you dirty old goat.'

'I keep telling you, darlin', that if the Good Lord didn't like dirt, he wouldn't have made so much of it.' Charlie snorted out a laugh, and said to Joyce, 'Pay them no mind.'

A short, sinewy man behind the bar grunted. 'I'd go with TJ on this one, honey. That hell-bound hound will sweet-talk you into buying an entire case of this goddamn overpriced salt' – he hiked his thumb over his shoulder at the display of bottled pink crystals glistening on the glass shelf behind him – 'faster than spit flies in the wind.'

'As if you don't get a cut of every bottle that goes outta here, Pete, you ungrateful pirate. TJ, darlin', please be so kind as to bring the lady a glass of water – Now, where did Danny disappear to?'

One of the three bar-stool sitters, a tanned and muscled blond in black-rimmed glasses, raised his hand as though he were almost sure he had the answer the examiner was after.

'Yes, Lucas?' said Charlie.

'Pete sent him out to sweep the kitchen.'

Charlie *tsked-tsked* his disapproval. 'Peter Scruggs.'

'The kid's gotta pay for his meals somehow,' said Pete with a defensive growl.

'Even though one of us already has?'

A man playing alone at a billiards table cleared his throat. 'We've had this discussion before, Charlie,' he said as he eased himself lower to line up a shot. He moved through the brightness of the table light suspended above him, and his dark bald skull gleamed, the creases on his khaki work shirt throwing peaked shadows across his back. What looked to be a pager was clipped to his belt. It seemed to be in the way; he took it off and laid it on the table rail. 'I told Pete the chores were OK. Danny likes to help out; earning his way is good for him.' He made the shot; billiard balls collided and dropped with a muted thump into various pockets. With a mumble of dissatisfaction at the outcome, he raised his eyes and stared directly at Joyce. 'What do you want with Danny?'

Charlie answered for her. 'She's looking for a seventeen-year-old boy.'

'Who isn't?' said TJ, smirking as she set a glass of ice water down in front of Joyce.

Joyce picked up the sweaty glass and gulped down the cold water, washing the taste of dust from her mouth. She drained it fast, letting a couple of the die-sized ice cubes slide onto her tongue, and then offered the glass back to the waitress. 'May I have some more, please?'

'Sure, but I ought to warn you that only the first one is free.' TJ took the glass.

'This ain't the time to be jacking up your tips, Miss Cortez,' said Charlie, pulling a chair out for Joyce.

The man at the billiards table rapped his knuckles on the felt-covered slate. 'I asked what you wanted with Danny.'

'I don't know,' said Joyce, sitting. 'My son has been missing for about two years now. My husband – my marriage is over. I have nothing left but to look for him. Someone said they saw him here.'

He rested the end of his cue stick on the floor and leaned against it like a staff. 'And you believe everything that you – Who are you? You have a name?'

'Joyce –'

'So, Joyce, do you believe everything you're told?'

'Duncan, why do you always have to be such a hard-ass?' said the man in the leather jacket, who sat between Lucas and the other guy at the bar. He swiveled his stool toward the billiards table. He had a dark, muttonchop mustache, and he wore the front part of his long silver-shot hair pulled back tight in a ponytail. An irregular plane of scar tissue ran from his right temple down his jaw and spread across his neck in an alluvial fan toward his chest. 'You heard the lady. She's been searching for her kid for two damn years. Cut her an inch of line, already.'

'An inch of line,' echoed the third man at the bar, a fireplug-shaped figure in a herringbone sport coat. 'Besides, I smell a good bet. Fifty says Danny is her kid. And that, ma'am' – he swiveled round to catch Joyce's eye – 'is meant as a vote of confidence.' He took a bite from a candy bar and chewed, absently toying with the row of gold studs in his left earlobe.

'Ozzie,' said the scarred man, 'what kind of jerk would take a bet like that in front of the mom?'

'In front of the mom? We don't know if she is the mom, Eugene,' said Ozzie. 'That's the foundation of the bet.'

'I get what makes for betting potential, Oz-man.'

'What makes for betting potential . . . I never said you didn't "get it"; what I was trying to point out –'

'Would you two shut up?' said TJ as she set the refilled water glass on Joyce's table. 'You'll have to excuse them. They're still sober enough to talk – What, Lucas?'

Lucas lowered his hand. 'Maybe someone should just go get Danny. You know, see if he belongs to her.'

'Hold on,' said Duncan. He laid the cue stick on the table and strode over to where Joyce was sitting. He grabbed a chair, swung it around, and straddled it. After adjusting the roll of each shirtsleeve, he rested his arms on the chair's slatted back. He steepled his fingers, bouncing them against his lips as he studied Joyce's face. Nervous under the scrutiny, Joyce tucked her hair behind her ears and smiled. He didn't smile back. He had a broadness about him, his posture, his features, and because he carried the aroma of cigar smoke, she immediately associated the deep brown of crushed tobacco with the brown of his skin. Determined not to fail this test, she held his gaze, focusing on the flecks of amber in his brown eyes. He leaned in a couple inches closer; she stayed where she was. She knew that he was looking for physical evidence of connection, and she was afraid he was going to sense how much she hoped he would not find it.

The severity of his expression relaxed. He leaned back. 'You resemble him enough, but that proves nothing.'

'Of course not,' she said, almost in a whisper.

'Danny!' Duncan shouted. A second later the door beyond the bar swung open, and a young man poked his head into the bar. Duncan motioned him over. 'Danny, come here.'

He pushed through the door and trotted over to Duncan's side. The fabric of his shirt, identical in color to that of Duncan's, draped loose from his shoulders to the waistband of his too-big jeans, cinched tight around his skinny middle. His hair had been cut by someone who had more ambition than skill; wispy, static-propelled layers flitted about his head. His cheekbones were too prominent, and the bridge of his nose zigzagged as though it had been broken more than once. He was attempting a goatee, it seemed, from the sparse bit of fuzz on the tip of his chin. His face was vacant of expression, but his eyes were bright and fixed on Duncan. 'I will be correspondent to command and shall do my spiriting lightly,' he said as he fell forward from the waist, his right arm sweeping in a grand flourish.

'I wish I could get him to stop with the bowing thing,' said Duncan as he turned to Joyce. 'Did you teach him to do that?'

Joyce stood without willing herself to do so. She said his name, or tried to, but it seemed she had forgotten how to breathe. 'I don't understand' was all she could manage.

She stared down at Duncan, who was staring up at her with undisguised skepticism. He crossed his arms over his chest; the gesture somehow altered the set of his face from that of suspicion to defiance. 'So, is he yours?'

Joyce shook her head, trying to clear it, and mouthed a word: *No*.

Danny straightened and blinked as though he'd just that moment noticed her. The corners of his mouth went down in a soft curve of genuine concern. 'Be collected. No more amazement. Tell your piteous heart there's no harm done.'

'I'm sorry,' said Joyce. She opened her hands, as if to push him away. 'I can't do this anymore.' She walked out of the Hoodoo as fast as her feet could carry her.

Four

TJ picked up the departed woman's water glass. She pulled the bar rag from her apron sash and began to wipe away the condensation rings from the table with tight, determined swipes. 'Heard Rachel over at the Hotel saying that that new puppy of theirs got tangled up in a mesquite. Poor baby is a mess of infection and imbedded thorns. Looks like they're going to have to put her down.' She stuck the cloth back under the apron sash and picked up the crumpled bit of paper the woman had left behind. 'You know, Mr Dupree, if your work here doesn't feel quite done, I know of a puppy you can take out and kill.' She marched back toward the bar.

'I'll take that under advisement, Miss Cortez.' Duncan glanced up at Charlie, who was giving him the eye. 'You heard the woman. She said herself that Danny isn't her boy. And considering what we've guessed of Danny's past, she ought to be damn glad he isn't.'

'True enough.' Charlie slipped a rumpled pack of Camel cigarettes out of his breast pocket. 'But she also drove out all the way from blessed Vermont thinking he might be. You might have shown a bit more solicitude in what must have been a heartbreaking disappointment.'

Duncan waved the judgment aside. His frame of mind had been barbed enough all morning, what with losing the calls to that SOB MacGruder and the fact he was hurting worse than anything a whole handful of generic Ibu-nothing could begin to touch. Even if the discs along his backbone were, this instant, to make their mystery shift into a few hours of pain-free alignment, even if MacGruder were, this instant, to head-on that rattrap wrecker of his into a tanker hauling 100 percent undiluted nitroglycerine, even if he, Duncan Dupree, had the power to snap his fingers, *poof*, this instant and make here and now the best of all times in the best of all worlds, he was not, repeat not, about to let himself be bullied into stupidity by the misplaced compassion of these sun-addled misfits. 'My first responsibility is to Danny,' he said. The kid was still there, swaying in that woozy way of his, from one foot to the other. Duncan cuffed him lightly on the forearm. 'You go on back and finish up whatever Pete wanted, understand?'

The boy snapped to attention. 'I am correspondent to command and shall do my spiriting lightly.' He bowed deeply from the waist, straightened, and ambled off toward the kitchen.

'You know, that bowing shit has got to stop,' Duncan called after him, checking to make sure the door had swung shut before speaking to the room in general. 'Any one of you standing here can give solemn, clear-eyed testimony to how this world is made and what it can do to you even when you're armed, ready, and watching. It is more than conceivable that one of these cross-country bottom feeders comes through Lágrimas, gets a look at our Shakespeare-spouting boy – and, figuring him for an innocent and us for a bunch of ignorant hicks, sends in a *mommy* to carry Danny off to God knows what.' He crossed his arms again and it hurt like hell, but that was quite all right because he was in the mood to inflict some pain.

'All due respect to your larger concerns,' said Charlie, 'but if that was indeed what she was up to, it was one mighty pitiful example of flimflammin'.'

Duncan could use logic, too. 'Rather than keelhauling me, you could be focusing some of this ill will on the unfeeling asshole who sent her on this rotten errand in the first place. What kind of shit would go and tell her they'd seen her kid in Lágrimas?'

'Ah, Duncan' – Eugene coughed – 'might be someone has.'

50

Duncan turned, gritting his teeth, his spine rotating bone against bone, to see TJ holding out a wrinkled strip of what looked to be black-and-white photographs. She swung it in her fingers, taunting. 'As much as I'd love to hear you say you were wrong about anything, Dupree, I'll settle for an admission that, just this one time, the rest of us may be right.'

Ozzie took TJ by her outstretched wrist and shifted the photographs so that he could see. 'May be right. These two do look familiar but hard to say they're a sure thing; the pix are awful bent up. The kid here does kind of favor our Danny.'

'Bring the pictures here,' said Duncan, rotating his grinding stone of a spine back to forward.

Lucas appeared at Duncan's elbow. 'Hurts a lot today, huh?' he said, working to smooth out the pictures a bit more.

'I've hurt worse,' Duncan said, telling the truth. Lucas pressed his index finger to the bridge of his glasses, pushing the frames against his flesh, and held them there for several seconds, as though he were trying to affix his glasses to his face with contact cement. He did this whenever he was anxious, which was often, and much of the time he carried the reddened imprint of the frames in the space between his eyebrows. It was one of an impressive assortment of idiosyncrasies that had garnered the guy so many competing nicknames that they'd gone back to calling him by his given name as a form of simplifying conversations that invariably went, *'I was talking to Bridges.'* 'Who?' *'Ears?'* 'Who?' *'Princeton? Fish Farmer? Sky Guy? You know, Lucas.'* Duncan rapped the tabletop, indicating Lucas should stop with the fussing and hand over the pictures, which of course he did.

Duncan tilted the strip, trying to get the light to fall around the folds and broken paper, but he saw the likeness of Danny straight off, no denying it. The girl pictured was a piece of tricked-out street trash, and both of them had the dead shark-eyes of dedicated addicts. In the near year that Danny had been living out at the yard, helping Duncan with the off-loading of derelict vehicles, stripping down and cleaning up parts, crushing the remains, in all that time, in all that work, he'd never seen the boy sip, sniff, or snort at anything. There had been none of the empty gestures that haunt the resurrected junkie like the corporeal echoes of old lives. No arguing Danny was troubled and hunkered deep inside the peculiar solace of his junkie-like repetition of lines from Shakespeare's play about shipwrecks and magical storms; *The Tempest* was all Danny had indulged in during the time Duncan had known him. He was damn sure of that. Duncan had, over the year, become as familiar with the threads of sound and meaning in that play as he had once been with the veins in his own arms, his thighs, between his toes.

'You see these two around town?' said Duncan, tossing the photos at Charlie. Charlie squinted, bringing the strip almost up to his nose.

'Just because I didn't see them doesn't mean they weren't here. Somebody placed them two here. Why else tell that poor woman you seen these kids unless it was true? Folks ain't that cruel.'

'Yes, they are. And would you compound that cruelty by leading her to believe her kid had come through here based on nothing but a hunch and some misplaced need to be *kind*?'

'Jesus, Dupree.' TJ snorted her disgust. 'I'm not saying we should have lied to her. But we could have let her know we'd be on the lookout for them. Have her leave a number where we could reach her, just in case. A little bit of encouragement. Would that have been so terrible?'

'If you're encouraging her into some sort of false hope, then, yeah, that could turn out terribly. The woman is looking for tangibles. Today she got one. She's not happy, but she knows where she stands.' He reached out for the photos, but Charlie tucked the photos in the pocket from where he'd taken the Camels. 'Go on, keep them,' Duncan said.

Charlie shook a cigarette out of the pack. 'I suppose any contradicting your worldview is a waste of breathing.'

'And with those unfiltered sticks you suck, you can't be wasting as much as a whisper.' Duncan chuckled until he reached for the cigar he was sure he'd stuck in his own shirt, and found it wasn't there. In his head, he could see exactly where he'd left it on the dashboard, the plastic tube shining in the sun. *Crap.* 'No point in grousing at me, Charlie; the woman's gone.'

'Was I grousing?'

'She's not gone,' said Lucas as he pulled at the top of his ear. 'She's still out in the parking lot. Her car won't start. It's going *whrrrrr-ump, whrrrrr-ump* like it isn't getting enough air to kick over. Can't you hear it?'

Duncan rubbed his thumb against his temple in an attempt to forestall the headache on its way. 'Yeah, Lucas, I hear it. I hear it saying, "Dupree, you are a chump."'

Pete called out from behind the bar, 'Sounds like she must have hit some dust and got herself mucked up.'

'That is indeed what it sounds like,' said Charlie. He stuck the cigarette in the corner of his broad grin. 'Be nice if someone who knew something about the infernal internal-combustion engine went out to give her a hand.'

'Hey, Pete, maybe you should call Gus MacGruder,' said Lucas. 'He'll come over and help her out.'

Christ, even loony Lucas had his number. 'The hell you will.' Duncan spread his already-sweating palms on the table and took a minute to gird his nerve endings for the ordeal of changing postures. In public he fought the pain, forbidding it to transmit its existence into noise or facial expression, and by doing so, managed to forestall the groans and grimacing privacy afforded. Duncan pushed against the table, and with only a small gasp that he tried to guise as a forceful exhale, he stood. He wiped his forehead against his sleeve. 'I'll take a look at her car, dammit. I had to go out anyway. Left my smokes in the truck.'

She had the hood up, and from the way she was standing, head down, shoulders going heave-pause-heave, Duncan could tell she was crying; the lack of sound told him she didn't want anyone to know about it. He could respect that. Fact was, he didn't want to know about it. If he were to sneak up on her in mid-sob, he'd be obliged to ask, and chances were she'd feel obliged to start telling. Only fair to both of them that he give her enough warning to collect herself. He headed for his truck at the end of the lot, whistling tunelessly over the feedback drone of pain, the piper's price for getting him from here to there at what might pass as a healthy man's gait. When he reached the rear end of the rollback, he allowed himself support by bracing his hand against the deck of the flatbed, nearly twenty feet of steel respite, as he made his way to the driver's side of the cab. He unlocked the door, opened it, and then with a technique so practiced it was second nature, he gulped his lungs full, held the air hard, and hands locked on the door frame, he hauled himself up on the running board and into the cab. The cigar was where he had left it, pressed up against the glass of the windshield. He grabbed it and eased himself back onto the parking lot, steeling himself against the pyrotechnics rocketing off his spine. He slammed the truck door with a 'Fuck you, bastard!' bang.

His breathing calmed. He tore open the sun-heated cellophane wrapper, bit and spit out the tip of the cigar, then chewed on the end for a few seconds before taking out his lighter. He puffed – embers flamed through the murky, bourbony smoke – and through the comforting warmth seeping through his chest, feigned gratitude for the questionable fashion in which the pain kept his memory sharp. It was an indifferent god's blessing, all right; pretty much everything in Duncan's life stayed exactly where he expected to find it.

The pleas of her dying engine started up again. He listened, drawing another lungful of smoke and exhaling it into the sky. From the sound of it, she wasn't going anywhere without a minimum of a couple hundred bucks of work. Well, that was something at least. He braced himself against the truck and

54

started out toward where he'd have to face her, red-eyed and voice breaking. He wasn't about to tell her he'd seen the photographs and that he understood these things, because even after all these years, he didn't. In fact, believing he could understand his cravings had only prolonged them, as though each time the needle had spiked his veins he was being asked to solve the riddle of his own existence. He never had the right answer, of course, but each fix had been like another chance at getting it. He had crawled after each additional chance hoping that, should he answer correctly, the question and the cravings would be silenced for good. The crawling had just about killed him off, and then he'd mistakenly crawled into the fist of merciless fate, which after slamming his idiot head into the wall of reality, made it clear, once and for all, the puniness of the question in the first place. The riddle of your existence? Heaven laughed. Hell, son, isn't getting from this hour to the next puzzle enough?

Movement in the side-view mirror caught her eye. He was coming toward the car. *Oh, please, please, just let me get out of here.* She jammed her foot against the gas, wrenched the ignition key forward. The engine responded with a fatigued warble. She tried again, if only to avoid acknowledging the finger tapping at her window. Neither course of action showed much promise. She fell back against the seat. The tapping at the window continued. She took a deep breath, swabbed at her eyes and nose with the heel of her palm, and then ventured a glance at him. He was now leaning against the Thunderbird parked next to her, chomping at a cigar and scowling with impatience. She lowered the window. 'I know. It's flooded.'

'Then you must also know you aren't helping matters any.'

Joyce looked back at the steering wheel.

'Not to mention you're killing your battery.'

'I'm making a lot of mistakes today.'

'And the day is only half done.'

'That's a happy thought.'

'I didn't mean anything by it,' he said, and she could hear him suppressing a laugh. 'I was trying to say you still have lots of time left –'

'I know, plenty of time to screw things up further.'

'That or improve upon the situation.' He pulled the cigar away from his mouth. 'Look,' he said, and she did, only to see he was gazing under the raised hood. 'I'm sorry Danny isn't your kid.'

'I don't think you are all that sorry.' That snagged his attention. He lowered his line of sight and fixed her with a raised-eyebrow stare of annoyed surprise.

'Oh, yeah?'

She tucked her hair behind her ears. *It's not this man's fault, Joyce; for once could you try to leave on better terms than you arrived?* 'Never mind. The last thing I meant to do was trouble anyone.'

'Do I look troubled?'

'It is obvious you don't appreciate my being here.'

He flicked the ashes from the cigar. 'You seem mighty sure of what's going on in my head.'

'And you seem mighty sure of what's going on in mine,' she said, raising an eyebrow of her own. 'I'm out here in the middle of nowhere looking for my son. Your Danny isn't who I'm looking for, I admit it. I made a huge mistake. Is that what you want to hear?'

'An understandable mistake. I'm just looking after the kid's interests, you see? He can't look after himself.'

She smiled at that, but her face felt tight. 'He's lucky then. It's good of you to be so –' She swallowed back the quiver of desperation in her voice. 'I'm sorry I bothered you with my mistakes.'

'Doesn't bother me.' He lowered his head, wagging it as he released a laugh. 'I simply came over here to help you out with your car troubles, but as you seem to be more interested in compounding the problem, I'm happy to leave you to –'

'It was like this when I got out here. I could smell the fumes before I was in the car.'

'So you –'

'Yes, I did. It never occurred to me what the fumes meant. This is a fairly new car. It's supposed to have some kind of computerized fuel-injection thing – the goddamn carburetor is smarter than I am.'

'Your car doesn't have a carburetor. None of the new ones do.'

'Fine. Great. Whatever. How could it flood out just sitting in the parking lot for ten minutes?'

'Under the usual conditions, you'd get this sort of problem after a dust storm.' He stuck the cigar back in his mouth. "Dust blocks the injector, so it can't close up all the way. You end up with a steady drip leaking into the chamber. No way that is going to clear on its own –'

'So, I need a new what? And how much is it going to cost?'

'You might be able to clean out the existing injector, but worst case, you'll need a new one. After that, you have to make sure there's no dust in the lines, no dust on the contacts or in the plugs, make sure dust hasn't settled in the sensors or choked up the intake manifold or worked –'

'In other words, I'm looking at buying another car.'

'In other words, if you don't stop interrupting me I'm never going to be able to tell you what it is you're looking at.'

Joyce nodded. 'I'm listening.'

'You heard the part about the dust storm?'

'Yes.'

'And?'

'And?'

He dragged his index finger over the roof of the car and then showed her the wedge of soft gray powder he'd picked up. 'Were you in a dust storm? Because under the usual conditions, we hear about them – at the very least, we hear about them.'

'It wasn't a storm. I don't think you'd call it storm.' Joyce went on to describe how she'd arrived in Lágrimas: losing her way in the clouds kicked up by the dozens of cars forging the unpaved back road after being detoured from the highway because of the accident –

'How many cars in the pileup?' It was his turn to interrupt. Throughout her telling, she'd noticed him leaning ever closer into the words, his eyes narrowing.

'I don't know. Someone said at least forty. It must have been quite a few to warrant closing down the highway in both directions.'

He grabbed for the clip where the pager should have been and wasn't. 'Both directions?'

'That's what they were saying – I think you left it – your pager? – on the pool table.'

'Did I?' He wondered if she had developed that one, too: the ability to make up for what she could not find by remembering the exact location of every other speck of matter that crossed her view. Perhaps, between the two of them, they could map creation in its entirety. 'Where was the accident? The closest exit? But you wouldn't know the roads around here, would you?'

She didn't get a chance to answer. He bolted upright and smacked the hood of her car with such force that it banged shut. 'Danny!' he hollered as he hurried back toward the bar, 'Danny, let's go! We got a job!'

In less than a minute, he – Duncan, she thought his name was Duncan – and Danny were dashing across the lot toward the flatbed carrier at the end of the line of vehicles. Joyce leaned out the window and watched as Danny, whooping joyously, his arms frenetic in their pumping, managed not to outdistance by a single step his – what? guardian's? employer's? – limping run. She'd seen Duncan's sort of herky-jerky haste before, back at the shipping company, and she knew what it meant for the runner: real pain and no choices. In the place where choices might stand stood instead ex-spouses or bookies or kids with terrible diseases or some other event that had caused the world to split apart into chasms of need that were impossible to fill and yet equally impossible to get beyond. You were trapped either way. She wondered the exact nature of the chasm this Duncan person was caught in. And as she wondered why she was wondering so intently about the situation of this one man, she noticed her right thumb and forefinger working the steering wheel.

Joyce pulled the keys out of the ignition, and, resigning herself to the reality that she wasn't going anywhere for a while, decided it was, at long last, time for a drink.

Five

'Yeah, yeah, I have the location. I heard. How many – hold on a second, Sophie.' Duncan slammed the radio transmitter back into its bracket and lunged across the cab to yank Danny, again, back inside the cab before the fool kid tumbled out the window. Left hand on the wheel, Duncan reached out – swearing at both the kid and the hurt charging along his nerves – and caught the boy's belt, then held on. 'Get back in here!'

Danny didn't hear or pretended not to. He was already near to sitting on the window frame, his hair and clothes whipping about as he threw his arms wide and shouted at the horizon in an attempt to motivate Shakespeare's crew, yet again, through the fearsome and apparently never-ending gale. They were doing close to seventy, and Danny was doing what Danny did when Danny was riled up: *Tempest,* act 1, scene 1, over and over, fast as his tongue could form the words. Since peeling out of the Hoodoo ten minutes earlier, Duncan had lost count of the number of turns through the scene, which seemed to accelerate with every recitation. Duncan, with every inch of his spine railing against the effort, dragged the kid back inside and dropped him on the seat; Danny made for the window again. As tempting as it was to imagine the resulting quiet of the tragedy begging to happen, Duncan would be damned if he was going to waste the time required to scrape up whatever might remain of a tête-à-tête betwixt Danny and the asphalt. He grabbed the kid back one more time. 'Sit still,' he said, his finger punching the air in front of Danny's face.

Danny, his expression one of fearful rapture, grabbed the dash-board with both hands, gaped out the windshield and began again. 'Boatswain!' 'Here, Master. What cheer?' 'Good, speak to the mariners; fall to't yarely, or we run ourselves aground. Bestir, bestir!'

Duncan picked up the transmitter again. 'You still there, Sophie?'

'. . . Heigh, my hearts! Cheerly, cheerly, my hearts! Yare, yare! Take in the topsail! Tend to th' master's whistle! Blow till thou burst thy wind, if room enough!'

'Yare. Yare.' The static broke up Sophie's giggle. 'Over.'

'It's my last nerve, girl. You break it, you've bought it. Over. Danny, shut up!'

'Don't tell him to shut up.' He could hear her earrings – tiny gold hoops, Duncan imagined, ticking against the headset he thought she must wear. 'You ought to be nice to the kid. I got a cousin who was sort of autistic, and it could be a lot worse. Besides, I think it's cool the way he does the different voices. And it's classy, too, the Shakespeare stuff. Over.'

'I'd be happy to have Danny come live with both you and your autistic cousin until you start hearing that classy stuff in your sleep like I do. Water torture on a hot day is still torture, baby, even if the drip-drip is the iced-down miracle juice from Christ's own crypt. Now could you get back to doing your job and give me status out at the site? Over.'

'Hey, you can take your teeth out of my ass, Dupree. It's not my fault I had to give MacGruder the up sign this morning; I am merely one shift of dispatch at Impound, and I'm lucky if I get a say in what goes on top of the next pizza we order. You know, I'm not even supposed to be talking to you. Your name has been crossed off the rotation, which means it's your problem because you went and pissed off the wrong guy – impossible as that is to believe. Over.'

'If you're done whining about the horrors of reaping a regular paycheck, could you please just give me the goddamn status? How many vehicles? Over.'

'Drive the fuck out there and count them yourself. Over. Oh, and once you're done with that, you can go fuck yourself, too. Over and out.'

Duncan pressed the Talk button a couple times – nothing but static. He looked over at Danny who was gesturing his way through another run of the scene, his voice nearly inaudible. 'Classy stuff,' Duncan said as he slipped the transmitter back in the bracket. 'Sophie's a regular Typhoid Mary of Happiness today, isn't she?'

Danny flung his head in a theatrical representation of disgust. 'A pox on your throat, you bawling, blasphemous, incharitable dog!' 'Work you, then.' 'Hang, cur, hang, you whoreson, insolent noisemaker! We are less afraid . . .' And on and on and back around to the beginning.

'That's right,' Duncan said, his words sinking beneath Danny's. 'We are less afraid.'

Joyce pulled herself up on the bar stool farthest from where the trio of drinkers still huddled at the other end. They offered her quick, sad smiles and then went back to watching the television set mounted in the corner. The sound was off; highlight footage from a variety of football games played out across the screen and with every tackle, kick, or completed pass, the three men would shout their approval or dismay, although it seemed they were never in consensus. The owner or cook or whoever he was came in from the kitchen, saw Joyce, and ambled over. He smelled of stale beer and hard work. He tossed a white paper napkin on the bar, and it slid across the black granite counter to stop just in front of her. She straightened it so that *Welcome*, the word printed on the napkin, was right side up and facing her.

He pushed up his sleeves. 'What'll it be?'

'I'm still thinking.'

'Don't think too hard, honey; we ain't one of them city joints. Don't got no blender; don't got no fancy glasses. I got short and I got tall.' He reached under the bar and pulled up a sample of each. 'If you're one of them martini types who can't drink her martini outta a tumbler, you're outta luck. More so, cause I got no vermouth. Haven't had no vermouth round here for almost five months.'

'Out of luck. That's me, all right.'

'You've had a rough one, I'll grant that.' He gave her a look of paternal indulgence and stuck the short glass back under the counter. 'OK, we're going tall.' He filled it with ice cubes and placed the glass on top of the napkin. 'Now what are we going to put in it?'

'I should have some orange juice.' Joyce ran her finger over the chip on the glass's rim. 'I'm getting over a cold and you know, the vitamin C – you know.'

'Hey, I don't care what you drink or why you drink it, so long as you got the cash to pay for it.'

'Cash, I have.'

'Then I have what you want.' He brought a nearly full bottle up from the lower shelf and set it next to her glass. 'Give me a second to scare up some OJ, and you're in business.' He headed back to the kitchen.

Joyce nodded. She studied the label, a densely ornate exercise in Cyrillic script and cartoonish bears. She didn't recognize the brand and was oddly relieved, as though the dive into an anonymous bottle might slip over the transom unremarked; at worst it would be a nostalgic drip of an icy nightmare rather than the failing floodgate of an undiluted hell. A shiver tripped across her shoulders as the chill of drinker's logic took hold.

The waitress bashed through the swinging door. She carried a plastic container of orange-tinted powder, which she placed on the bar next to the vodka bottle. '*Wa-la.*'

Joyce picked up the container, shook it. 'I was waiting for orange juice.'

'And here it is.'

'Is this –'

'Yep.' The waitress filled the glass with vodka. 'The traditional Hoodoo Screw. It's how they get the astronauts into space.' She handed Joyce a spoon.

'But this is California. I thought you had orange trees everywhere –'

'This is the Mojave. It's a desert? No magic orange trees around here.'

'Of course.' Joyce considered the permutations of spoon, powder, and tall glass full of vodka. 'I'll need some water.'

'Between you and me' – the waitress lowered her voice to a conspiratorial hush – 'the vodka's a bit, um, *weak*. You have enough water in your glass right now to irrigate an orchard.' She laughed. 'Oh, and Charlie has your pictures. He's out back having a smoke; he'll be right in.'

'I'm not going anywhere.'

'Neither am I.' TJ leaned on the bar, shrugging her shoulders so that her fluorescent orange curls bunched about her ears. 'Mind if I talk to you about them? The pictures?'

'I don't think I'll be minding much of anything in a few minutes.' Joyce slid the drink powder aside and wrapped her hands around the glass, twisting them into the sweat of condensation, getting a good first grip.

'The last thing I want is to lead you down another dead end, but we' – she tilted her head toward the men at the end of the bar, and they immediately went back to pretending rapt interest in the silent TV – 'we think it's possible that your son and the girl in the picture did come through Lágrimas.'

'What makes you think that?'

'The photographs. Those two look very familiar. We're not sure or anything, but it is possible.'

Joyce found it difficult to meet the frank pity in the young woman's eyes; she looked down at her drink. 'Possible. Yes, I guess it is.' She tightened her hands, squeezing the glass to steady its sudden shaking. The ice cubes shifted. 'Thank you. You're very sweet, but it's all a misunderstanding. They wouldn't have been passing through. He said he'd talked to them; he thought they lived around here.'

The waitress made slight bobbing movements with her head. 'Who is *he*?'

'Just someone who felt he owed me some sort of kindness. You wouldn't know him. He stopped here for lunch a couple weeks ago on his way back east. He said that's when he saw them, here at the Hoodoo. I don't know why I even believed him. His name was Jake something. Poor kid. He'd flunked of out magic school –'

'Oh, my God.' The waitress's eyes went wide. 'I do remember him. I remember. Dove and bunny tricks. Jake, the bad magician.'

Joyce didn't feel the glass shatter. She was only aware that her hands were burning, and she was holding nothing but ice and blood.

The Highway Patrol officers at the roadblock motioned Duncan toward the median where they were gathered around a patrol car, talking. He idled, the truck's engine chugging pleasantly, while he chewed on what was left of his cigar and waited for them to give him clearance to proceed. Danny was declaring, for the fortieth time or so, that all aboard should 'sink with th' King,' his fist raised in exaltation. Duncan focused beyond Danny into the distance where the dust was boiling along the makeshift detour road. Vehicles vanished whole, as though folding into a thick soup. No wonder that woman's car choked. If that's what she put it through, it was going to take more than a couple hundred in parts and labor to get her rolling again. Add that to whatever he could scavenge from the wreckage ahead, and the day might prove worthwhile after all.

The CHP guys were still chatting, laughing it up. They weren't anywhere near moving the cruisers so that he could pass, and they weren't going to indicate he should just off-road around them. They were, goddammit, stalling him out. Some of these officers he knew, not well, but he'd worked with them enough to have established a little two-way professional respect. Professional respect this was not. 'We are definitely on somebody's shit list,' he muttered to Danny, who was at the top again summoning the Boatswain. Duncan rolled down his window and banged on the exterior of the door. Five sets of mirrored sunglasses turned their attention to him.

'Arpel? Is that you?' Duncan tried to force a shade of jolly between his pain and his burgeoning frustration. 'Your wife have that baby yet?' If he could get Officer Arpel away from the pack, get him over to the truck and talking, Duncan might be able to coax some information out of the brother and find out just what the hell he'd done to so completely piss everyone off. Arpel, who was standing with his foot up on the front fender of the cherry-top, said something to the pixieish female officer next to him, and the two laughed. Arpel smiled at Duncan, a bright, fake smile that made him look like a fucking CHP recruitment poster. The smile said Arpel wouldn't come over to talk – wouldn't or couldn't. 'Not right, not right,' Duncan said to Danny, who was ordering invisible men about the invisible besieged ship. 'This just isn't right.'

'Down with the topmast! Yare! Lower, lower! Bring her to try with the main course!'

Damned if I'm about to go begging. 'OK, then,' Duncan called out the window, 'since you don't seem to be needing my services, I'll be heading on back to Lágrimas.' Careful not to flinch through the effort, he rolled up the window, slow and smooth. He put the truck in gear and wheeled it across the median. Headed back in the other direction, he kept checking the rearview, swearing he could still see Arpel's shit-eating grin.

TJ insisted she could handle this one; it wouldn't be necessary to call Doc Freemont. This news seemed to relieve Pete, who seemed to fear the implications of getting the medical establishment involved. 'Anyway, you can't sue me,' he said. 'You can't. Look around you. This is all I'm good for.' He paced the length of the bar while TJ tweezed slivers of glass from the cuts on Joyce's right palm. It stung; reflex compelled her to try yanking her hand away from the sting, but the long-haired man with the scarred face, Eugene was his name, was holding her forearm flush to the bar. TJ plucked. Joyce winced and shot an angry glance at her captor.

Eugene made an exaggerated frown of hurt feelings before he winked. 'Trust me – it's Joyce, right? – trust me, Joyce, watching only makes it worse, so don't.' He moved his head so that it blocked Joyce's view of the procedure. What she saw now was the intricate topography of scar tissue that claimed the right side of his face. He must have sensed the inspection because he said, 'You got two ways to wreck a bike ride real fast: fall over or run into something. I did both.'

'Did both,' said Ozzie as he popped the last bite of yet another candy bar in his mouth and leaned in to watch TJ's work. 'You can also have the fuel tank burst and go fireball on you.'

'I was talking about bikes in general, Oz, not specifically refer-ring to my Hog. But you're right. I did all three.'

Pete's litany continued. 'You can't sue me. It ain't worth it. This is all you'd get. Please.'

'Please. Don't. Stop.' Lucas pressed his frames into his forehead. 'Come on, Pete, like you haven't been looking to dump this place for years. Do us all a favor, ma'am. Sue him and his salmonella back to Oakland. Hey, Charlie.'

Charlie had apparently returned from out back. Joyce couldn't see him, but she could smell the dregs-dull tobacco smoke as he came closer to the bar. 'Who went and hit who?' he said.

'Nobody got hit. Too early for that.' TJ wiped the blood off the tweezers. 'Some of Pete's damn cheap barware exploded. OK, get ready, Joyce; this last one is in there deep.'

Joyce inched forward to see how deep but decided against it and instead scanned the main part of the room, her sight flitting from one thing to another in search of an appropriate diversion:

the slowly rotating ceiling fans, the glut of papers, signs, and photographs cluttering the walls, the grimy grout between the floor tiles, the pool table, the – *count them quick*, twelve wooden tables, each with four wooden chairs – the OUT OF ORDER sign on the jukebox, the OUT OF ORDER sign on the pinball machine . . .

'Got her, Eugene?' said TJ.

Hands at Joyce's wrist and elbow tightened. 'Got her.'

'Sorry about this,' said TJ just as a spike of pain rocketed up Joyce's arm with such ferocity that her stomach rolled in nausea. Sparkly pinpoints danced in her vision, throwing fairy dust everywhere.

'And we're out.' TJ raised the jagged, bloodied shard, still pinched between the tweezers, into the light for Joyce's inspection. 'Now, we just have to bandage you up. You can let her go, Eugene.'

Eugene released his grip and stepped aside. 'You did good.'

Joyce flexed her fingers, making the cuts gape and bleed. None of it, the blood, the throb of insulted flesh, the hand, or even the will to move it felt like it belonged to her. It was as though she had finally, finally drunk herself into a state of exile outside her own skin. But, she hadn't taken so much as a sip. It was this place, this moment in time; it was the knowledge of having missed him by a few dozen hours and the immensity of gratitude that came with the knowledge. She balled her fist, squeezed it, eased it open. The lines in her palm ran red.

'Oh yeah, Joyce, that's helping,' said TJ as she tore open the packaging on a large square bandage. She covered Joyce's palm with the bandage and began wrapping it taut, round and round, with a roll of gauze. Her face took on a cast of uncertainty as she worked; every so often she'd pause to glance up at one of the men who were watching the process as though taking a silent vote. Finally, decision made, she shrugged and sighed and went back to wrapping. 'All right, Joycie, here's my theory. Jake, the bad magician, was here; we're sure of that. I wasted an hour trying to teach him basic bar tricks. Klutzy little dweeb. Good tipper, though. Jake says he is absolutely certain he saw your kid and the *chiquita* at the Hoodoo? I say we believe him. Jake said they live around here? I say we believe him again. That doesn't mean they're locals, mind you; there's a hell of a lot of area around Lágrimas to live in. But all of us thought they looked familiar, right? To me, that says they've been here more than once' – TJ secured the end of the wrapping with tabs of adhesive tape – 'and that means there's a chance they'll be back.'

Joyce examined the bandage, the faint darkening crescents where she still bled. 'What sort of chance?'

'Good chance,' said TJ.

'Decent chance,' said Eugene, in a correcting tone.

'There's also a chance they'll never come in here again?'

Eugene nodded. 'That's the bitch of it. No guarantees. But I'd take the bet that they show. Long as we keep it open-ended. It's not too probable they'll be walking in here this afternoon. They're not regulars. We know that on account of we're the regulars.'

'We're the regulars,' said Ozzie, 'if by regular you mean that except for the salt co-op and the occasional shower, we have no reason to be anywhere but here.' He paused as though he were going to laugh, but didn't. 'You leave us a way to reach you, and when they show up, we'll sit on them 'til you get here.'

Charlie came over and pulled the strip of photographs from his pocket. He laid them down on the bar beside the towel, which was smeared with red and scattered with the pieces of glass TJ had extracted from Joyce's hand. 'If you could bear to leave these pictures with us, darlin', it may further the cause.' Joyce stared at the images of her son and Maddie; the crumpled paper lent a monstrous quality to them both.

'I can't,' she said, almost to herself.

'Well, that's fine. I understand. Perhaps you could see fit to send us –'

'No. I can't leave. My car is kaput. I couldn't drive anyway with my hand like this, well, not for a while. It's not like I have some-place else I have to be.' She looked up at the ceiling fans, letting them dizzy her into a decision. 'It's my birthday,' she said, feeling as though an explanation was required. Joyce pushed herself off the bar stool. The room felt floaty, insubstantial, as though the Hoodoo and its inhabitants were part of an uncoalesced dream. 'I left my purse in the car.'

'We got it, darlin'. Don't you worry about the tab.'

'Speak for yourself,' said TJ. 'I saved her a trip to Larkin Emergency. Gratuities are in order.'

Joyce gestured that they'd misread her exit. 'I've got cash.' She reached the door but turned back. She sought out Pete, and as the gates of possible escape crashed shut around her, she smiled. 'All of it,' she said, speaking loud enough to be heard over the din of collapsing options inside her head. 'How much do you want for all of it?'

The drive back to Lágrimas had been one long, repetitive invent-ory of outright missteps and potential misunderstandings, but compartmentalize and tally as he might, Duncan couldn't identify any act grievous enough to get himself blacklisted.

'My permits, my fees are all up to date and in order,' he said, tapping at the stickers on the windshield. 'Can't be the bureaucratic shit. Must be political, right?' Danny, who had fallen into a sulk, kept grumpily mumbling the contemptuous rants of magic-blighted Caliban.

'This island's mine by Sycorax my mother, which thou tak'st from me. When thou cam'st first, thou strok'st me and made much of me; wouldst give me water with berries in't; and teach me how to name the bigger light, and how the less, that burn by day and night; and then I loved thee . . .'

'Yeah, I know.' Duncan talked over Danny's grumbling, because there would be no shutting him up. 'But you are no more pissed to be coming back empty than I am, believe me. Giving my place on the rotation to MacGruder is a statement. That much I'm sure of. Why the guessing games? Why don't they just come out and say it? Hell, Impound told me that MacGruder hasn't gotten a call in close to three years; no one trusts the bastard – parole boards be damned. Why today? Why him instead of me?'

'. . . and here you sty me in this hard rock, whiles you do keep from me the rest o' th' island.'

'Well, you can't fix a thing when you don't know where it's broken. That's all I'm saying.' They had reached the edge of Lágrimas's dry lake. Duncan wanted to make straight for the yard, get on the horn, and find someone willing to read aloud to him from whatever page in the *Big Book of Entrepreneurial Screwups* might be applicable to his situation. But his education would have to wait long enough to make a quick run by the Hoodoo to scoop up Vermont's dust-plugged Saturn. Monetarily at least, the day wouldn't be a total write-off. He might recoup enough for the rollback's fuel, and some groceries. She was probably good for a lot more than that . . .

'If I weren't such an ethical idiot,' he said, gritting his teeth against the hot-tempered scolding of his spine as he worked the steering wheel through the turn into the Hoodoo's lot. More turning, more grousing, he turned the truck so that the rollback mechanism, when rolled back, would hit the gravel right at the rear wheels of the disabled Saturn. This brought the truck's front grill almost edge-on with the Hoodoo's tiny front patio. Satisfied with the position, he threw the shift into Park and sat, breathing, waiting for the pain to subside enough to move on to the next phase of the operation. He kept his hands tight on the wheel and stared hard out the windshield at the Hoodoo's front door. The protests of muscle, nerve, and bone began to fade to an angry mutter. It was then he noticed something was missing, from the building. The FOR SALE sign had been taken down, leaving behind only a rectangle of darker coral paint. Pete had relettered that thing only a couple weeks ago; why would he – Duncan looked in the side-view mirror at the backward VERMONT lettered in white on the green license plate. He looked at the ever-blathering Danny whose thin face was now flush with an aggravated emotion Duncan could appreciate.

'What does she think she's doing?'

Danny was jabbing at himself, pointed fingers into his own chest. 'You taught me language, and my profit on't is, I know how to curse. The red plague rid you for learning me your language!'

'We're going to get ourselves rid of something, all right.' Duncan killed the engine. 'Let's round up this loony broad and get her back on the road.'

Six

The Hotel was the largest building in what the locals called downtown Lágrimas. It was a two-story structure with a covered porch that ran the breadth of the building's front. The white paint on its clapboards was wind-worn, exposing dove-gray patches of weathered wood. Only the red neon of the VACANCY sign in the front window betrayed the illusion of long-gone Wild West legends and brought her to this present of exhausted confusion. Joyce stood in the shade of the porch, suitcase in her good hand.

She had watched the rollback diminish into the distance, her Saturn piggybacking along for the ride. He was going to take it out to his garage, give it a look, give her a call. It was about all he'd said to her in what she believed to be the longest five minutes in the history of timekeeping: the five minutes it took to drive – Duncan, Danny, Joyce, and Joyce's suitcase, all squished together in the cab – to the Hotel. Duncan was making no effort to veil his unhappiness with the change of ownership at the Hoodoo. Although it was beyond Joyce why he should be so perturbed, he spoke to her in minimal syllables and only in response to requests for information. Even making allowances for the discomfort she assumed he was managing, he had been more than distractedly curt; he had been angry.

'How long do you think it will take to repair my car?'

'Can't say.'

'Are you the mechanic who's going to do it?'

'I am not a mechanic.'

And this before they'd even hauled the car up the inclined deck, a procedure accomplished by Danny's enthusiastic scrambling about as he pulled the cable from the winch behind the truck cab and hooked it to the Saturn's undercarriage. The audience of Eugene and Charlie shouted instructions that Danny showed no sign of hearing. Duncan supervised silently, his lips clamped over the end of a cigar. No matter where she stood, she couldn't escape the odor of the smoke; it was making her head pound. She hoped that he would extinguish the hateful thing before the ride into town, but she was not about to make a request that was guaranteed to be refused.

Of course, when they piled into the cab, Danny shoehorned in between them, Duncan didn't put the cigar out, didn't put the window down. Once they were under way, she'd started to crank her own window open, and he'd barked at her.

'Don't.'

She assumed he didn't understand that she simply could not breathe; she went ahead and lowered it anyway, at which point Danny scrambled across her lap to hang out the window and bellow courtly orders to sailors on a sinking ship. It took Duncan's pulling and Joyce's pushing to get the boy back in the vehicle and seated again.

'Why?' she'd said, still panting from wrestling the deceptively strong frail-framed kid. 'Why does he do that?'

'What?'

'We split, we split! – Farewell, my wife and children! – Farewell, brother . . .'

'That. Why does he do that?'

'Because *that* is what he does.'

Other than the terse instruction to wait for his call, the rest of the three-mile ride consisted of Duncan's smoking, Joyce's willing herself not to retch from the smell of it, and Danny's robust *performance* – no other word for it – of what sounded to be a shipwreck involving multiple characters.

*   *   *

76

The Hotel's lobby was a sunny, crowded space of mismatched furnishings cluttered with children's toys. The air was sharp with the garlicky and peppered aromas of a recent meal. Joyce waited at the front desk, called out 'hello' a couple of times, and finally gave herself permission to do as the sign on the counter suggested. She tapped at the domed bell with her bandaged hand, gently, until it rang. She waited, reading the names – pen on masking tape – under each pigeonhole of the mailbox behind the desk. She waited a bit longer and rang the bell again.

A door banged at the rear of the building, followed by the sound of hurried steps. An angular woman in dark braids came in apologizing, brushing dust off her hands and onto her tiered denim skirt. She wiped at her face as though fearing dust had caught in the fine lines left there by sun and time. She had been out back, she explained, at a funeral; they'd lost a puppy a couple hours earlier, and her children were channeling their sadness into rites befitting the death of a king.

'How many kids do you have?' Joyce tried to make conversation as the woman bent straight from the waist and cleaned off the pointed toes of her boots.

'I stopped counting at five,' she said, lifting herself back to vertical with the grace of a dancer. She said that her name was Rachel, and before Joyce could return the introduction, Rachel announced that she already knew of Joyce, mother of a lost son, driver of a sick car, new owner of the Hoodoo Bar and Grill.

'It seemed like a good idea at the time,' said Joyce. 'It's about my son. Just a hunch – nothing is finalized, you know.'

'Tell that to Pete. Or rather, don't tell that to Pete. He'll try to throw himself off the water tower. Again.'

Instead of expanding on that detail, Rachel went into what sounded like an oft-repeated description of the Hotel as more of a boardinghouse most frequented by itinerant youth who'd work the salt co-op for a few weeks to earn a bit of cash and then move on. For that reason, rooms were let by the week or the month. Rent included kitchen privileges but no meals unless you were sick or Rachel found you pitiable for other causes, which she did not list. Given Joyce's unique situation, however, they could come up with a day-to-day deal, as it shouldn't take Pete more than twenty-four hours to pack up his few belongings and vacate the apartment at the bar.

'There's an apartment at the Hoodoo?'

Rachel blinked. 'You mean you bought the place without looking around?'

'Nothing's finalized.'

'Do you know anything about the restaurant business? About business at all?'

Joyce, in increasing horror at her foolishness, could only imperceptibly shake her head.

'Christ.' Rachel laughed, but not unkindly.

'I'm not bound to anything. There's a three-day back-out clause; buyer's remorse. I'll go back later and tear up the offer.'

'You put it in writing?'

'I wrote a number on a cocktail napkin.'

'Solid as a contract with Satan in these parts. Tearing it up would be the rational act – if you can get it out of Pete's paws,' she said, still laughing as she slipped a key from one of the mailbox bottom sections. 'I'll pile up some mattresses under the water tower. Hope you don't take this the wrong way, but to go and buy the Hoodoo without even looking at it – that's something only one of us would do.'

'What's that supposed to mean?'

Rachel spun the key chain around on her finger. 'No one ends up here in Lágrimas by way of good decisions. So, Joyce, my friend, welcome home.'

The room was spare but comfortable, outfitted with a bed, bureau, and desk in the same mix-and-match thrift-store style as the lobby. She had a tiny private bathroom but no phone; only the long-term boarders had access to the telephone rooms for which they paid a premium. She was, Rachel told her, free to use the telephone downstairs. The room was situated on the second floor, in the front corner of the building. She had windows on each of the exterior walls. The plank floor had a subtle slope that lent the impression of walking downhill toward the open windows, which were tall and narrow and covered in yellowed shades with tasseled pulls. Joyce raised the shades farther and looked out onto the town, if it could be called that.

Four sun-beaten automobiles lined up single file in front of the building across the street, some kind of general grocery. Faded paper banners in the windows announced special pricing on hamburger and bread as well as new hours for the post office. Up against the building was a bank of locked mailboxes like she'd seen set up at condo and apartment complexes. Next to the store was a gas station with three rust-stained pumps in front of a white cinder-block cube with one huge picture window. A small satellite dish for television signals angled off the back of the roof. Joyce could see a vending machine for soda radiating cool blue light in the otherwise dark building. A bit beyond the gas station lay a hodgepodge of a trailer park with more satellite dishes, cinder blocks, and sun-dulled metal. She could see laundry flapping on sagging clotheslines and every so often, small children dashing about. Rachel had told her about the coin laundromat on one side of the Hotel and the hardware store on the other side. The water tower, which stood behind the Hotel, cast a giant daddy longlegs–spider shadow onto the road where Joyce knew it would inch longer as the afternoon wore on, as though trying to sneak unseen out of town. Who could blame it? Lágrimas proper had so little to recommend it that the locals might waylay errant monsters if only for the questionable entertainment in provoking the odd and the dangerous.

She became aware of the aching pulse in her hand. No wonder – she had clenched her fists again. She uncurled and wriggled her fingers. The bandage was no more spotted than earlier; the bleeding had stopped.

'At least I didn't drink,' she said to herself. The pain climbed in degree as though to underscore the larger reality: *No, you astounding idiot, you tried to buy the entire bar. Rip up the offer. Plead yourself insane. Get out of here before –*

A sudden, muted bang made her jump. It was a backfire, that was all, she told herself as she held her injured hand to her chest, feeling her heart skitter back toward a normalized rhythm. She surveyed the street, looking for the source of the sound. None of the cars in front of the grocery had moved; no vehicles at the gas station. Nothing moving or threatening to move on the main street, the only street of Lágrimas. The bang sounded again, closer this time. She leaned against the window glass and saw a truck speeding into town. Fingers of blue exhaust trailed up behind it. Another backfire popped. The truck, a rust-colored old wrecker, whizzed past the Hotel. *There must be an accident somewhere,* thought Joyce as she lowered the shade once more. Odd that there should be more than one auto business in a place this size. The wise thing, the *good* decision, would be to contact this other guy – MacGruder had been the name painted on the truck's door – after she got the estimate from Duncan. A second opinion might save her some money. She hoped Duncan wouldn't be offended by the notion, but too bad if he was. He was a businessman, and this was just business. She didn't owe him a thing.

It was then that she remembered she'd left the bird's-eye maple box filled with talismans in the glove compartment. She could see it happen, see him rummaging for the manual, see the box tumble forward, see the secrets spill. Joyce was seeing her secrets rush away from her as she left the room and rushed downstairs to find the phone.

After they let the woman off at the Hotel, Danny fell into one of his rare quiet moods where, although still – always – running lines from the play, he only mouthed them, his lips working silently except for the deep whistling inhales of air required for some of the longer speeches. Duncan, grateful for peace, suspended his red-alert vigilance over the kid for the first time that day. He stubbed out his cigar in the ashtray and just drove. Four and seven-tenths miles lay between the hotel and the dirt road that took them to the scrap yard. Dust devils spun like ghostly tops along the roadside, held back from crossing by the force of sun-heated air rising off the asphalt. Far overhead, scavenging ravens rode the thermal drafts that allowed them to hunt carrion without the energy expense of flapping their wings. The weed and brush dotting the hardscrabble earth looked particularly brittle to Duncan, as though it were desiccated down to the root. He feared the first good storm would strip the soil of what remnants of life it now supported. It wasn't true, he told himself, but he feared it anyway. He put both hands on the wheel and let the droning roar of his shifting bones drown out the trepidation.

Danny shifted, too, so that his back rested against the door. He pulled his feet up on the seat, dragging dirt across the vinyl upholstery as he adjusted them for comfort. Duncan smacked the kid in the calf. 'Feet on the floor, Daniel.' Danny made a harumphing sound of displeasure but complied. Duncan swept at the dirt, trying to corral it into a pile before herding it back to the floorboard. He noticed Danny was peeking at something clutched tight in his hand.

'Give it up.'

Danny pulled it out of reach.

It was going to be like that, was it? 'Don't you growl at me, boy. I want to see what's in your hand. Right now.' Duncan flashed him a stern look.

Danny withdrew into the farthest corner of the cab and cracked his grip an inch to reveal his treasure: Vermont's strip of photographs.

'How the hell is she going to find her kid if she can't even keep up with his damn pictures? How did you – That's not yours, Danny.' He glanced over at the boy; Danny was back in rapt study of the much-abused scrap of pictures. Duncan would be the last in line to volunteer he had an inkling as to what was happening in this kid's head, but the way he was staring betrayed more than idle interest. 'They're not pictures of you, Danny,' Duncan said, softening his tone in deference to the boy's confusion. 'It isn't you, if that's what you're thinking.'

Danny sighed. He spoke to the photograph, low, beseeching: 'Admired Miranda! Indeed the top of admiration, worth what's dearest to the world! Full many a lady I have eyed with best regard, and many . . .'

'The girl? That's what you're stuck on?' The sign for the scrap yard came into view; Duncan slowed the rollback, more mindful of Danny than the left turn he'd made maybe ten million times. 'They're not pictures of you, and that is not your girlfriend. No Miranda. No admired. Got that?' Danny's posture had not altered, but he was staring out the windshield. Duncan followed his line of sight. His foot squeezed the brakes, and he brought the rollback to a dead halt in the middle of the road, mere feet from the driveway to his home and business. He sat there for a long time considering the view. But that wasn't going to get the question answered, so he pushed open the door. He climbed, slow, stiff, out of the truck – 'Stay here, Danny' – and forced himself across the road to touch the reality he hoped he wasn't seeing.

The signboard, shimmying in the wind, had been spray-painted over in slapdash strokes of still-wet and dripping red so that Duncan's careful lettering of LÁGRIMAS SALVAGE AND SCRAP had been almost obliterated. It appeared that an attempt had been made to hatchet through the two-by-six posts to which the sign was bolted, but for whatever reason, the ax man had relented. Duncan's mailbox had proved a more achievable target, and it lay toppled, the sheet-metal box battered until nearly flat. The red flag was up. He walked over to where it lay and squatted next to it – his back crying for mercy. The hinges on the mailbox door had been smashed close to unworkable, but with one good yank, the whole door came clean off.

An envelope had been shoved into the box. He worked it free from the folds of metal. The envelope was not sealed and bore no address. It contained a greeting card, an old one you'd have to search out in the bins at a thrift shop. The illustration was in the style of thirty or more years earlier, a sugar-and-spice girl child blowing soap bubbles from a wand as her stuffed toy rabbit looked on. A rollicking script announced that the sender was 'Wishing You Happiness on Your Special Day.' He opened it. On the inside was glued a small square of yellow note paper with large block printing: LOWER THAN A HORSE THIEF.

Duncan inhaled hard and shielded his eyes. Up the road he could see the matte sheen of afternoon sun on the dead metal sea of the scrap yard, a little more than a mile from where he stood. It was most likely safe to continue, he reasoned. If they – whoever they were – had set out to ambush him on his own ground, they surely would not have left him this warning of their presence on his front doorstep. Duncan heaved his groaning body back to vertical and read the card again before ripping it into several pieces and giving them to the wind.

He hobbled back across the road to the rollback and – breathe, brace, pull – swung himself back into the cab. 'We may have some trouble,' he said to Danny.

Danny nodded. 'My master through his art foresees the danger that you, his friend, are in, and sends me forth – for else his project dies – to keep them living . . .'

'I appreciate your wanting to help here, Danny, but I'm going to need you to stay –'

The pitch of Danny's voice slid up an octave as he sang: 'While you here do snoring lie, opened-eyed conspiracy his time doth take. If of life you keep a care, shake off slumber and beware. Awake, awake!'

'Stay awake. That's the plan,' said Duncan as he put the truck in gear. He made the turn toward the yard and whatever might be waiting for them there.

Seven

'You can try,' said Rachel as Joyce dialed the number. Rachel
used the remote to mute the volume on the lobby's TV so that
Joyce could better hear the telephone. Joyce counted twenty rings
and let it go on ringing uncounted more times before giving
up.

'No one's there,' she said, hanging up the receiver.

'Not necessarily.' Rachel pushed at the buttons on the remote,
cycling through the channels on the still-muted television. 'Duncan
is – how shall I put this? – employing an unorthodox business
model.'

'He doesn't answer his phone?'

'Oh, he'll answer, but only if you're calling at a time he's speci-
fied. Otherwise, he calls you.' She settled on a station broadcasting
footage of wildfire leaping up a hillside. The flames lapped at the
stilt supports of houses jutting out into midair. The image changed
to that of an attractive blond newscaster wearing too much eye
makeup. A caption came up on the screen beneath her: ARSONIST
STILL AT LARGE. Rachel made a *pffft* noise of dismissal, and said,
'Because without help, the mountains wouldn't burn every year,
anyway?'

The screen door at the Hotel's entrance creaked open. TJ came
in, followed by Lucas. Both of them carried cardboard cartons
printed with a line drawing of a tear blossoming into a rose. Over
the drawing curved an arch of words: LA FLOR DE LÁGRIMAS. TJ's
stilettos ticktocked her across the floorboards to the front desk.

She hefted her carton, bottles rattling inside, onto the counter and laughed. 'Your salt delivery, ma'am.'

Lucas stacked his carton on top of TJ's. 'Invoice is in this one.'

'Grand,' said Rachel through a good-humored sneer. 'Now I'm all set for the notoriously busy salt season. How much will the co-op charge me to stop sending this stuff over?'

'You ask that every time,' said Lucas.

'And I'll keep asking –'

'Excuse me,' said Joyce, trying to address her immediate concern. 'I have to get in touch with Duncan. I left something in my car. Something I need.'

'You'll never get him to pick up,' said TJ as she rubbed the back of her head. 'You want to go out to the yard? I can run you out there.' She yanked at her scalp and pulled the entire mass of orange curls free. She shook out the wig and ran her fingers through her peat-brown hair until the wig-flattened strands loosened to hang lank and sweat-damp against her neck. 'Give me a second to clean up, and we'll go.'

Before Joyce could get far enough beyond her surprise to express her thanks, the girl had kicked off her heels and was bounding up the stairs.

'TJ's your neighbor,' said Rachel as she tore the tape off the top carton. 'Couple doors down the hall from you.'

'Oh.'

Rachel laughed. 'The wig? TJ has a theory – TJ has lots of theories. This one holds that in isolated establishments such as the Hoodoo, where the same folks show up day after day, a new wait-ress makes better tips simply on the power of her novelty. That's why every couple of weeks, TJ becomes a "new" waitress.' Rachel started unpacking the bottles – tall, narrow cylinders with a Mason jar-type metal clamp over the lid. A small pamphlet was tied to the clamp with a red string. 'Whether you buy into the theory or not, she's doing something right, because the girl is pulling down enough with that one job for rent here, plus a car, plus tuition.'

'She's a student? Of what?' said Joyce.

'Law,' said Rachel as she went to work on the next carton.

An electronic chirping sound started close by. It was coming from Lucas, who was standing beside Joyce. He lifted his left wrist to show her it was a signal from his watch. He didn't shut it off, only sighed and said, 'The fish would need to eat now.' He went to sit in front of the silent pictures of the inferno unfolding over the television screen.

Joyce turned her confusion to Rachel, who smiled and continued unpacking the salt bottles. 'I don't know because I don't ask. Anyone. Anything. Ever. I don't ask why people show up in Lágrimas; I don't ask why they leave; and I certainly don't ask why they choose to stay. I take it on faith that everyone – *everyone* – who ends up here is here for a reason. Would you look at the dust?' She held up a bottle of salt to the lengthening shafts of afternoon light and flicked a cloth at the lid. A stream of particles fountained into the light, swirling, slowing, drifting away on unseen currents like newborn stars.

'How's that hand?' said TJ.

'It hurts.'

'I bet.' TJ steered her Thunderbird out of its parking spot with her right wrist slumped over the wheel. She had taken off her makeup and twisted her hair up with pins and a clip so that it sprung like plumage off the back of her head. She wore jeans and a sweatshirt emblazoned with *UCLA* in letters faded from many washings. 'Sorry the car is such a mess,' she said as she slipped on a pair of night-dark glasses.

'I appreciate the ride,' said Joyce, trying to find a place to settle her feet amid the empty diet-soda cans, french-fry boxes, and notebooks. The dashboard was strewn with Post-it notes scrawled with names and phone numbers and the www-dots of Internet addresses. 'Do you have to commute all the way into Los Angeles for school? Rachel told me –'

87

'Rachel tends to shorthand information.' TJ hit the accelerator, and the car gave an almost joyous shudder as it sped up. 'I'm getting an associate's certificate as a paralegal through an on-line distance-learning deal, and *then* I'm going to get myself out of ol' Grim Ass and into a job at one of the big firms in L.A. and have them foot the cost of my J.D. at UCLA. Then I'm going to be rich. Happy ever after all the way round. What are you smiling at?'

'You remind me of someone – never mind. It's wonderful that you have plans. I hope it all works out the way you want it to.'

'Why wouldn't it?' TJ glanced over, her expression one of authentic curiosity.

'Things happen,' said Joyce. 'Life happens.'

'I know. Isn't it great?' TJ double-clutched the next shift, and the car jolted into the next gear. Faster.

They whipped past the trailer park, and Joyce glimpsed a couple of the children, golden in the late light, playing chase among the windblown shadows cast by sheets on the line. Beyond them the blue of the sky had deepened in shade and distance. The day was folding down into evening. She felt suddenly desperate to not talk anymore about the future; she chanced another wholly unpleasant topic. 'This Duncan person seems very angry with me.'

'He does? Yeah, well, I guess it would look that way to the uninitiated. I've developed a tolerance for him.' She broke into a throaty laugh at some private joke. 'Here's the basic rundown on Duncan Dupree: Get beneath that abrasive, ill-tempered demeanor, and you'll discover, in actuality, one abrasive, ill-tempered human being. Charlie says Duncan, on a good day, has all the charm of a short-circuiting cattle prod. It's not only you; Duncan is like that with all of us, all the freakin' time.'

'All except Danny.'

'Ah, but Danny isn't one of *us*. OK, Duncan may have been particularly hard-assed this morning. My theory is that his dander was up because you are a blunt-trauma reminder that somebody out there does have a legal claim to Danny, and someday that somebody might roll into town. Although if Duncan were to ask me – and he won't – considering the conditions in which he found Danny, I doubt the asshole responsible for the kid would have the nerve to show himself, but with assholes you never – Uh-oh.' TJ slowed the car. A signboard strafed with trails of red paint stood beside a rutted dirt roadway to their left. TJ cranked down her window as though the glass might be interfering with her vision. 'OK. This isn't good,' she said as she made the turn and cranked up her window before the dust got in.

'What's wrong?' said Joyce, eyeing the felled mailbox and the hacked stub of a post they were passing on the right side of the road.

'Probably nothing; kids from the trailer park found a can of spray paint or something like that.' TJ let the car roll forward, tapping the gas only enough to keep them moving slowly toward the acreage of abandoned vehicles up ahead. 'But the local brats know better than to provoke Duncan. So what's this mean? I'm not sure.'

'Maybe we should come back another time?'

'We have to see if Duncan and Danny are all right,' TJ said. She leaned over the steering wheel as though she might have spotted something, then she settled back in her seat.

Joyce became aware of pressure in her right foot and realized her foot was jammed against the floor, trying to bring the car to a stop. She willed it to release, and in doing so, bumped a pile of cans. The cans tumbled about with a tinny racket that made Joyce straighten with a start.

TJ noticed. 'You're scared?'

'Maybe. A little.'

'That's good. Frightened people pay attention.'

Joyce tried to swallow but found her mouth and throat had gone dry. 'Pay attention to what?'

TJ bobbed her head and the plumage of her hair bounced. 'It's obvious Duncan has secrets, and as Charlie says, a man with secrets is a man with enemies. What kind of secrets? The betting line down at the Hoodoo is that he's killed someone or stolen something and he's hiding out in Lágrimas until the heat blows over. But that's crazy; his money depends on keeping in close touch with the Highway guys. Hide in plain sight might work for party games, but it outright sucks as tactical defense. My theory is that he's in some witness-protection deal. It's the only explanation that makes sense. You have this smart, educated man who's managing the aftermath of some terrible injury –'

'His back? From the way he walks, I thought it might be his back.'

'Yeah, his back, but no one knows what happened there; secret number one. So you've got this smart, educated, mysteriously injured man who decides Lágrimas – *Lágrimas* – is the only option he has. That's suspicious in itself. Now, once in Grim Ass, smart, educated man bunkers himself out in a scrap yard with a variety of firearms he is actually trained to use. He's a pro, Joyce. Add to that the fact he answers his phone only by appointment; he answers personal questions never. He keeps a police scanner next to his bed, but he never sleeps. As one of my professors would say, "What defensible assumptions can we make from the evidence presented?"'

'Maybe we ought to go find some help?' Joyce searched the view of flat, stubbled terrain for an indication of where quick assistance might come from.

'We are help.' TJ leaned over and pulled an automatic pistol from under her seat and slid the magazine clip into place by hitting it against her thigh. She looked over at Joyce. 'Don't worry. I know what I'm doing.'

'One of us should.' Joyce blinked, disbelieving. The yard was only a few hundred feet off. She could see her Saturn up on the flatbed of the truck, which had been parked – both of the cab doors flung wide – off to the right of a sort of garage building. The three bay doors of the garage were partially raised, revealing only shadow behind them. Any other view of the building's interior, what would have to be the office, was blocked from sight by the closed slats of the venetian blinds over the windows. Off the right side of the building, a good thirty feet away and down a slight slope, was a mobile home with faded green siding and white shutters at the windows. It was raised off the desert floor on a foundation of cinder blocks. On the other side of the garage, set somewhat behind the building, stood a massive piece of machinery painted school-bus yellow. The front of the thing was a massive rectangular plate on which the stenciled label EZ-Crusher offered a pithy explanation of what the machine did. A short-necked crane sat next to the crusher. The claw device that dangled from the crane's cable swung in the wind like the hook on one of those grab-the-prize games that were impossible to win. The prizes here lay as row upon row of dusty, derelict automobiles slouching on wheel hubs stripped of tires.

TJ rolled the Thunderbird up directly behind the truck and cut the engine. 'First we wait,' said TJ, almost in a whisper. She had the pistol pointing up, her left hand bracing her right wrist as she looked from side to side. 'We wait to see if Neb's around.'

Joyce wriggled down in her seat, trying to get out of the woman's line of sight as well as her line of fire. 'Neb?'

'Nebuchadnezzar. The dog. Big, fucking mean, feral shepherd that roams around Lágrimas.'

'You're going to shoot a dog?'

'If I have to – Oh, don't go all Humane Society on me. It's not a pet. It's feral. The dog *eats* rattlesnakes, Joyce. I'm not making this up; Neb has a kind of immunity to rattler venom. But it's made him loco. He's eaten so many snakes that venom is chugging through his psychotic doggie system; it's in his saliva. A minor bite, hell, one smacky doggie kiss, and you're hauling ass for the nearest antivenin outlet. Bad enough the poison fried his brain, but it also paralyzed Neb's vocal cords, so he can't bark or growl anymore. You can't hear him coming until it's too late. The dog shows, I shoot.' TJ nodded in assent to herself. 'Fortunately, it's never come to that.'

'This is ridiculous. I don't believe any of this.'

'Belief is not a prerequisite for how things work around here.' TJ twisted around to check out the back window. 'Neb should have heard us by now. Must be off hunting or someone else has already capped him.' She cracked open her door and called. 'Neb!'

'You're calling it?'

TJ shushed her. 'I want Duncan to hear my voice so he knows we're around and that he needs to look twice before he starts shooting. Hey, Neb! Here, boy! Come see me, baby! Come see Tequila Jane.' She pushed the car door open with her foot and stepped out onto the dirt. With the pistol raised to her shoulder, TJ stalked toward the garage bays in steady, measured steps. Halfway there, she pivoted back toward the Thunderbird, her head cocked. 'You coming, Joyce?' TJ all but yelled her name.

Joyce quickly polled the few remaining centers of her better sense and shook her head hard. TJ shrugged, and said, 'Your choice, but statistically *inside* a car's not the best place to be in situations where crossfire is a possibility.' She grinned. Joyce's better sense rendered its earlier poll unacceptable; votes were recast. She found the door handle.

The cab of the rollback provided no information. 'But they left it in a hurry, right?' said Joyce. 'The doors are still open. They were in a hurry.'

TJ laughed beneath her breath. 'Nice try, Nancy Drew. The doors are open because Duncan wouldn't want to risk the sound of closing them. Let's check out the office.'

Joyce glanced at the tightly shut blinds pressed flush again the window. 'I'm not sure that's a good idea.'

'We can't decide that until after we've done it. Try to relax, Birthday Girl. I have studied.' TJ, pistol in a double-handed grip, sidestepped toward the office door, tilting her head to indicate Joyce should follow.

Joyce crept close behind TJ, trying to remember the seemingly centuries-ago conversation with the girl. 'You said *paralegal*, right?' she whispered, as they continued forward. 'Not *para-military*.'

'Have you been to a courthouse lately?' she whispered back.

'They have you take classes for this?'

'No, silly. I learned this like everyone else does. On television.' TJ grinned over her shoulder, and Joyce saw herself twice reflected in the sunglasses.

'You're joking. Please tell me you are joking,' said Joyce. TJ giggled.

They reached the door, taking a position to the right of the plain steel panel with its gray factory finish. Joyce flattened herself against the cinder-block wall and tried to get some control over her breathing. She watched out the corner of her eye as TJ palmed the doorknob. 'Locked,' she said. TJ fished a bobby pin from her hair. She bent the pin between her teeth and after a few seconds of jiggling it in the lock, a click sounded. TJ withdrew, waiting, gun ready. When nothing happened, she said, 'It's clear.'

'You're sure?'

She reached over and pushed the door so that it opened slightly. 'I am now. Your basic bad guy would have shot at that in a second. But just in case . . .' TJ jumped in front of the door, shuffled a few steps to build up momentum, and fired a roundhouse kick into the steel panel that sent the door flying wide. She fell to one knee on the threshold, arms rigidly sweeping the gun in an arc through the darkness. Slowly, her arms loosened. She stood, bounced on her toes, and turned, grinning at Joyce. 'I told you.'

Joyce saw the shotgun barrel sliding past the door jamb before she realized what she was seeing, and before she could even whimper a warning to TJ, the muzzle was resting on the skin of the young woman's temple. At the contact of gun metal to flesh, TJ flinched and went rigid. 'Hey, Duncan.'

The barrel lowered. Duncan came out of the office. He reached down and pulled the automatic out of TJ's hand. 'Cortez, you are not only dead at this point; you died embarrassed at your own stupidity.'

TJ yanked her sunglasses off her face. 'I wasn't that inept.'

'Yes, you were.' He tucked the pistol in his waistband, glowered at her, and then turned the glower to Joyce. 'I said I'd call, didn't I?'

Joyce, on the verge of hyperventilation, gulped at the air and nodded.

'My car. I left something.'

He pursed his lips and nodded. He called back toward the garage. 'Danny!'

Danny ducked out from under one of the bay doors. He trotted over, his color high and his eyes huge and shiny with excitement. Danny went into his sweep of a bow but was forestalled in midbend by Duncan's hand against his forehead. 'I will be correspondent to command and do my spiriting gently,' Danny said to Duncan's boots.

'The lady wants something from her car. Climb on up there and fetch – What is it?'

'A small wooden box in the glove compartment. It's rather fragile. I'd feel better if you'd let me get it.'

Duncan pushed Danny back to upright. 'Danny knows how to be careful –'

'But does he even understand –'

'That was English he was speaking, wasn't –'

'Of course I recognized it as English. What I meant was –'

'Again with the interruptions. Do you interrupt everyone like this?' He turned to TJ. 'Does she do this to you?'

TJ slitted her eyes, cocked her head as she chewed on the stem of her sunglasses. 'You know, Duncan, I haven't noticed.'

He pulled a cigar from his shirt pocket. 'Danny understands

94

everything said to him. But he speaks *Tempest*. Shakespeare? He speaks only in lines from that play.'

'*The Tempest?*' Joyce blinked. *Something's coming.* 'Why?'

'Why?' Duncan tore off the end of the cellophane, blew into it, and slid the cigar out. 'Like I said before, no *why*. Just is.'

'I didn't mean to insult anyone. Please. Let me get what I need from the car. It will take two seconds and –'

'And given the kind of day you're having, you'd fall off the deck, bust your ass, and I'll lose my liability coverage.'

'Now who's interrupting?'

'Danny, go get – What was it? Yeah, the small wooden box from the car up on the rollback. Make it quick.' Duncan stuck the cigar in his teeth. Mercifully, he didn't light it.

Danny loped off to carry out his instructions. Joyce took a couple of steps after him. She wanted to call out a reminder to be careful, these things were fragile, but stopped herself for fear of conveying another offense of mistrust in the boy. She watched him clamber up the back of the flatbed and into the passenger side of the Saturn. A second later he lifted the box high into the light, and Joyce, certain he was going to drop it, called out that yes, that was it, and thank you. Danny was about to leap down from the deck when he seemed to have noticed something else inside the car. He went into the backseat and came out with the brown paper bag in which she had hidden the beer. With the bag clutched to his chest, Danny jumped. He hit the ground and stumbled as his boots slid on the dirt, but he found his footing and loped back to Joyce, where he stood, too close, breathing hard.

He held the box out to Joyce, which she took, careless of the pain it caused to grasp it tight in her bandaged hand. He gingerly tendered the bag. She swallowed and nodded and took that, too. 'Thank you,' she said. But the boy stood there breathing his hot, coppery breath into her face. His eyes were green-gray rims around the dark islands of his pupils, which seemed unnaturally large. *Dilated* was the word. Dilated pupils were what the attentive mother would remark.

'Thank you, Danny,' she said again.

95

'Come on, Danny,' Duncan said in a tone of gentle admonishment, 'the rest of it.'

Danny grumbled some unintelligible sequence of words before producing the strip of photographs from the back pocket of his jeans.

He let Joyce take it from him, but she had to tug it out of his grip. The pictures were so bent up and torn as to be nearly useless. 'How did you get these?'

'You must have left them behind in the rollback earlier,' said Duncan from behind her, all the gentility withdrawn from his tone. 'Danny doesn't take what isn't his. He doesn't steal.'

'*Danny es un ángel,*' said TJ. She bounded over to the boy's side, threw her arms around him and kissed his cheek. '*Danny es mi amante verdadero. ¿Sí?*' They were about the same height, Danny the taller by a couple inches at most. He didn't return her embrace, and although he was still muttering angrily, he didn't seem to mind TJ hanging on his shoulder. She was smiling. 'Get what you needed, Joycie?'

Joyce heard the question but couldn't answer. She looked from TJ and Danny to the pictures and back again, understanding in that instant what Jake the bad magician had in truth seen, whom exactly he had spoken to. It was TJ and Danny that Jake had mistakenly recognized from the photograph that night at the gas station. Why hadn't she seen it earlier? It was an honest mistake, but one that had steered her life down an unexpected path. The path came to a dead end here in this moment. She could wait for him here, and these good people would wait with her, and no one would think to condemn her when he never, ever showed up.

'This is all I need,' said Joyce, her voice sounding far away inside her own head. 'But if I might beg another favor from you, TJ?'

'Don't beg. It's your birthday.'

'Could you take me back to the Hoodoo? I want to get a look at exactly what it is I'm buying.'

Eight

TJ had deployed her full arsenal of logic: She had been trying to help him and if she'd screwed up, then hey, it was his fault because he was her teacher after all; wouldn't it make more sense to use the situation as a learning experience? Point out her errors, get her ready for the next time?

'No next times, TJ. You're not getting the gun back.'

Her head bobbed as she reassessed her approach, then her eyes brightened with mischief. She sighed, her body melting with her breath as she batted her lashes, and she bit at her lip and tugged at her sweatshirt so he was certain to see her breasts heave when she sighed in increasingly heavy disappointment. 'I know I was stupid. I won't do it again. Please. Please, Mr Dupree.'

It was her impression of Charlotte Cox – or maybe Hillary – one of the notorious twins. TJ had captured the infamous Cox come-on perfectly and must have known it wouldn't work. Her personal ethics, TJ's rules of engagement, wouldn't allow her to exercise her real and impressive skills of seduction in this matter. She probably realized that engagement wasn't going to do her any good, either.

'No. We agreed it was for target practice, period.'

'I said please.'

'I said no.' Duncan chewed at the cigar, letting the second-rate tobacco juice seep between his teeth and down his throat. God-damn, what he wouldn't give for one, just one decent smoke. Cheap cigars were depressing, almost as depressing as watching the Vermont woman standing off in the shadows near TJ's

Thunderbird, cradling that paper bag like a child against her chest. She had her hurt palm wrapped tight around the box, probably some reminder of her lost boy, and she was still doing that nervous, hair-behind-the-ear tuck she had been doing earlier, but she had to use her little finger, crooking her arm high so as not to hit herself with the box. The way she moved had slowed, as though she were caught up in her thoughts. Something had happened there, a few minutes earlier, when she'd been hassling Danny about the photograph. Duncan had seen the shift in her posture, the sudden softening in her shoulders, as though her bones had weakened and were no longer able to support the full weight of her living. Now she had her eyes focused downward on her dirty shoes, no doubt to avoid the unwavering gaze of Danny, who, doglike, seemed to believe that staring at a person would eventually sway them to his will. He wanted the photographs back. He wasn't getting them.

TJ bent forward an inch to smooth the flap over Duncan's pocket and button it. She straightened his collar. The girl was playing chicken. 'What if we run into Neb?'

'You told Vermont about Neb?'

'She has a *name*. If Joyce is going to live in Lágrimas, she needs to know about Neb.'

'I don't believe she is going to be living in Lágrimas.'

'And she doesn't believe in Neb, which makes the two of you even.'

'Either way, you'd better get Vermont out of here before Danny stares a hole straight through her head. She can't afford another one.'

'You are being awful rough on her.'

'And you all are feeding her tainted hope by letting her think her kid might turn up in Lágrimas.'

TJ toed the dirt. 'We didn't expect her to go and buy the Hoodoo. We just wanted to make the day up to her somehow. She drove twenty-five hundred miles for nothing. It's her birthday, dammit.'

'Everybody has one.'

'That would be every human body, Mr Dupree, sir. Let her spend a couple days in Grim Ass. You work on her car. We'll work on her. By the time you get that Saturn moving, you'll have to drive it up the road to catch up with her sprinting back east. Ozzie even has a pool going as to the exact hour she splits. He's got a few squares left, if you want in.' When he didn't jump at the invite to throw his money away, she kicked a small pebble that pinged and ricocheted off the office door. 'Other than your foul mood, is everything OK out here?'

The depth of concern in her voice surprised him. Duncan glanced at the shotgun leaning against the door jamb. 'OK as things ever were. You hearing anything about Gus MacGruder?'

'He hates you; you hate him. The usual. Should I be hearing more than that?'

'Nah. I'll handle it. Business situation.'

She narrowed her eyes in suspicion. 'Okey-dokey. I guess we'll be going.'

'Wait. You're from around here. "Lower than a horse thief" – does that mean anything to you?'

'Riddles? If I guess right, do I get a reward?'

'You are not getting the gun back, TJ.'

'In that case, you might not be getting your reward.' She brushed her shoulder against his chest. 'So, what? You're serious? OK. I thought nothing was lower than a horse thief. You'd hang for it in these parts – a long time ago, of course. You been out thieving horses, Dupree?' He didn't answer her. 'Still love me, don't you?'

'As much as I ever did.'

'How much?'

'No gun.'

She grinned at him and stalked off toward her car, walking on her toes, ass swaying. The Cheshire cat, thoroughly pissed off. She'd make him pay for this one, and that was something to look forward to.

TJ started up the engine, had it gunning before Vermont had shut the passenger door. The Thunderbird shot back, surprising Danny so that he leapt out of its way. TJ kept it in Reverse until she'd gained enough speed and then – he could see her hand, feel it, kneading the shift, waiting – she dropped it into Drive. The Thunderbird snapped into a 180-degree spin and roared off in a cloud of dust and exhaust.

He heard the squeal of tire rubber on asphalt and saw the flash of headlights, still pale in early evening, as the Thunderbird sped back toward town. He called to Danny, told him to finish closing the bays. Duncan hefted the shotgun and went back into the office.

He flipped on the lights. The incandescent bulbs in the overhead lent a false warmth to the imitation-walnut paneling and plastic window blinds. It was one of those questionable blessings that he'd been able to forestall TJ's seeing what had happened here. The last thing he needed was her entertaining the drunks at the Hoodoo with her overheated descriptions of how his files had been trashed. The wrong ears might be present. The wrong heart might be cheered.

It was business-motivated; it had to be. The first place he'd checked was the house and not a dust mote of home had been disturbed. So this was business, or they wanted him to think it was business. He skirted the toppled, beaten filing cabinets, trying not to leave boot tracks on the spilled papers as he made his way to his desk. He could see the tidy stack of mail the vandals had left on top of the mess they made of his paperwork. Kind of them to rescue the junk mail, and the bills, from the mailbox before they beat the crap out of it. As if he wouldn't have made the connection between the damage out front and in here, where his couch had been slashed, the poly-fill billowing from the ripped gashes and now drifting in mounds about the smashed-up computer tossed in the corner, and the grill and filter torn from the air conditioner – and his chair; goddamn them, his chair. After the icy realities of his past and his addiction had demanded the foreswearing of painkillers and forced him into hiding a good light-year away from physical therapy, the chair had been his one concession to the weakness of wanting comfort, an eight-hundred-dollar, custom-built, twelve-point positioning wonder stuffed taut with a space-age foam that melded about every gnarled twist of his knotted spine with the supple grace of a gifted lover. The trespasser had knifed the chair, rending the brown twilled upholstery from headrest to lumbar pad. Spongy space-age foam bloomed at the wound like keloid tissue. The chair now resembled what it was designed to embrace. He had to believe the mess was made for its own sake; those who might have cause to search Duncan's office would also know Duncan was of keener mind than to keep anything worth taking out here. But his chair? That was just fucking mean; it was the simple meanness of the act that made his gut go watery with fear.

One by one, he heard the garage bay doors ratchet down on steel-wheeled tracks, then the echoing bang as each hit the concrete floor. Danny came in through the door that connected the office to the bays. He took a long look around the ransacked room. 'These are not natural events; they strengthen from strange to stranger. Say, how came you hither?'

'I don't know why, or what exactly has turned on us, Danny. I have to think for a while. Here's what we're going to do in the meantime. We're going to leave this bedlam lay until morning. We're going to head on back to the house, and I'm going to heat up what's left of that chili. We'll dump it over some spaghetti, toast us up a few pieces of garlic bread, and have us a supper like every other night.' *And then you'll go to sleep, and I'll sit up until dawn with every lamp burning. I'll try to keep the shadow out of corners where masked men with iron rods wait in ambush. I'll stare into those corners and wonder why mercy couldn't have allowed for a small error of estimation and made them whale on a bit longer, or harder than necessary, enough to finish it; sever the cord and cut me free of sensation. My scarred veins will burn and the demons welded, iron on bone, to my back will thrash and scream. There will be no mercy. Just like every other night.*

Duncan pushed back in the recliner and adjusted, again, the dime-store magnifiers up and down his nose, trying to find the distance from lens to page that would allow him to read his Haynes guide for recent-model Saturns. As annoyed as he was with that Vermont woman, he was feeling gratified by the prospect of mucking out her car's fuel system, and not just for the money it would bring in. He *needed* work the way he used to need other diversions, and tonight he needed work more than ever. Vermont's car was the mooring on which he could tether his dangerous, wandering thoughts. He understood the substitution principle he was operating on, how identifying – naming – each element of the car's system failure allowed an inference of control over the failings of the world's bigger systems. *Fix what you can, buddy; fix what you can.*

He had already gone through the section on the Saturn's fuel injection and exhaust mechanics, and even though he hadn't raised the hood on the vehicle, he had surmised what he was dealing with by the nature of the symptoms: it was a throttle-body injector deal, a step up from the classic carb model. Probably a basic cleaning and system flush would bring it back. Not as much moola as a rebuild, but hey, if he could get her running in a hurry, it might be just the nudge of momentum necessary to get her moving on out of town.

That settled, he turned to the section on the clutch and drive axles. It had nothing to do with Vermont's situation; everything to do with his own. He liked to study the diagrams, the exploded views of the clutch disc assemblies. It was an odd comfort; he could grasp his own injuries, his own exploded disc assemblies, when considering these indifferent juxtapositions of metal parts. Pictures of the human spine – and he had seen many, both in diagrams and his own X rays – never seemed to explain it to his satisfaction. Bone and nerve and muscle and the interconnectivity were too organic, too human to be the source of his suffering. How could a man's own body betray him like that? No, these photographs and drawings of metal interlocking with metal, the wear and tear of too much friction in a badly lubricated system, the grind of contact between parts designed never to touch spoke truth to his sense of having had an essential part of his physical self replaced by a foreign, inorganic, and uncaring linkage of ill-functioning mechanics. It made the paradox comprehensible. *This isn't me hurting me.* Over the years he'd stopped equating the exact position of one day's discomfort with his chipped T-3 vertebra or the surgically tended traumas that had befallen T-5 through L-2 or the discs that lay between them or the facet joints that permitted or did not permit movement; these days it was bent fingers on the clutch's pressure plate or a broken tooth on the flywheel or pitting on the cage. If only one of these junkers he hauled in and stripped down could provide the necessary replacement parts.

That wasn't going to happen. He closed the book and let it drop to the floor. A hollow discomfort knocked at his belly, not so much hunger as a disembodied need for food. Answering it wasn't worth the effort of getting up. Food had become even more of a problem over the past few weeks. He pulled at the waistband on his shorts, looser still. He'd dropped more weight; the pain had a way of stealing his appetite or making him sick with what he did get down. The pain had been getting worse over the past year, but he'd also been thinking more than he should have been. Thinking about Danny. Thinking about those who might come looking for the boy and the unavoidable connection to thinking about who might come looking for Duncan himself. The shrinks in rehab had warned him about how the pain, the way it *felt,* could be altered by his mental state, his memories, his emotions, none of which were ever top-of-the-charts. He'd given up quick on the positive thinking and meditation prescriptives, finding it next to impossible to focus his thoughts, to 'let it go' when his body was under assault. You don't meditate through a war; you fight. Against the shrinks' advice, he fought it. He counted any minor advances as a victory. Tonight he'd done pretty good at dinner by sticking with plain spaghetti, a bit of olive oil, some bread. Given the state of his office and the MacGruder crap and everything he could read into those two events alone, the fact that he'd managed a simple, little meal was a big-time, capital-*V* Victory.

The heating pad was starting to heat. The thin rods of the space heater on the floor were popping back to life, starting to glow scarlet. Outside in the dark, not too far away, a pack of coyotes were singing to one another with those weird yelping cries of – what? *I'm hungry? I'm horny? I'm alone?* With the coyotes prowling Lágrimas, the cry would be *Dumpsters full at the trailer park! Somebody splurged on ribs! First come, first served.* Around here it was more likely to be first come, first shot – whether you walked on four legs or fewer. It was easy to make a mistake when it was dark and the clanging metal of tipping trash cans reminded you too much of iron bars hitting concrete. *It's easy to make a mistake, isn't it, Danny?*

Danny was curled up fetal on the foldout bed. He fell into sleep each night like a plumb bob through a vacuum, mumbling all the way down the passage from the play that Duncan called the boy's prayers: Prospero's 'Our revels are now ended' speech. It was indeed the stuff as dreams were made on, rounding the day in a little sleep and much snoring. For a child of such slight build, his snoring was damn near operatic in its basso profundo reverb. Tonight he had this sort of bleat going toward the end of each snore, so that he sounded much like a bear regurgitating live sheep. He was doing that twitchy dance step he did when he was dreaming, where his fingers and eyelids trembled and his feet worked the blankets as though he were running. *Chasing rabbits* is what you say when it's a dog dreaming; when it's a kid, you worry about what might be chasing him.

Duncan often wondered if the monster chasing Danny through sleep was Duncan himself, the man who came a split second shy of pulling the trigger on him, having mistaken his scrawny, pale haunches as belonging to those of some coyote come pawing through the precious, all-mighty-it's-mine garbage. A fortunate parting of the clouds from over a near-to-full moon had brightened the world enough to prevent a terrible, terrible mistake. 'Hey!' is what Duncan had shouted, and 'What the hell do you think you're doing?' on the assumption the trespasser was one of the perpetually stoned hoodlums from down the road. The pale figure wrestled himself out of the trash can and stared at Duncan. The moonlight reflected greasy white off the kid's hair, his wide, shining eyes, the knobs of his shoulder bones as he panted shallow breaths. He had a rind of that morning's breakfast cantaloupe in his hand; it appeared his knuckles were bleeding. He was all but naked, his butt and balls covered by a filthy pair of stretched out briefs. The stink of him hit Duncan's nose – the stink of sick, dirt, and the primal metallics of real terror. It was an olfactory express elevator straight down to the place where Duncan's memory ossified and filled with marrow, and he was on the concrete of the warehouse floor, his shinbone protruding, his backbone fractured, unable to get up and away from the hell that awaited. That was the point. That was the lesson. Duncan snapped back, snapped out. He kept the shotgun aimed. The kid was cowering near the trash can, his eyes darting from Duncan out toward the yard where the moon was running silver over the gutted automotive carcasses.

'You got a name?' he said to the kid. 'You from around here?'

The kid was shaking from cold and fear. Duncan remembered how one fed the other and figured it was the reason he was shaking, too.

'Can't go sneaking around a man's place like this. Not out here. You nearly got yourself shot – What?'

The kid was saying something – low, broken, maybe just to himself, but he was talking.

'Come again.' Duncan dropped the barrel of the gun as incentive. 'I can't hear you.'

The kid, eyes still darting, raised his voice: 'Be not afeard: the isle is full of noises, sounds, and sweet airs that give delight and hurt not. Sometimes a thousand twangling instruments will hum about mine ears; sometime voices that, if I then had waked after long sleep, will make me sleep again; and then, in dreaming, the clouds methought would open and show riches ready to drop upon me, that, when I waked, I cried to dream again.'

Duncan knew those words, had read them, had studied them in a long-ago life of libraries and lecture halls, yet in the shock of hearing them from such an improbable mouth, he was unable to recall anything but the author. 'Shakespeare? That's Shakespeare.' If the boy had planned to distract him with the recitation, it worked. In Duncan's momentary disorientation between sound and source, the kid took advantage and hightailed it for the yard.

The next morning began a game of hide-and-seek conducted with a most serious purpose. If that kid was holed up somewhere in the yard, Duncan had to flush him into the open. There'd be no operating the EZ-Crusher until the kid was out – the crushing trough was at ground level and as open as a drive-thru lane at a burger joint. Duncan could see the piston-driven plates drop, shove, and smash into a tidy rectangle of wreckage the very automobile the kid could have chosen as a nest. Crushing was income, however, and Duncan could not afford to wave the scrap buyers aside for endless weeks while that crazy kid made himself at home. Duncan had to find him.

Thin, high clouds veiled the day, and for this Duncan was thankful; it was hot and windy, but he'd been spared the convection-oven effect of direct sun hitting the closely packed junkers. He walked among the wrecks along the haphazard network of hard, dry paths. He checked rat-eaten backseats and sprung trunks. After an hour of searching, he started to think he'd imagined the whole encounter. *Tell it again, Dupree, the one about the garbage-scarfing wild boy who sang Shakespeare at you.* Several times, he considered giving up, writing it off to a somnambulist's bit of fantasizing. And then he'd see the crusher go to work, the first plate falling on top of the car, the second cramming metal in from the side, the third compressing the length from the rear; he'd hear the noise of the diesel engine powering the pistons, the sighing squeals of twisted, breaking things that would drown any sound of human voice until it was too late and the crushed vehicle was popped, bleeding boy blood from the ramp. *EZ.* Duncan shook off the image and went back to searching.

About noon he found, in the back of a late-model station wagon, a wad of old blanket, some empty stew cans of a brand Duncan favored, and a gnawed-up cantaloupe rind. Outside the wagon, near the wheel hub was a mass of human stool, pale and fetid. Duncan surveyed the yard. 'You want something to eat?' he called. 'I'm not going to hurt you.' He waited, hoping for a telltale movement or sound. When nothing surfaced, he yelled, 'Stay the hell away from that crusher!' He continued searching for as long as his legs held out.

That night he left a couple of juice cartons filled with water, a few sticks of beef jerky, and a cellophane packet of dried apricots out on the lid of the trash cans. He then spent the longest part of the dark sitting awake in the recliner, listening for the slightest trembling clatter of trash-can metal. He must have dozed, because suddenly the windows had gone gold with sun.

He went out back to check. The food and water were gone. Not taken by the coyotes; they'd have savaged the cartons and wrappings right there. The kid was real and he was still around. Duncan dressed in his work khakis and packed up an old boot box with more dried meat, fruit, a jar of peanut butter, a package of saltines. He filled a gallon milk jug with water. He set out again, headed for the station wagon.

The sun was hanging hazy and low over the hills. The wind was down, so the morning heat had a touch of humidity to it, lending the desert air a rare sort of heaviness. The day was off to a sulk. He made his way through the wrecks, listening to the scratch and scurry of rodent claws against metal. A supple little chuckwalla dashed out from under a Chevy Nova. The dust-colored lizard stopped in Duncan's path and blinked its dinosaur eyes, tongue flickering, before dashing on ahead as though leading the way.

Duncan reached the station wagon. The blanket was there but wadded in a different corner than yesterday morning. The juice cartons of water lay in tatters, as though the kid had drained them and then ripped the paper apart to get at whatever few drops of water might hide within. Duncan slid the boot box into the wagon, put the water jug on top of the box to weight the lid shut. 'I brought you more water,' he yelled. 'You have to be careful out here, boy. There's sharp stuff and broken glass. You could get yourself cut up real quick. And the snakes. Watch out for the snakes. And scorpions. And –' Why not do it the same way that adults of Lágrimas had been tethering their wanderlusting young to the homestead for generations? 'And Neb.' Duncan started toward the center of the yard, better for his voice to carry. 'You've heard about Nebuchadnezzar? Dog used to guard hell's own front gate, until Lucifer fired his ass for being too damn mean.' He listed, loudly, Neb's legendary characteristics of size, silence, and snake-poisoned spit. 'So it might be wise for you to come on out of hiding. Come on up to the house and let me get you a proper meal – before Neb makes a proper meal of you.'

He thought he heard the creak of a door hinge or car spring. He waited for a minute: rat scurry-and-dig, nothing more. 'All right. I have to be getting to work, but if you should change your mind . . .' He began the trek back toward home. Again came the creaking of a hinge or spring. This time closer. Intuition told Duncan not to turn toward it, to keep walking away. The creaking stopped. A hood or trunk slammed shut. Then came a voice.

'These be fine things, and if they be not sprites. That's a brave god, and bears celestial liquor. I will kneel to him.'

Duncan tried to move slowly, not wanting to scare the kid off, not wanting to miss him, either. But before he'd completely turned, another voice sounded. This one gruff and slurred: 'How didst thou scape? How cam'st thou hither? Swear by this bottle how thou cam'st hither . . .' The drunken voice, Duncan discovered, also belonged to the kid. He was standing on the roof of a rust-rotted Gremlin, clothed in the same dirty underpants and now sporting the blanket from the station wagon as a cape, the way small boys pretend to be superheroes. He had the water jug open, and after taking a swig, he proclaimed grandly how he'd washed ashore on this 'butt of sack which the sailors heaved o'erboard, by this bottle, which I made of the bark of a tree with mine own hands since I was cast ashore.' He drank again, spilling water down his dust-caked body. It traced runs of suntanned skin down his jaws, his neck, his chest. He shook his matted head and wiped at his chin, smearing the dirt around the sparse fuzz of beard on his face. He laughed, and his voice slid down to the wonder-struck tones he'd first used.

'I'll swear upon that bottle to be thy true subject, for the liquor is not earthly.'

Drunken voice: 'Here! Swear then how thou escapedst.'

Third voice, comically stupid, equally drunk: 'Swum ashore, man, like a duck. I can swim like a duck, I'll be sworn.'

First Drunk: 'Here, kiss the book.' The boy drank. 'Though thou canst swim like a duck, thou art made like a goose.'

Second Drunk: 'O Stephano, hast any more of this?'

First Drunk: 'The whole butt, man: my cellar is in a rock by th' seaside, where my wine is hid. How now, mooncalf? How does thine ague?'

Wonder-struck voice: 'Hast thou not dropped from heaven?'

And on he went. Duncan didn't dare interrupt; he couldn't tell if the boy was performing for him or had forgotten Duncan was present. The voices cycled; it was a scene from Shakespeare, of that Duncan was certain. He knew these words. Much about drinking and books and monsters: credulous monsters, puppy-headed monsters, scurvy, abominable, and ridiculous monsters. The Second Drunk was going on about howling monsters, and suddenly the boy broke into song.

> No more dams I'll make for fish,
> Nor fetch in firing at requiring,
> Nor scrape trenchering, nor wash dish.
> 'Ban, 'Ban, Ca-Caliban
> Has a new master: get a new man.
> Freedom, high-day! High-day, freedom! . . .

'*Tempest*,' Duncan said, as the elements clicked in connection. 'Caliban is the monster in *The Tempest*. It's Caliban who "cries to dream again." You're doing the scene where, where two of the sailors . . . Stephano, you said Stephano . . . and wait, wait, Tinquilto, Trinkquilo, something like that . . .' Duncan realized the boy was unimpressed with his recognition, apparently unmoved by Duncan at all. In fact, he had begun again, from the top.

'These be fine things, and if they be not sprites. That's a brave god . . .'

The absurdity of the situation hit him, and Duncan lost the sound of the boy's voice in the roar of his own laughter. Oh, goddamn it did hurt to laugh, each guffaw like thunder to a lightning stroke of pain. But what could he do? Here was this near-naked kid covered in sores and dirt standing on the roof of a junked car, his voice cycling through the words of two drunks and the sea monster they'd run into. And it was Shakespeare. How could you not laugh? 'What are you doing?'

'O brave monster! Lead the way,' said the Second Drunk, with a flourishing sweep of his thin, dirty arms. Duncan's sight followed to the place the boy pointed.

'The house? You ready to come inside?'

* * *

110

The steady drip from the garage's exterior spigot and the moisture-darkened earth beneath it suggested answers to some of Duncan's questions: specifically how the kid had managed to last during the heat of the day. The boy must have been taking water at night or when Duncan was away on a call. Who knows how long the kid had been out there?

Duncan wrenched the connector onto the spigot and straightened out the coil of hose. He turned on the water to a fairly strong flow. He turned to the boy, who stood a few feet away, visibly anxious and still yammering the inventory of monsters. Duncan felt the water: cold – or as close to cold as it was going to get. He held out the burbling end of the hose to the boy. 'You want to do it? Clean yourself?' Duncan mimed washing, the way he had mimed to the kid to remove his briefs and the blanket cape. 'Look, son, I can't put you in the shower like you are. All that dirt will block the plumbing.' The boy reached, without moving his feet, and carefully accepted the water. He pulled the hose in toward himself, staring as it splashed over his hands and forearms. He was still talking.

'By this good light, this is a very shallow monster!' said the Second Drunk, Trin-something, as the boy lifted the water to his head. 'A very weak monster! The Man i' th' Moon? A most poor credulous monster!' The water poured down over his face as he spoke. He inhaled some and started to cough but kept talking. The water flowed, over his shoulders, his chest, the tiers of his rib cage; the surface dirt was dragged downward, and blotchy, sun-browned skin emerged. Wonder-struck: 'I'll kiss thy foot. I'll swear myself thy subject.'

Stephano, the First Drunk: 'Come on then. Down, and swear!'

The boy turned; the hose snaked up around his feet. He held the hose to the back of his neck. The Second Drunk said, 'I shall laugh myself to death at this puppy-headed monster. A most scurvy monster! I could find in my heart to beat him . . .' Water rolled down the gully between his shoulder blades. He moved the water;

more of his back became visible, and what Duncan saw raised such a howl of old ghosts that for a few seconds they drowned out Duncan's senses altogether.

The water tracked along the raised, welted scars on the boy's back as though it were being guided through a series of interlocked troughs. The welts began at the top of his spine and fanned out to cover his back and buttocks and the top of his thighs like the blanket cape he had been using to cover them. The instrument of infliction had varied; fine slashing hash marks were layered over and between broad swaths.

'. . . An abominable monster!'

Shift of tone: 'I'll show thee the best springs: I'll pluck thee berries; I'll fish for thee, and get thee wood enough. A plague upon the tyrant that I serve . . .'

'Who?' said Duncan, taking a step closer, beginning to sense the shape in the outlining edges of what he had been hearing. 'Who is this tyrant you're talking about? Who did this to you?'

'. . . A most ridiculous monster, to make a wonder of a poor drunkard.' Water splashed. The earth muddied where his raw, blistered feet turned and tangled in the hose.

'Who did this to you?'

'Farewell, master; farewell, farewell.'

'Who?'

'A howling monster! a drunken monster!' Danny fell into Caliban's song.

Duncan shut off the water. 'Who did this?'

The singing quieted to a mumbling. The boy, naked and wet, considered the last dribbles of water and sighed. He looked over at Duncan, bereft.

Doctor Milton Freemont settled his big haunches at the cramped dinette in Duncan's cramped kitchen and went over his notes, making irregular clicking and sucking noises with his dentures. Occasionally, he glanced toward the bathroom, at the far end of the house. He'd wag his wedge-shaped head in amazement and go back to his notes. The boy had been in the shower since Freemont had examined him, a process that had proven an exhausting series of biting, spitting tantrums exploding with furious Shakespearean monster talk, all of which ended with the boy breaking free of Duncan's grip and escaping to the shower stall at the other end of the house. Duncan, fed up and aching, had turned both faucets on full over his head. The water seemed to calm him. So there he stayed. Duncan was certain the kid was going to empty the well. Through the thin panels of the shower door, Shakespeare rang, but it seemed to Duncan that each repetition of the scene was faster, as though something inside the words was gaining velocity.

Milt was tapping his pencil on the table, working the yellow stick like a metronome set to a dirge, first lead, then eraser, then lead. He was one of those big men who moved hesitantly, as though his size were a costume he had just now tried on and he had yet to adequately gauge his space; through innocent misestimation, he might knock over your grandmother or your Ming vase – and as a result he'd have to feel horrible about things. Milt hated when things felt horrible. Duncan figured that's why the man had gone into medicine. He tapped a bit longer and then erased a few words with the pink eraser on the pencil's end, blew the rubbings off the paper, and wrote something new.

'I appreciate you coming out like this,' said Duncan, which was as much hospitality as he planned to offer. He leaned against the counter hard so that the press of the edge into his back, just below his belt line, produced the sharp sort of sensation that sometimes confused his brain and stifled the reception of neural outrage. He was damned if Freemont was going to see him wince. The doctor would haul out a prescription pad and, because he could see Duncan felt horrible, would sign off on a first-class ticket to the last place Duncan could afford to go. 'Bill me extra for the house call.'

Milt looked up from his notes. 'Nonsense. Under the circumstances, what else could we have done? Can't believe the boy's in as good a shape as he is – given everything I saw. The resiliency of youth, I guess. When he's done cleaning up, I'll take him out to stay –'

'He's not going anywhere.'

'Duncan, he needs attention, and you know it. The boy has been hurt, and not all of the injuries are physical. On top of that, you have to assume somebody is looking for him.'

'That is what I'm assuming, and that's why you can't make him easy to find.'

'He's a minor – fifteen, sixteen max, a child. The law says he needs a legal guardian.'

'And what is the law going to say if the legal guardian is the one who embossed those stripes onto his flesh? If he got away from someone, what do you think will happen when that someone gets him back?'

Milt hung his head and ran his palms across his scalp, smoothing what was left of his hair. 'What do you want me to do, Dupree? His behavior suggests schizophrenia of some sort or a high-functioning autism. Maybe some trauma-induced fugue state. He may need medication. He definitely needs more experienced care than I can give him. I'm a fucking dermatologist. His acne flares up, I'm there, but hell, the Shakespeare – You're sure it's – OK, I'll take your word for one, but all that "celestial liquor" and "hast thou not dropped from heaven?" – shit, that's gotta mean something.'

'Of course it means something, Freemont. It means exactly what it sounds like it means: He's happy to be found; he's grateful.'

'So these monsters he's talking about –'

'They're the ones that look like you and me. Your everyday, ordinary monsters.'

'Right.' Milt put the pencil down. 'You know, if he were to get some rest, eat well, build up his strength, he might be able snap out of this and fill us in on his history.'

'True.'

'You can't hide him or pretend he isn't here, Dupree. Wouldn't be right.'

'And I wouldn't do it.'

'If official missing-kid notification turns up, we'll have to call him in.'

'Debatable.'

'No, not debatable. I won't keep him a secret, but I won't put him up on the wire, either. We'll wait awhile to see who comes looking. Fair enough?'

'Fair enough.'

Milt stared off at the bathroom. 'I don't think he's going to come out of that shower as long as I'm here.' He squirmed and shoved himself into standing. He handed Duncan a sheaf of prescriptions. 'Antibiotics. Vitamins. Cortisone for those rashes. You can have them put under your name.'

Yes, that's what he needed, his name looping through a pharmacist's database. That would be the first place they'd look. 'No. No scripts in my name.'

Milt exhaled. They'd had the 'Let me prescribe something for that pain' argument so often that Milt's sigh was sufficient to convey his side of it. 'Well, you'll have to come up with a name for the boy, or Margaret won't fill them.'

'I'll tell Margaret he's my sister's kid.' Duncan took a cigar out of the packet he kept by the sink. 'Let her think one of yours has taken up with one of mine and sullied the bloodline. That ought to put her ladyship grocer back into whatever crypt she crawled out of.'

Milt studied his prescription pad, making it clear he felt horrible to be part of such a horrible world. 'Yeah, jeez, people. What can you do?'

'Being that we ended up in Lágrimas, I think we've answered that one.'

The doctor ducked his head in concession. 'And being that we're in Lágrimas, you got to know that once Margaret has those scripts, the stories start. By supper tonight, my kids are going to be pestering me to find out if it's true some crazy, bare-assed wild boy brought old Nebuchadnezzar to heel.'

Duncan flicked his lighter to flame and raised an eyebrow at Milt. 'Daniel.'

'Who?'

'That's his name. The crazy, bare-assed wild boy who – Didn't you go to Sunday school?'

'I went.' Milt shrugged. 'Daniel, it is. Daniel what?'

'Caliban.' Duncan puffed on the cigar, filling up the tight space with smoke. 'Until someone tells us otherwise, he's Danny Caliban.'

That had been a year ago, last August, and since then no one had come into Lágrimas looking for any more than the fastest way out of town. Not until today, when the dams against the past had broken open and flooded the streets with a thin, sweaty sheen of apprehension: Vermont, MacGruder, horse thieves. Duncan was too smart to think these events were connected to one another by any fashion other than interpretation; he had also been on the planet for a hair over fifty years, long enough to learn that the mind tends to think its way toward safety, even when safety itself is a trap. The resemblance between Danny and Vermont's missing kid? The CHP giving the widely despised con artist MacGruder a day's worth of Duncan's business? The 'horse thief' question taken in context of what Duncan had been and what it cost him? All of it rolled back into what Duncan could surmise from the junkie stares in Vermont's pitiful strip of photographs. It was as though Duncan were under siege by forces he couldn't name or even see, but he could feel them, the cold-forged edge of their intent along every inch of his spine.

Danny rolled over in his sleep, snuffled, and cried out softly. Duncan strained to catch the sound of something spoken, but Danny had gone under again. Sometimes he hoped that during the inadvertent vigils insomnia provided, he might catch Danny's guard down; the boy might talk in his sleep, might give voice to words of his own and thereby a hint of who he was, where he came from, and what had happened to him. Other times Duncan hoped that he would never have to learn any of Danny's history because he already knew how it would read; he had pretty much the same lines written in his skin.

Duncan turned up the setting on the heating pad as high as it would go. Over in the corner the scanner crackled with distant staticky laughter. He closed his eyes and tried to remember sleep.

Nine

Something is coming. Joyce sat up, sweating, her breath catching and burning in her chest. She called out for Paul, reaching to shake him awake. Her hand hit empty air; she nearly fell to the floor. *Where am I?* She fumbled for a bedside lamp, found one, and got the knob turned in spite of her shaking hands. The lamp threw a frail yellow glow onto the room, and as her mind spun successively slower pirouettes, Joyce saw the wooden box on the nightstand. She began to remember. *Lágrimas.* Her breathing quieted. She checked her watch; she'd left it on her wrist because the room had no clock. It was nearing four. She had been in bed less than an hour.

She shoved her hair out of her face. Had she really called out Paul's name? She'd been dreaming about him, about home, and it hadn't been a bad dream at all, at least not in the beginning. Was he wondering where she might have gone? Had he reported her missing? Was he calling friends or Joyce's sisters or anybody – or was he simply relieved? He'd miss the money she'd taken, and that might be enough for him to send someone out to track her down. She shook her head at her own unfairness. Certainly, Paul couldn't bear all the blame for ending the marriage. He had, like Joyce, been washed overboard and left flailing without anything to hold on to. What choice did he have, really? If he'd tried to hold her up any longer, they probably both would have drowned. Maybe he'd finally gotten the message: She wasn't interested in swimming any longer. Still. She should get California plates on the car as soon as she could. That should go at the top of her growing list of things to do.

She threw off the blankets, extras that Rachel had brought up when Joyce commented on how cold the night was. Now the sheets and her thin cotton nightgown were soaked with sweat. Her stomach bubbled acid, and the disorientation in her head had gathered itself into a sullen pulsing ache just above her left eye. If she hadn't known better, she would have sworn she'd been drinking.

But she had not, even though she'd spent more than eight straight hours at the Hoodoo watching the denizens of Lágrimas knock them back. For Joyce, it had been water. That was it. Nothing more. Not even so much as a sip, when, after last call, Pete proposed a toast to Joyce by opening a bottle of champagne so old and cheap, the bubbles had deserted it and the cork had to be wrenched out with a pair of needle-nose pliers. Charlie, Ozzie, Eugene, and Lucas, the regulars who apparently had after-hour privileges – that or nowhere else to go – they and TJ had passed the bottle, lifting it in Joyce's honor and solemnly wishing her the best on this her birthday and in all future endeavors. The solemnity was due in part to the fact that the lot of them were in varying degrees of drunkenness, but most of it was their resignation to failure as they had spent the better part of the night trying to talk Joyce out of what the general consensus, minus Pete, held as 'purified, drop-dead, out-of-your-mind lunacy.'

The anti-sales campaign began on the way back to the Hoodoo, after the adventure at the salvage yard. TJ slowed the Thunderbird and just about coasted through downtown Lágrimas. 'What a fucking pit,' she muttered with stage-whisper articulation. 'Look at this place, Joyce. I mean, open your eyes and look at it.'

Joyce looked at TJ instead. 'Do you have kids?'

'No, thanks be to whatever spirit is in charge of that one.'

'Until you do have children, you won't understand.'

'I don't need kids to recognize a bad idea when I see one. If

120

– When your boy shows up, him or the girl, we'll call you. Immediately. You have to trust us on that. Most everyone around here is lost, one way or another; we bust ass to help out when it looks like somebody's going to get found.'

Joyce shook her head. 'You don't understand.' TJ twisted her lips into a pout of frustration, but Joyce could feel the strategies reformulating. TJ withheld her next argument until they were in the Hoodoo and she had pinned Joyce down at a table under the pretense of applying a clean bandage to her hand.

'This is what *you* don't understand,' she said as she wiped the dried blood from Joyce's skin with a cotton ball and hydrogen peroxide. 'The Hoodoo is not a neglected gem in need of a bit of polish. You aren't going to paint this place a nice happy color, make some cute curtains, put together a chichi Southwestern bistro menu, and get the Vegas crowd to stop for a snack on their way to or from financial ruin. Ask Pete. These people – look at them, Joyce – these people are your customers. They're salt harvesters. They stand in the sun and drag boards across evaporation pools to scrape up what's been leached from the surface, or they trowel it out of brine veins that run through the mud below the crust. It's hard, awful work – and it's a co-op. No protection; no guarantees. They wash it, they bottle it, they advertise it, and they ship it out. They do everything, and at the end of the week, they split up whatever's left of that week's sales, take it home, and say grace over their boxed macaroni dinners to thank heaven for the rich-bitch gourmet princes and princesses of the world who can drop twelve bucks on half a pound of pink salt – one of whom I plan to be someday. I'm not going to end up like these people, who can't afford to spend an extra nickel on their breakfast for a bit of cilantro in their eggs – it's all I can do to seduce them into a decent tip.'

'Pete's managed; I'm sure I can. You will stay on, won't you? You will work for me, won't – Ouch!'

'Oh, did that hurt?' TJ snarked a laugh. 'Good. I wanted to make

121

sure you had some functioning sense left. This is going to be enough for you? Is it? Day after day of this? The grill. The deep fryer. The burnt-fat smell that gets so deep in your pores, no amount of soap can wash it out? You want the piles of dishes? The empty beer bottles? Unclogging the puked-up toilet –'

'You're worse than my mother trying to talk me out of marrying my husband.'

'A marriage you *can* get out of, honey. The Hoodoo is forever.'

'Pete's getting out.'

'Pete has apparently traded in what he tries to pass off as his soul.' TJ taped off the ends of the clean bandage. She turned around, and called, 'Hey, Pete. Tell Joyce how long you've been trying to sell this dump.'

Pete was behind the bar getting a beer for Charlie from the tap. 'I don't know. Not very long.'

'You don't know?' TJ crowed. 'You tell her or I will.'

'A couple – OK, Cortez, five, maybe six years.'

'Maybe seven. Now tell her how long you owned it before you decided to put it on the block.'

'Around a month, I guess, but don't let that put you off, Joyce – I was bound by circumstances that I had not made allowances for.'

'Like reality.' TJ opened her palms and offered up the obvious.

Joyce laughed and patted the girl's arm. 'You are very sweet to worry, but you can stop. All right? I'm doing what I need to do for reasons that mean something only to me. It will work out. If you still want this job, it's yours. Other than that, my decisions are mine.' She smiled and tried to affect a convincing certainty. 'Now, maybe you could show me around the kitchen? Rachel said there's an apartment out here?'

'This isn't about just you.' TJ threw the tape back in the first-aid box. 'Your stubbornness is endangering us all. You're going to bring down *el búho*, you know that? The Owl will come rip up Lágrimas, and it will be your fault.'

'The what?'

'God's Owl, *el búho de dios*. If you are going to stay, you should probably know that Lágrimas is an ancient battleground in a war against the demonic spirits. It is holy ground, and when a traveler who doesn't belong –'

Joyce waved her to a halt. 'Never mind. No more. I've dealt with tactical defense and dust storms and snake-dogs and spontaneously shattering glass today; I don't need owl stories or tales of demonic anything.'

'You do need to know what you're getting yourself into.'

'Which is why I would very much like to see my kitchen. Now, please.'

'Yep,' said TJ, 'the traveler who won't listen. That's how it always begins.'

Within seconds of pushing through the swinging door, Joyce's mental list-making machine lit up: *item one – industrial degreaser and disinfectant, one fifty-gallon drum. Better make that two.* The kitchen appeared to have been the site of its own demonic showdown. Pots bubbled on the range top, filling the room with a blandly scented steam. Joyce followed along as TJ played car-show hostess, making dainty hand movements as she ran down the failings of each appointment: the blistering heat of the grill; the unreliable freezer; the iced-up fridge; the eons-old oil in the deep fryer; the thumping-bumping flow of water into the rust-stained sinks; the potholes in the floor – caused by actual falling pots – that had been filled in over the years with a paste of grease and dirt. Dust was on everything, glued in place by hardened grime.

The dust-and-grime theme continued into the apartment, which was situated off the kitchen through an archway hung with a stiff canvas curtain. Joyce took only a cursory tour of the place; it felt awkward to be in the rooms of a man she didn't know. Open boxes were lined up along the uncarpeted plank floor. No money yet, nothing official signed, and yet Pete was already packing. She wondered if he planned to leave behind any of the furnishings, simple and few as they were. The front room was a tiny parlor with a couple of chairs and a coffee table and a floor lamp. Beyond that, through another curtained arch, was a small bedroom with a single window, a single bed, and a single chest of drawers. The closet-sized bathroom was accessed through the parlor and located so that it shared the plumbing of the Hoodoo's one public rest room.

'Seen enough?' said TJ, when Joyce came back into the kitchen. TJ was sitting on the edge of the long table in the middle of the room.

'It needs some work, but what doesn't?'

TJ inhaled deeply, and shoved her sweatshirt sleeves up to her elbows. 'OK. This is the last thing I wanted to do, but I owe you the truth. Earlier today, when you came in, we may have been a mite too optimistic when we were laying out odds on your son –'

'I know. You were trying to be kind. You are trying to be kind now. It is highly unlikely he'll come through Lágrimas again. I know.'

'Then what the hell are you doing? It's not like you're some sloshy old booze sponge who thinks she's swan-diving – splash! – into the fountain of eternal oblivion –'

'Of course not,' said Joyce.

'Out of some insane kind of hope? You're going to play this place like it's a lottery ticket or a point spread? You're hoping you get lucky and he'll walk through the door?'

'I said that I didn't expect you to understand.'

'Good,' said TJ, 'because I don't. I do not understand the *hope* thing.' She rubbed her eyes and left faint smudges of mascara beneath them. 'I'm going back to the hotel to get ready for work. Work, I understand. You coming?'

'I'll stay here, I think. I have lots of planning to do.'

Pete said that tonight anything she wanted was on the house. 'Which would mean that I, being the house, am paying for it,'

124

she'd said, and asked for water. The place was filling. Sweaty tired men and women in clothing streaked with dust and slate-blue mud trudged in alone and in groups. They settled at the bar or at the tables and waited for the beer that Pete poured without having to be told. Joyce smiled in return for the overt stares they gave her as she wandered about the Hoodoo, cataloguing her new possessions, deciding what would stay, what would go. The same blue mud showed up in finger and fist prints on the many petitions that were tacked to the Hoodoo's walls. The petitions were asking for support in opposing something called the Desert Protection Act – even though it had been passed in 1994. The act made the Mojave National Preserve into a national park, the rationale being to help preserve the wilderness area. A noble undertaking, Joyce thought. But the columns of signatures beneath the long, passionate arguments on the petitions attested to local belief that to declare the land protected would only bring in those social elements that require and provide protection: souvenir hucksters, campers in RVs, and rangers with rule books and citation pads. In other words, civilization – and civilization was what a lot of these people, judging by the number of signatures, had been exiled from or sought to escape. The Mojave, in its inherent unfriendliness to humanity, enforced its own rules, thank you very much. Those who lived here were proud of having made a tenuous peace with the desert. They respected it absolutely; in return, it let them do as they damn well pleased.

Other than the petitions and clippings, the Hoodoo displayed a collection of juvenile postcards of the 'I got my rocks off at Yosemite' and 'What a set! Greetings from Grand Teton' variety. What looked like children's watercolors of sunrises with cacti hung near the front door, while pictures of odd rock formations taken from nature magazines and set in dime-store frames filled the wall between the out-of-order jukebox and the out-of-order pinball machine. They'd been mounted so that page numbers and captions were visible; a quick scan of this information informed her these were famous examples of desert hoodoo, rocks that had eroded into columns with spectacular and eerie effect. Some of the formations seemed familiar, especially the one called Icarus Ascending: Dawn at Balanced Rock, in which a 3,500-ton boulder perched with impossible delicacy on a jagged pillar of stone, seventy-three feet tall. It was so familiar that for a minute Joyce thought she might have been there, but the caption said it was in Utah. She was certain she'd never been in Utah.

She recognized few of the songs on jukebox, only those that had blasted for hours from her son's room. No hurry to fix that. The pinball machine was of a billiards theme, which seemed redundant, given the actual billiards table a few feet away.

The balls were racked, ready to break across the burgundy felt. No one was playing. The mahogany table appeared to be an antique; unnecessarily ornate for Joyce's taste, it featured legs carved in the shape of buxom nudes who supported the table on their heads, gold fringe on the pockets, and mother of pearl inlay along the rails. A rectangular lamp with a green glass shade hung over the table on brass chains. It was as though someone had transported the whole setup from a Victorian bordello. It sat among the utilitarian furnishings of the Hoodoo with a sort of self-conscious audacity, overdressed for this party and proud of it.

Joyce was running her hand over the felt, when Charlie, empty beer mug in hand, came over. 'You play, darlin'?' His words wafted on a cloud of beer breath.

'Long time ago, and not well,' she said. 'Maybe now I'll have a chance to practice.'

'Not without permission. This here is Duncan's table. He owns it.'

'And he keeps it here?'

Charlie nodded, his head hanging as though it were too heavy for his neck. 'Dirty out at the yard, he says. Not enough room, besides. And the Hoodoo'll stand up to a big wind better than any building in Lágrimas. It's a beautiful table, don't you think, darlin'? Beautiful.'

'Yes, well, it's very old. Probably quite valuable.'

'Duncan will never sell it to you. Somebody gave it to him as a gift. Woman, we think.'

'I don't intend to buy it; I was wondering how old it is.'

'Eugene!' He turned, and used his mug to signal the man with the scar. 'Eugene, how long has Duncan had this table out –'

'No,' said Joyce, 'I meant, how old is the table itself?'

Charlie didn't hear her; he just kept waving Eugene forward with his beer mug, as though he was trying to guide a plane on a tarmac. Eugene staggered a bit in approach, favoring his left leg. 'It's Duncan's table,' said Eugene on arrival.

'I've been told.'

'He had it brought out when he first came to town – like what? – eleven years ago? It's for his back. Some doctor told him he had to stretch his muscles, you know, on a regular basis; you know, exercise, so he'd keep his mobility. And that's why Duncan shoots pool. You can tell it's killing him some days. He won't play no one; says he's not interested in the game, only in the shots.'

'He's playing pain is what he's doing,' said Charlie, gazing into his empty mug. 'He's playing the pain like pain was a double-dealing hustler and he knows up front he's going to lose. Playing pain on this beautiful table.'

'That's kinda poetic, old man,' said Eugene, patting his shoulder. 'Why don't you go get Pete to draw you another round. On me.' Charlie raked his fingers through his hair, muttered some thanks, and wove his way back toward the bar. When he'd gone, Eugene pulled at his mustache and leaned in toward Joyce. 'You'll have to excuse the old guy. He gets kinda sentimental when he's had a few.'

'He's all right.'

'Charlie? He's the best. Top-shelf. That's what's so weird about it – that tenderhearted old coot . . .' Eugene's voice drifted off as he aimed an imaginary gun and made two whispery *ka-pow* sounds. 'Not that he wasn't in his rights, not that at all. Man's got a right to defend his place. Says so in the Consti-fucking-tution. It was a long time ago, but I still have problems seeing it, you know. Sweet old Charlie deadeyeing them trespassers, giving them both barrels straight in their faces. Couldn't even identify the SOBs afterward; they were just a couple of raw-meat lollipops by the time the authorities got there. I just have a hard time imagining it. You know what I mean?' He stroked his mustache and looked down at Joyce, his expression one of earnest, drunken contemplation.

'Yes,' said Joyce, when she realized he was expecting an answer. 'Yes, I have a hard time imagining it, too.'

His face brightened at her agreement, and his grin raised ridges in the scar tissue. 'What you drinking there? Can I buy you another?'

'Water, thank you. And I'm fine.'

The grin fell. 'Water's no good. How am I going to talk you into coming home with me if you're only drinking water?' He loomed over her longer than she cared for, until finally the realization dawned on him that she was not interested. His shoulders dropped and he limped back to the bar.

Within the hour, the red-wigged TJ was back. Dressed again in flounced skirt and heels, she swung in from the kitchen, cymbaled a couple pots lids together, and announced that Pete was in the kitchen. She sashayed from table to table, scribbling down orders until she cornered Joyce, suggesting Joyce try the meatloaf, as it wasn't nearly as bad as she might have heard. Heading back for the kitchen, TJ pointed Joyce to an empty seat at the bar between Lucas and Ozzie.

She slid onto the bar stool; each man herded his respective bottles and mugs closer together. She told them not to worry, she had plenty of room, but she knew the gathering wasn't out of consideration for her comfort. She remembered quite precisely that nervous sense of propriety over one's drink, and she put her water glass on the bar as evidence that she, too, had something to lose.

TJ brought out Joyce's meal, a plate heaped with slabs of oatmeal-augmented ground meat covered in ketchup, with a scoop of glutinous potatoes and a pile of gray-green canned peas on the side. 'I recommend lots of salt,' she said, 'if taste means anything to you, that is.' She set a shaker of plain white regular salt on the bar. 'The Hoodoo can't afford to use Lágrimas pink. Just more helpful information, Joyce – and speaking of information: Lucas, honey, you know everything, right?'

He blushed, pushed his glasses up, finished chewing, and swallowed. 'I wouldn't say that.'

'OK, you know more useless stuff than anyone else in Lágrimas.'

'That would be more accurate.'

'What is lower than a horse thief?'

'A riddle?'

'That's what I thought, but if it is, it's not mine. Here's the deal' – she went on to retell the events at Duncan's that afternoon – 'and that's what he asked me. What's lower than a horse thief? I got a feeling from the way he asked that the vandalism might be connected. The horse-thief thing and his feud with MacGruder – he was asking if I'd heard any news about MacGruder.'

'News about MacGruder?' said Ozzie. 'Haven't seen him around here since he made parole.'

Lucas dropped his voice into a slow-witted monotone: 'Hell's bells, Your Honor, I was as surprised as anyone to learn them was stolen cars, yes I was.'

'MacGruder?' said Joyce, not at all sure she wanted to get closer to Dupree's unpleasant business problems. 'He has a tow truck?'

'A tow truck,' said Ozzie as he set about peeling the label from his beer bottle. 'He used to have big place closer to the interstate. Turns out he was running a chop shop.'

'More local history for you, Joycie,' said TJ, leaning in. 'OK, the cops knew it was someone out this way, but MacGruder had already planted evidence so that if they came looking, they'd look straight at Duncan, which is what happened. Cops bust the yard, go through everything, find nothing, but they keep Duncan under surveillance until about a week later when the overnight shift of stakeout guys on their way home stop at MacGruder's for coffee and walk right into a delivery of – mm-mmm, good – fresh, hot stolen vehicles. MacGruder pleas out by naming his suppliers. Major car ring goes down, and he does one year and a month out of the five he was given. Moron that he is, he comes back here, and ever since, he's run his little roadside car lot and stayed the fuck out of Grim Ass.'

Lucas's wristwatch beeped. He glanced at it before shutting it off. 'The fish,' he said, frowning. 'Anyway, that right there could be the solution to your riddle, TJ. If a horse was a means of transportation. Modern transportation is the automobile. Trade out the terms: what is lower than a car thief?'

'The one who rats out the thief to save himself?' TJ shook her head. 'That would be MacGruder, not Duncan. Everyone knows that. Besides MacGruder's been out for nearly three years, so why go for vengeance now?'

Joyce cleared her throat. 'Horse has other meanings.'

Lucas and TJ exchanged a glance, which Joyce read as his silent question and her quick response. 'No,' said TJ, 'I don't think that's it.'

'I don't think that's it,' said Ozzie, 'but I'm willing to entertain wagers.'

TJ smacked him lightly, the tips of her fingers glancing off his skull. 'I am willing to entertain that the three former Mrs Ozzie Mendozas will show up en masse to beat you senseless if you gamble away their alimony again. Sure thing.'

'Sure thing,' said Ozzie.

From behind them a group of men yelled, 'TJ!' in unison.

'Oops. I've been ignoring my fans – aw, shut up, you guys. I'll be right there.' She winked at Lucas as she left. 'You get any more ideas, you let me know.'

Lucas pushed at his glasses. He got off the bar stool and followed TJ down the length of the room and kept on going out the front door into the dark. Joyce turned to Ozzie, who in his sport coat and jowly weariness looked like a third-rate salesman experiencing an interminable slump. The multiple ear studs he wore in both lobes threw the salesman impression into a downward curve toward desperation. He gave her a grin and raised his bottle in salute. He didn't take a drink; he appeared to be on the verge of speaking, so Joyce waited, but he said nothing, only smiled and stared. It got to be unnerving, so she shrugged, and said, 'So what's with Lucas and the fish?'

'What's with Lucas and the fish? No one knows.' He took a long drink from the bottle, emptying it. He then pulled a bag of chocolate kisses from his coat pocket, offering her one. When she declined, he opened the bag and started shucking the chocolates free from their foil like beans from the shell. 'You can ask him – he'll be back in a minute after he's done checking on the stars. He says that some of the stars are moving too fast, and we may have gravity problems, which means we're going to have problems with time. According to Lucas, here and now are coming apart at the seams. Says he has inside info.'

'That's –' she stopped herself from continuing.

'That's' – Ozzie continued for her – 'Lucas. And the fish? We've all asked about the fish, but asking seems to make him very sad, so we gave up. Lucas is a genius – legit. His IQ is something like two-twelve, and he's as sensitive as a virgin's cl – Pardon me, he's real sensitive. Too smart and too tightly strung, that's Lucas's problem. That or he's crazy. He's no trouble to anyone; he's quiet and tends to keep to himself most of the time. We try to be real nice, real gentle with him on account we figure he's about a hair's breadth from taking up serial killing – if he hasn't already – and we'd like to stay on his good side.'

'You're kidding, of course,' said Joyce.

'Of course,' said Ozzie, popping a handful of chocolates into his mouth. Grin.

The Hoodoo emptied more slowly than it had filled. At two A.M. TJ locked the door and complained about still having to study later. Pete brought out the champagne. They drank. Joyce made a little speech about how grateful she was for their concern and that she had appreciated all the effort to scare her off, but their stories of curses and demons and disaster were for naught. She was staying. She asked Pete if he might accept a few dollars less on the place if she gave him cash for the transaction.

'The whole thing?'

'Every last penny. Cash. Tomorrow morning.'

Pete dashed across the room and threw his arms around Joyce and kissed her cheek as he whirled her about in a cloud of body and food odors. He let her go and kissed her again and jumped about, throwing victory punches at the heavens. TJ pointed at him and laughed. 'Joyce, you sure you want to stay someplace that feels this good to leave?' *Yes.* Eugene muttered something and Ozzie echoed it back: 'purified, drop-dead, out-of-your-head lunacy.' *Quite probably.*

'I should have told them,' she said aloud to the shadows of the hotel room. *Yes, but where would you begin?*

Joyce went into the bathroom and turned on the light. She opened the mirrored medicine cabinet over the sink. The six beer bottles were where she'd left them, tucked in at angles on the narrow metal shelves. She shut the mirror and had to face her tired, frightened reflection; she and the reflection turned away from each other quickly. *I should have said something about MacGruder's truck. If it escalates, the man might be in real danger. And the boy. The boy. You have to do it for Danny.*

She put her sweater on over her nightgown. The door to her

room creaked more than she remembered; she tried to be quiet, not wanting to wake anyone unnecessarily. She padded quickly down to the room TJ had gone into after saying good night. No light shone from under the door. Joyce knocked, waited, knocked again, louder. No answer. TJ must sleep with the same intensity she brought to her waking life. Well, it would wait until morning.

And what happened the last time you thought your problems could wait until daylight? Joyce stiffened against the memory, refused it entrance. She would have to call out there herself and do it right now, just in case. Waiting cannot always be forgiven.

She crept down the staircase into the lobby. Rachel or one of the boarders had left the television on, the sound still muted, still running film of the ridges of flame devouring the mountains to the west of Lágrimas. The blue flicker of the televised fire seemed only to accentuate the gloom, and Joyce was grateful for the tiny brightness of the electric candle Rachel left by the telephone for those who might need to make calls during the night. The phone number was still on the message pad where Rachel had written it down. Joyce picked up the receiver and took a deep breath, reassuring herself that the man couldn't possibly dislike her more than he already did. She dialed the numbers. It rang. And rang. She decided she'd let it go on ringing until he picked up.

It took a couple minutes, but the ringing quit in midtone. 'What?'

'I apologize for waking you, but –'

'Who is this?'

'Joyce.'

'Who?'

'You have my car? Vermont?'

He paused, then came a sound like he'd dropped the phone and a muffled barrage of swear words. 'I told you I'd call when it was ready, didn't I?'

'Yes. But this isn't . . . at the Hoodoo tonight I heard about . . .

133

well, I saw MacGruder's tow truck come through town. I thought you'd want to –'

'MacGruder in Lágrimas? When?'

'This afternoon. About fifteen, maybe twenty minutes after you dropped me off at the hotel. He whizzed through like he was in a hurry.'

'You're sure about this?'

'Yes.'

More muffled sound, as though he was covering the receiver to talk to someone else. 'I appreciate the information. I'm not surprised. It's a business situation; so not a concern for you.'

Joyce swallowed. 'I heard something about your situation tonight. I also heard about the horse-thief question.'

'Goddammit, TJ. Your mouth will –'

'Don't be angry with her. She's only trying to help by coming up with an answer –'

'She's the one who needs the help –'

'I just wanted to say that maybe no answer is the right one, not in the normal sense. Maybe the question itself is the point.'

He drew a deep breath, not speaking, while he seemed to consider this. 'OK, Vermont, enlighten me.'

'I used to work for a shipping company, very small, privately owned –'

'The abridged version?'

Joyce gripped the phone tighter. 'My boss and his wife divorced, a real bitter, vindictive breakup. He'd had her sign a prenuptial agreement so that if the marriage fell apart, she couldn't touch the business – and that was, of course, where all his money was. Since she couldn't benefit from it, she decided he wouldn't, either. She whispered some questions in the wrong ears, nothing big, just small, quiet uncertainties about shipment theft and employee problems. She let imaginations take over from there, and in no time the rumors were mushrooming: He's running drugs, guns, illegal workers. You can imagine how it played out. Clients got

134

wind of the stories; their nerves broke and they went elsewhere. The business slowed down; driver layoffs followed. The established clients, the ones he'd built the business with, started to doubt the stability of the company. For their own protection, they took their contracts to someone else. The whole company collapsed.'

'Tough break.'

'But the oddest part was that his most trusted, long-term employees – and I was one of them – we who worked there every day were dead certain the stories were false, and yet, we kept asking ourselves why was this business failing? The reasons we came up with were worse than any of the original rumors.'

He sighed. 'And the horse thief is the wife?'

'No. The thief is the question itself. What could be lower than the lowest thing out there? What's the worst betrayal you can think of? You don't need to have an answer; people will think up their own. And even when they know those answers are lies, it's next to impossible to prove something *isn't* happening.'

'Go on.'

She closed her eyes. 'Forgive me for what I'm about to suggest, because in my situation, I, more than anyone, want to believe a stranger might take in someone – you have Danny, a teenage boy, a child, living out there with you, right? Alone, right? In an isolated place, right? And he's obviously, um, dependent on your generosity. What do you get in return?'

He didn't answer. She could almost hear his disgust for her and her ideas coalescing at the other end of the line.

'Mr Dupree? Duncan?'

He hung up without saying any more.

TJ pushed up from where she had suspended herself to get her ear closer to the phone. She took the phone from his hand and set it on the table, which was a stretch from her current position, straddled over him, a knee wedged between each of his hips and the chair arms. She came back to center and braced her arms against the armrests. Her perfume was an expensive oriental spice fragrance she wore sparingly, so he could only catch the full spectrum of it when she got very close. She sank again, her breasts grazing his belly, and the spices filled his head – coriander and cinnamon plus an edge of the wildfire smoke that traveled from the other side of the mountains when the wind hit them right. The combination of fragrances suited her, but even with the swiveling pull of inner muscle that the girl ought to patent, he knew it was a lost cause. Hanging up the phone, he'd hung up his inclination as well. She realized the same. She scrunched her nose up in consternation and blew a puff of breath upward that fluttered the nylon strands of her ridiculous red wig. 'That was a real mood killer, huh?'

He ran his hand down her inner thigh. 'You heard?'

'All those nice things you said about me?' She sat up straight; the shift in her weight altered the path of sensation down his back. Same pain, different place. She must have seen it in his expression, because she tilted forward a bit to lessen the pressure. 'Yeah, I heard most of it.' She kept her voice low. Even though she had woken Danny enough to guide him, sleep-blind and mumbling lines about Ariel, into the bedroom that would be Duncan's if he were able to lie prone, and even though Danny's snores were rumbling through the walls, she was careful about these 'therapeutic' visits, as she called them. Danny had a sweetly chaste crush on the girl, and TJ wanted to protect both Danny and his reverence of her. She yawned; the thin straps of her satin camisole drooped over her shoulders. 'Do you think Joyce is on to something?'

'Doesn't matter. If she distilled it down to that, someone else will soon enough. That or something worse.'

'Worse? Earlier tonight, she was making all sorts of connections with different meanings of the words.'

'What words?'

'Horse.' TJ traced her fingers along the paths of old scars snaking up his arms. 'Danny can't stay out here anymore, can he?'

'No.' He brushed TJ's hand away. His head rang with the sound of iron rods clanking against the concrete as the attackers threw aside their weapons and ran. Did it always have to come as an ambush?

'The Freemonts will probably take him in.'

'For a day or two. Then Milt will get the heebie-jeebies about harboring a runaway, and they'll call in Social Services. I can't put Danny in that system. It will kill him.'

'Rachel has the room; she has kids, so maybe –'

'Rachel has too many kids as it is. I'm not ready to guarantee that Danny can be trusted around –'

'Joyce.' TJ jerked upright. 'That's why she's here. That's why she showed up when she did.'

'Wait a minute, Teej –'

'Don't you see it? She needs her son. Danny needs a place to stay. There's more than coincidence at work here.'

'TJ.'

'She's buying the freaking Hoodoo. It's perfect. Man, I love it when the gods opt for obvious. Look at it, Duncan: I tried to talk her out of it. We all did. Eugene told her about happy adventures with Charlie – and then he hit on her. Ozzie presented his "Lucas is a serial killer" theory. Lucas was, you know, Lucas – he was making Ozzie's case for him. After our little performance, I thought Cinderella would be hot-wiring a ride to get out of town before midnight. But she only smiles and stares at us with that same shiny expression. Until this instant, I thought it was because she was certifiable. Hell, I told the woman she was *búho* bait.'

'What if she is?'

'It's called gratitude, baby. Give it a try – or the Owl just may come who-whoing for you.' She poked him in the chest with two of her elegant fingers. 'It works, Duncan. Even you must see that. It works. It's the only option that does work. He'll have structure and supervision, and it's the most damn public place in town. No secrets at the Hoodoo. I'll be there to keep an eye on him. You'll be able to see him whenever you want. He can keep the drunks away from your pool table. It will be his official job. Oh, don't frown at me like that, Dupree. The spirits have sent you one of their weird cross-wired gifts. Take it before they change their minds.'

It might work, but – 'You seem mighty sure Vermont's going to agree to this.'

'I am.' She squirmed down on him for emphasis. 'Joyce has no choice. It's what she came here to do – Ooo . . .' TJ's eyes brightened, and she eased back down, forearms on the armrests, fake red hair and satin-covered nipples feathering along his chest. His lungs filled with allspice and ginger and the woody smoke of faraway fires. TJ laughed. 'I think someone just got happy again.'

Entr'acte: Abby

I am here to tell you the truth. You know, before you start making assumptions. Whether or not you believe me, I can't do anything about that. But, for whatever it may be worth, everything I'm about to tell you is true – which is not the same as saying it actually happened.

Six years ago, when I was eleven, I had an accident with a magnifying glass in the vacant lot at the end of my street. I was looking at ants, the tiny red biting kind, for a 'Nature in My Neighborhood' journal we were keeping as part of our environmental-studies project. I'd followed a grasshopper all the way up Madera Canyon Drive, although it probably had no idea my interests were limited to that of a sixth-grade class assignment. It probably thought I was chasing it because I was hungry. I was hungry, but by age eleven I was getting good at figuring out how to not feel what I was feeling. I exiled hunger from my belly, sending it to pace around the edges of my mind like one of those cage-crazed animals we saw on field trips to the zoo.

The vacant lot filled the curve of the cul-de-sac and spread out in a pie-shaped wedge until it hit the upward slope of the next hill. It was a rocky but level space covered with weeds and prickle plants. The air was full of chirping insect sounds. I had my notebook and pencil and the magnifying glass I'd borrowed from my mother's cross-stitch stuff – she uses it for enlarging patterns and undoing mistakes. I lost my grasshopper in the vacant lot; it escaped me, disappearing in the rustling brittle grasses. I was trying to hunt it down when I spotted the ants. Fire ants, they're called. They swarmed in curlicue lines around the tufts of brown grass to get to whatever was inside the lunch bag someone had dropped out there. The lunch bag was what they were after, but it took me a while to track down the hole in the crumbly earth where they were coming from. I felt tingles on my feet, crawling on my ankles and bare legs. I kept thinking the ants were on me, inside my socks and shoes, trundling blind up my thighs, up under the cuffs of my shorts. I slapped at myself and jumped around. I must have looked like a dork. But I didn't want even one on my skin. A single fire ant won't bite; it waits until a bunch of its buddies are on board, and then through some sort of ant ESP, they bite simultaneously. They got on me once when I was little and playing at a friend's house. I learned real quick how they earned their name. I screamed and screamed until my friend's mom came and turned the garden hose on me full blast to wash them off. My skin, where they'd bitten me, went sunburn red.

In our nature journals, we were supposed to note all our observations of the habitat. I wrote:

Habitat: Vacant Lot
Fire ants
Crawling
1,000,000 (approximately)
Madera Canyon Drive
Weeds
Garbage
Hot

We were supposed to draw pictures of what we saw, but fire ants are itsy-bitsy things, hard to see even if you get real close. I supposed they looked like every other ant out there, but I wanted to see if I could see their fire teeth. I wanted to be precise.

I scouted the edges of the swarm around the lunch sack, to find one of those loner ants you always see weaving around away from the group, and found a tiny little guy teetering along the bend in a blade of grass. I scrunched up a page from my notebook – it made a kind of bowl – and used the point of my pencil to knock the ant off the grass, catching it in the paper. Piles of rocks were scattered about like some of the younger kids had been playing in the lot, the way we used to play here. I used one pile of rocks as a stand for the bowl so that I could hold the magnifying glass in my left hand while I drew with my right. I squatted down and used my thighs as a table for my notebook. The ant scurried about the crinkles in the paper while I looked through the lens and drew and looked and drew.

Really, I was surprised how fast the paper caught flame, so surprised I think I might have shouted a swear word. I mean, I understood what had happened. We'd been doing the sun-and-magnifying-glass 'experiment' every year since second-grade science, but in school it seemed to take more time, forever in fact, for anything to ignite – and you hardly got a chance to see the flames before the teacher doused your creation. I suppose it was that prior experience of create-and-kill that had me stomping on the flaming paper and the captive ant, stomping everything down, out, drowning it in the dirt.

The second fire, a few minutes later, was not an accident. The idea welled up from what I used to call, when I was little, the dark of my brain. It was the place I thought I went when I slept, a theater space where dreams were projected – like movies. The ideas from the dark of my brain never felt like new ideas; I would not say inspiration had come up from behind and hit me. Dark-of-the-brain ideas feel more like remembering something I've always known. At that second, in the vacant lot, I seemed to remember that me and the fire ants had – as they say in the movies – some unfinished business. A score to settle. Here was the perfect opportunity.

I angled the pinpoint of sunlight onto the lunch bag. The

ants steered clear of that spotlight, I tell you. The bag started smoldering, and I could smell something like grilled hot dogs – baloney sandwich, I bet. The ants were scattering fast by this time, and as the flames chewed away the paper, I heard a tiny, crisp popping sound. I wonder if ants have a way of screaming.

I realized that most of them were going to escape, which didn't seem quite fair, as this was an exercise in long-overdue justice. I pulled up a handful of stiff brown grass blades and stuck them into the flames. I sprinkled the burning grass over the ant streams. That turned out to be a bit more effective than I'd hoped.

I'd avenged myself with the ants, all right. I'd also, by the time it was over, taken out eight acres and forced the evacuation of my street. We were lucky. The woman who lives in the house next to the vacant lot happened to walk past a window at exactly the right second to see me running through the lot, the flames fanning out behind me. She called the fire department. We were lucky. The wind was down, so the flames had munched away at the scrub on the hillside kind of lazylike. A small fire, by local standards. We were lucky. That's what my parents said, after the fireman and police had taken my statement and scolded me about the magnifying glass by saying that they were supposed to teach us about these things in school. We were lucky, my parents said. *We could have lost you.*

I had to write letters of apology to every one of our neighbors. And thank-you notes to the firemen. So that was luck?

Me Now
Abby
17 years old
Madera Canyon High School
Boyfriend: Not yet
Parents: 2
Siblings: 1 brother in college

Things I Don't Do
1. Drugs
2. Drink: booze or coffee
3. Smoke: weed or tobacco
4. Sex
5. Eat: red meat, french fries, candy, or breakfast, in hopes of staying thin enough so that someone will want me for #4 without first needing #'s 1, 2, or 3.

Things I Do
School
    a. Language Arts
    b. Biology II
    c. Calculus
    d. Drama: Class and Club
    e. Art History
    f. American History
Homework – I've been on the Honor Roll every semester since seventh grade.
Jobs: Pretzel Factory and baby-sitting
Exercise: Run 5 miles every day; bike; lift weights; swim
Drive my car to work so I can earn the money to pay for my car.
Set stuff on fire.

I think I may have screwed up. I'm sitting here in my aunt's kitchen trying to read a chapter of a history assignment on the first transcontinental railroad and how it changed the American economy and culture. I can't concentrate. I keep seeing the detectives as they walked past my locker, giving everybody and everything that sneaky sideways glance movie detectives use. It was right after lunch. We knew they were police; I mean we all knew – ant ESP – cops were on campus before they'd cleared the front desk. The Lockdown alarm rang – the code is two blasts – pause –

one long blast – repeat, not to be confused with the Fire, the Earth-quake, or the Someone's-Got-a-Gun alarms. Lockdown means you can't leave the building until they give the All Clear's long, steady, ear-breaking blast. The Lockdown alarm is always followed by lots of groans and swearing and slamming of locker doors; people have jobs to get to, places to be. Those of us with classes went off to class, like always. The detectives cruised around the halls for about thirty minutes. They talked to some teachers, including Mr Hommerson, who was giving us this very history assignment when the detective called him out of the room. He was gone for only two or three minutes, which could only mean a sort of roundabout questioning. The detective then came back in and took this long, slow look around the room. Thank God for all those improv exercises Old Lady Donetelli has us do in drama. I was able to look the guy right in the eye and not even blink. Acting innocent. Oh, yeah, they are looking for something, even if they aren't quite sure what – or who – it might be.

It's me they're looking for. They've been looking for a while. I can't help but see it in the newspapers. They're not sure I even exist; it's only speculation, but they've picked up a sort of pattern and regularity in some of these fires: small controlled burns on windless days. Hence my nickname: the Careful Arsonist. That's the best they could do? Let me tell you, the first time I saw that in print and realized it was me, I had to run to the bathroom. I threw up. It was awful. After a while, it became easier to deal with; I was glad they understood that I didn't want to hurt anyone.

Not that I'm keeping a scrapbook of clippings. That would be sick. I've done some research and learned that the experts believe that what I do is a 'plea for attention.' The fuss of a fire makes me feel important. I don't think so, Mr Expert Guy. It's not attention I want; I have too many people looking too closely at too many parts of me as it is. In fact, it's the exact opposite, when things are burning, people tend to *stop* paying attention to me – they look at the fire. They remember how big and uncontrollable the world is, how helpless we are, how stupid our lives can be. After the fire is out, for a while at least, an hour maybe, they stop the inventory of how pretty, how smart, how productive you are or are not, and they are happy for the sheer luck of not losing you. For a few minutes, you have a value for just standing there, upright among the ashes, just breathing, a value that outranks the house or car or job. It doesn't last long; soon, usually by cocktail time, you're back to what you were, another collection of pieces in the exhibit of their highly prized stuff. You would think that by now they'd smell the smoke on me.

Apparently, the detectives think they've smelled something, found some piece of something left behind at the last one. They just haven't figured out which one of us it belongs to. They've probably decided it means I want to get caught. They'd be wrong on that one, too. Uncaught is what I'm trying to get.

CAREFUL ARSONIST GETS CARELESS? That was the headline. I felt badly about that last one. I still do. Careless, yep. Madera was an impulsive fire, kind of like the ant thing; it got away from me. Big, uncontrollable, helpless, and stupid.

Madera Canyon Drive dumps out onto Little Diego Road, which winds on down the foothills, picking up the incoming traffic off these residential side streets before it merges into Big Diego, a four-lane boulevard banked on both sides by aging strip malls. Every year, the stretch makes the top ten on a bunch of environmental-disaster lists. You name it, Big Diego has it, sometimes twice. Everyone I know is working there – our parents use it as academic motivation: *Do you want to spend the rest of your life working for minimum wage on Big Diego?*

Six weeks ago – six weeks tomorrow, to be exact – I had just finished my shift in the roll-twist-salt pit of despair that is the Pretzel Factory – oh, go on, guess where it is – and I was heading out back where they make us pretzel slaves park our cars. We're up against a corroded stretch of bent and buckled chain-link fencing intended to keep the junior-high brats from pushing the Dumpsters

145

over the edge of the ravine. Thus thwarted, the brats take the trash bags out of the bins and hurl them individually over the fence. The bags split and spill. Everything rots down there. We get coyotes and rats. It's lovely.

Six weeks ago, tomorrow. It was one of those nice days we get in late September. Still hot as the ovens in the Pretzel Factory, but the smog wasn't so bad that your lungs felt bruised by every breath you took. The building next to the Factory had propped its back door open with a folding chair. I heard voices coming from inside, two guys arguing. It was one of those arguments where it's clear the issue is already settled. It's won and over, but the loser won't give up. I recognized the voice of the owner – the obvious victor. He has a very formal way of speaking that sounds completely fake, but he seems nice enough. He was doing that emphatic thing with his voice that nice people resort to when they realize that 'nice' isn't getting the job done. The loser was crying; his words were choked and broken, so I couldn't recognize him on sound alone. I was sure I must have seen him. A lot of them were just impoverished students for whom a pretzel and a soda were the big meal of the day. We pretzel slaves weren't 'nice' to the magicians. Actually, we sort of treated them like the bad jokes they were. I was kind of taken aback by how emotional this guy was. I know, it was rude listening in like I did, but I swear it was the first time I'd heard a man, outside the movies, cry like that.

'Please. One more chance. I can't go back like this. Please let me stay. I'll practice; I'll get better.'

'You have the desire, my friend, I'll give you that, but you don't seem to have the requisite skills, the requisite *adroitness* for the work. I am sorry, but it would be unfair, it would be wrong – worse, it would be *immoral* to take any more of your money.'

Not take any more of his money? He was getting dumped. If it weren't for the guy's heart breaking, I would have laughed out loud. I mean it's a school for magicians in a strip mall on Big Diego. The Academy Arcana? Christ, the place exists to take

146

people's money. In exchange, they might land you a gig as one of those cheesy restaurant geeks who slink up to the table and ask the birthday girl if she'd like to see some card tricks. How about a balloon animal, honey? How sad is that?

My eyes went blurry with tears. Why was I crying? Here was somebody begging to be given a second chance in strip-mall hell. It wasn't sad. It was pathetic. He was flunking out of loser school. I wiped my eyes and went on home.

No one was there. Not unusual. The kitchen counter was piled with partially unpacked shopping bags from the Real Mall. (See what they did there? It's like, 'Take that Big Diego, we're a *real* mall,' but they jazzed over the insult by pronouncing it Spanish-like: Ray-al. Clever, huh?) Mom had been scorching the credit cards at La Cuisinerie again. She took cooking classes over there. She was into Tuscan at the time, and the fridge was reloaded daily with fresh pastas, peppered bacon, and weird crap like preserved figs. She kept a big jar of oil-cured olives on the top shelf that made me think of mummified eyeballs. Mom had clay pots of herbs lining the windowsill and wine bottles cradled in baskets of yellow straw and hefty loaves of bread singed crisp on the crusty edges. I wished then, as I wish now, that it was OK to eat, but I resisted; resist, because when love finally comes, it will feel like food – what else would love feel like? – and then I can be full and thin at the same time. I've yet to meet anyone who made it work the other way around.

I finished unpacking the bags to see if she'd brought anything good home, maybe some chocolate; nothing restores my confidence like saying a big old *No* to a hunk of dark semisweet. Well, almost nothing. Alas, a braided rope of garlic cloves, a tube of saffron threads, white peppercorns, more herb seeds, a cylindrical bottle of rock salt. The salt was in one those old-fashioned bottles with the metal clamps that's supposed to make it look special instead of like what it is. Salt. Although this stuff was different; it was pink, sort of pink. I held it up to the sunlight coming in the window.

Pink, all right. The label declared it to be WORLD-FAMOUS FLOR DE LÁGRIMAS GOURMET SALT. La-di-da. The label explained that the salt was 'hand-harvested' by 'a cooperative of artisans' called *paludiers*. You have to love the gourmet-food racket; find the foreign way to say anything, and add ten bucks to the tag. The label went on to explain the pink color was from beta-carotenoids – a source of important beta-carotene vitamins – left behind by bacteria; I stopped there and reminded myself to stay away from the saltshaker. Bacterial pink salt? That's what she paid – gasp – twelve dollars for?

The bottle came with a card, light beige in color, tied to the metal clamp with a piece of red string. On one side of the card was printed a map of where the salt came from, along with an invitation to stop by Lágrimas and tour the facilities. Yeah. Right. Sounded like a fourth-grade class trip if I ever heard one. The other side of the card presented 'The Legend of Playa de Lágrimas.' Ooo – stories. I grabbed a diet soda from the fridge and sat cross-legged on the floor to read.

Long ago, when water was here, a people made their home in this valley, for it was soft and green and thick with life. Among these people, as is the way of people everywhere, a man fell in love with a woman. She loved him in return. They promised their lives to each other.

One morning, the man went off to hunt food. Day passed into evening. He did not return. His young wife, stricken with fear, set out by moonlight to find her husband.

Near dawn, she came upon his body. Not a mark was upon him, no injury, no cause for his passing. She lay down in the grass beside him and held him and wept. Her tears rolled to the earth and ran together into a pool that grew with her grief until it became a small sea.

For many days and nights, she lay with her dead love, weeping. She would have lain there forever, had not the most

148

ancient of the gods wandered by in the guise of a coyote. He saw the lake of tears and laughed. 'Surely, child, you will flood the valley with all this weeping.'

'Have the gods no pity?' she said. 'Can you not see that I have lost my love, my husband, the reason for my entire life?'

'Pity, we have,' said the coyote, 'and we do see.'

'Then rid the world of its sorrow,' she sobbed. 'Take pity on us and take away our tears.'

'If that is what you wish,' said the coyote before continuing on his way.

The woman's weeping ceased. Her heart felt lighter, empty, like a dried gourd. The lake of tears was gone. Gone as well, the soft green grasses. The young woman found herself embracing nothing as she lay among a dry scattering of bones. Choking dust swirled about her on the broken, salt-crusted ground. 'What have you done?' she cried after the coyote, her horrified voice barely able to escape the gusting wind.

'Only as you asked,' the coyote said, his laughter returning. 'This is the world without sorrow, child. This is the world without tears.'

Weeping. I thought immediately, of course, of that poor sobbing dweeb getting his butt kicked out of magician college. The idea appeared right then, perfect and shining and whole, an island of fire surfacing from the dark of my mind. I'd do the magic school. I'd set the Academy Arcana to flame, and the loser dweeb, wherever he might be when he heard about it, would feel lucky. Saved by his own failure. And if the Pretzel Factory caught an inferno by association, I would have saved us both.

I didn't plan it out much except for figuring that it would have to wait for Sunday when the stores opened later and the Academy was closed. As Sunday got closer, however, I kept thinking that I had no way to be sure the buildings were completely empty. I didn't want to hurt anyone. And honestly? I wasn't confident I could start a building, get it going small and quiet and keep it going until I got far enough away. The buildings have alarms. Nature doesn't. I scaled back to the tried and true; I'd start the ravine behind the buildings. What with all the garbage and the dried grass down there, I'd only have to squint at it and think angry thoughts to get it going. I felt much better, more sure of myself. But my trusty magnifying glass was out. Early in the day, the sun wouldn't be high enough. Later? I couldn't just stand around at lunch break throwing laser beams from the sun into the kindling. *What are you doing, Abby?* Nope, that wasn't going to happen. Still, it wasn't going to be difficult. It wasn't rocket science.

The plan was this: Sunday, I get up at four-thirty, as I usually do, for my run. I dress in warm-up pants and put on the long-sleeve T-shirt I wear when it's too cool to be out in only my sports bra. I tie my shoes tight and knot an old bandanna around my head as a sweatband. I do some warm-up stretches for my sleep-tightened muscles. I hate the static stretch stuff, the hold and breathe and count of it, but I pay later with cramps and shin splints if I skip limbering up. I gulp down a carton of orange juice and then grab my water bottle and go out into the garage where I fill it to the top with gasoline from the can my dad keeps for the lawn mower. I take a book of matches from the box of supplies we keep in case of earthquakes or whatever.

I must be pumping more adrenaline than I can feel, because my feet are flying; I sprint the entire way. Thirty-five minutes, a new personal best. By the time I reach the parking lot, I am huffing and puffing and I feel the pulsing heat of the flush in my face, but I also feel the calm, the undeniable correctness of what I am about to do. The breeze, slight when I left home but stronger now and building, cools my skin. I double-check to make sure I am alone. No cars. The sky is getting to the first blue of morning, and the sun is rosy-gold between the buildings, beautifully soft on the hillside on the other side of the ravine. Here in the parking lot, the buildings kindly provide a cloak of shadow for my work.

It doesn't take long. I get the water bottle under the lower edge of the fence at a place where it bows from being bumped by a delivery truck. I unscrew the lid. The fumes bring water to my eyes. God, I'm thirsty. I give the bottle a tiny shove so that it will tip onto its side and roll over the edge and down the slope and into the paper-studded scrub, spilling a trail of gas as it goes. I light one match and set it to the puddle where the bottle first fell. A sweet little *tha-wump* sounds and the blue-footed flames race down the trail. A few seconds later a much more robust *Tha-Wump* erupts with a bright flash. Abracadabra!

A flock of dung-colored sparrows explodes out of the ravine. Above their panicked chirping I can hear the happy rice cereal–snapping of plants crinkling up in flame. It is started. I toss the lid to the water bottle over the fence, likewise the rest of the matches, and I start jogging toward home, the breeze, really more a wind now, chilling my sweat-dripping body.

Nothing went the way it was supposed to. The people who live high on the hillside in houses that cantilever out into midair on those ridiculously perilous stilts slept in late or went to church or idled on the wrong side of their homes. No one was watching. Someone was supposed to see the flames and call it in; someone always does; I plan for that. The wind was supposed to stay low and harmless, not become a full-scale Santa Ana gusting upwards of fifty miles per hour. The fire was supposed to stay in the ravine, not break free as windblown embers of garbage or branches that would burst into full flame on browning lawns and sun-baked roofing or explode in the tinder-quick stands of pines. It was like a giant Fourth-of-July sparkler had gone off over us and it was raining stars. The canyon burned for days and days. Firefighters trucked in from all over So-Cal and later from out of state. It kept getting around them and over them. Big Diego burned. Little Diego burned. The mountains beyond burned and kept burning for over two weeks. I lost count of the final number of acres, although I do remember the houses. I managed to burn down fifty-seven houses, including my own. The local papers and the televisions ran damage totals, the injured, the property loss. No one died. Everyone said for that we'd been lucky – very, very lucky.

I tried to confess. We were throwing things into the car to evacuate and I tried to tell them that this was all my fault. I kept yelling at them, 'This is me. This is mine. I did this.' My mom, who was still in her bathrobe and crying, kept yelling back, 'It's not your fault, Abby. How could this be your fault?' Even as I drove my car out behind theirs, through swirling vortex tunnels of smoke, I kept screaming that this was all my fault until I couldn't hear myself above the sirens.

So we're living with my aunt and uncle and three cousins for a while until we see what the insurance clears, what we can rebuild. I have my car but no job. I have a ton of homework that I can't focus on, and I have nightmares about being swallowed by monsters. After today, I have reason to believe that those nightmares are about to come true. I believe those detectives are going to believe every word I tell them, and I will tell – unless I'm not around to ask.

I can't work right now. I close my history book, one of the few things of 'mine' that is left because my schoolbag was in the car at the time we fled. *Fled* is the only word for it. I slip the card I've been using for a bookmark into the fold of the book's spine. It's the card from the salt bottle. I pull it down below the edge of the pages so that no one will see it – even though, at this point, only I understand its significance. The print is wearing off from my fingers running over it for six weeks, as I considered the invitation. It is an invitation. Says so right here in worn blue italics: *You are invited to visit Lágrimas.* They've even provided a map to show me where it is, in a remote crook of an anonymous Mojave valley. Hours away. I can be there by suppertime if I leave right now. I will only be making matters worse, of course. They'll start wondering why. Confessions will be remembered. They'll believe me best if I run.

A world without tears? Sign me up for the whole tour, Lágrimas. *Fled* would be the word.

II. Strix

One

He was sneaking over the threshold of sleep, just about inside, when his ever-vigilant gatekeeper tripped the alarm and had him ejected from the sanctuary of his own home. Duncan was jolted once more back to wakefulness. Third time that night. He decided it was time to quit trying and get up. Braced for the usual protests from the usual places, he reached for the lever that would contract the recliner back into standard chair configuration. Except for a bit of stiffness in the muscles, his back had no complaints. Second morning in a row. That's over twenty-four hours without pain, which, for Duncan, felt like twenty-four hours without gravity. He eased himself out of the recliner and straightened with a fluidity of motion he found frightening.

The pain did this occasionally, made these dramatic departures without any clue as to why or what he'd done to bring the big exit on. He used to fall for it, too. He'd believe. He'd strut and stretch and shout in celebration only to be cut down by its door-busting return. *Gotcha.* A young doctor at the pain-management clinic had given him theories. He'd paid attention because she had long legs, a kind smile, and because she was so new to the reality of her work, her eyes still held voluptuous depths of hope. She had faith, and he was desperate to be converted. She'd sat close, bent over her clipboard, and while chewing on a piece of wintergreen gum, told him in those earnest tones doctors use when they're explaining from book learning as opposed to body knowledge, that pain was a complex event of stimulus and interpretation. Sometimes, in chronic cases such as his own, the pain sensors in the brain, overwhelmed by the ongoing input, get locked in the On position so that pain is experienced even when the stimulus isn't present.

'You think I'm making this up?'

'Oh, no, Mr Dupree,' she said, 'it's real. Your pain is real.' For that, he loved her, instantly, completely, would have married her on the spot if she'd have had him. He told her that, and, bless her, she didn't laugh. She shook her head with great sadness. 'It's going to be difficult for you. More difficult than it is for the others, and for the others it is hell.'

He'd grown smarter about it, stopped trying to figure out if these miracle hours of reprieve were a gift or a perverse form of torture, like allowing prisoners of war to think they've escaped. Over the years, the question had evolved away from the *why* of things to the *what*. And then *What next?* had become *What now?* Slowly the questions died out all together. He had learned to accept that he was in the direct path of colliding forces larger than his understanding. God may not play dice with the universe, but He sure shot a mean game of pool.

And the shots God had taken over this passing month had bordered on the tricky, show-off stuff a hustler indulges when he's decided to let it tip that not only have you been had, but there's nothing short of your own damnation that you can do about it. Danny was living with Vermont, four and a half weeks now – no sign of her own kid yet; Danny was going far to fill in that blank, too far, from how she'd taken to mothering him. That was a worry, but what could he do? For the time being, Vermont using Danny as a surrogate was Danny's own best insurance until Duncan could care for the kid again himself. From the looks of things, that was going to be a while. Business was still off. Sophie assured him he was back on the rotation at Impound, but the two-way stayed hushed; the pager didn't buzz. The scrap end of things kept him busy enough; he was spending most of the day crushing, working the claw on the crane to grab and drop so that the yard was being screechingly transformed from a chaotic jumble of automobile carcasses to pyramid stacks of rectangular metal blocks. The maze was rising up and changing shape, a different, more useful configuration of walls. He was building a battlement.

The phone rang. He reached for it, resting his hand on the receiver, waiting. The ringing continued.

He felt a confrontation of some sort coming, and that wasn't just his daily dose of paranoia taking hold – in the pain's absence he was better tuned to the prickling pitch of unease in his gut. The phone rang on. He had to answer. He had agreed to be available to Vermont for problems that – Danny being Danny – might arise, and he'd promised Danny he'd be there whenever the kid needed. Being there meant answering the phone.

He picked up midring, put the receiver to his ear. 'Yeah?'

Breathing. A swallow. And then the quiet click of disconnection. See, this was the tribulation: it wasn't the kid or Vermont calling most often; it was these calls from no one, the listening before the hang-up. *I know where you are, Dupree,* the silence said, *and I am watching.* Lágrimas phone service didn't provide such luxuries as caller identification features that could tell him these calls were from a pay phone or an unknown number with an unknown name. Unknown, maybe, but Duncan could guess. Might be MacGruder marching on in his adolescent campaign of intimidation. Might be someone else. Any one of many someones who hadn't heard that Duncan was no longer carrying anything for anybody; he had nothing. They'd taken it all. What the fear told him was that some fateful magnet had drawn the filaments of his past out of their proper place, buried in time, and had dropped them in a forge to be melted down, reunified. A needle. A crowbar. This was why he was happy Danny was elsewhere, nagged and nattered at. The yard was no longer a safe place. It had become a part of the world.

Joyce woke coughing. Her mouth was caked with the salted-wool taste of Lágrimas dust. A bad case of old Grim Ass grit-'n'-spit.

Charlie had warned her off sleeping with the windows open on certain nights. But even after a month in Lágrimas, she had yet to develop a sense for the subtle turning of currents that would send a wave of dust off the dry lake, down the road, into town.

The night before, she had stood out under the stars while Danny brought in the NEW OWNER, NEW HOURS, NEW MENU sign Eugene had built for her. The sky had been cold and clear, the darkness layered with gossamer sheets of stars. She'd held her arms out, like a weather vane, and waited for a nudge of what the others felt in the barometers of their bones. Her inability to anticipate the shifting currents in the wind only reminded her again that even though the place was hers, she was as much an outsider at the Hoodoo as anywhere else. It was the unreadable weather and TJ slipping, unthinking, into Spanish with the customers and the jargon of the salt co-op and Danny's wholly recognizable yet uncrackable code. Being surrounded by all these languages she couldn't speak had made her daring in silly ways. She would have been willing to bet – and a dollar to Ozzie for the exercise – that this night she could leave her bedroom window cracked to the mid-November chill that assuaged her homesickness for Vermont. At least she wasn't required to admit this foolishness to anyone.

Through the window she could now see the night softening with the milky glaze of the emerging day. She pulled the dust from the corner of her eye with the tip of her little finger and checked the clock. It was five-fifteen, time to commence the ritual of bribing her body out of bed with promises of a nap after the breakfast rush. *Back under the covers for an hour. I swear.* She knew she was lying, but she shoved back the comforter and got up anyway.

The morning's cold held no nostalgia for her except, perhaps, the suddenly fond memories of a certain cranky old oil furnace that had groaned and rattled as it blasted hot air through the vents. The electric baseboard here in the apartment was no match; its *ping-pingy* noises were annoying, and the heat it provided was meager at best. Joyce pulled off her nightgown and raced the cold to get her body into underwear, jeans, and shirt. She threw on a sweater and shoved her feet into her grease-stained mules.

She pushed aside the canvas curtain. The sitting room, where Danny slept on the foldout sofa Duncan had contributed, was a part of the Hoodoo's original structure. It was protected from the wind and caught each day's spillover of kitchen heat, which dissipated slowly through the building's thick walls. The room was quite comfortable; if only she could convince the boy of that. She turned on the floor lamp, but she already knew he wouldn't be there. Danny was dealing with a homesickness of his own.

She went out into the kitchen and switched on the overhead fluorescents. They flickered to life, making a feeble mirror of the window over the sinks. Joyce saw herself reflected in watery greens against the brightening lavenders of the dawn. On the sill were the six bottles of beer she'd emptied down the Hotel sink after TJ had shown up at her door with Duncan's proposal: that Joyce look after Danny for a while in exchange for Duncan's repairing her Saturn. The arrangement was simultaneously more expensive and beneficial to her, but the idea had her spinning with emotional vertigo for hours. In an effort to steady her nerves and as a private toast to second chances, she'd dumped her traveling companions. The bottles now served as inelegant vases for six fake sunflowers that shone sallow in the cold electric light. Joyce hit the brew switch on both coffeepots, grabbed a sponge from the dish rack, wiped the dust off the grill. She yawned, loudly, before taking one of the long stick matches from the metal shelving next to the grill. She struck the match and proceeded to light the pilot flame on the main burner.

The rushing swoosh of gas into flame was a warming sound, and the quiver of heat from the gas jets gave her a shudder against the cold. Nevertheless, in an hour the heat raging from the grill would have her fantasizing about defrosting the freezer, her bare arms and neck sprinkled with ice chips as she hacked away. She went to the big refrigerator near the back door and pulled out double cartons of eggs, a box of bacon rashers, and a half-gallon paper carton full of premixed pancake batter. She lined these up on the table to the right of the grill.

And now her *favorite* part of what had become the morning ritual. She pulled the sweater tight and shouldered through the swinging door into the bar. Without taking her eyes off the still, dim space of the Hoodoo's main room, she found the wall switches. She flipped on the lights. The overhead fans began a lazy rotation. Joyce took the stiff-bristled broom from its corner by the door and began her daily search for uninvited guests: rats, lizards, snakes – with rattlers and without.

Behind the bar the raised platform of slatted wood flooring, designed to let spilt drinks and dropped ice fall beneath the path of the bartender's feet, was clear. Nothing hiding in the overflow catch beneath the beer taps, no snakes coiled in the ice bin or sleeping on the chipped black granite of the bar itself. Well, none of the usual sort; she put a near-empty Johnnie Walker bottle back on the shelf and flipped on the bar lights, halogen spots illuminating the fairy-tale city of pink crystal towers that made up the salt display. She had yet to sell a single one. The arrangement of salt bottles served best as armature for the nightly weavings of inoffensive spiders. These she flicked away with a dampened bar cloth.

Satisfied with the pest-free state of the bar area, she ventured out onto the terra-cotta tile flooring of the main part of Hoodoo, checking beneath each of the twelve tables, in the seats of each of the forty-eight wooden chairs. She ran the broom behind the broken jukebox and the broken pinball machine. She broomed the sills of the narrow gun-turret windows, working her way toward the pool table where Danny slept. The cocoon of the blanket he'd dragged in with him had fallen to the side, and now he was fetal-curled, stark naked, against the cold.

Joyce used the broom to reach over him and grab the loop in

160

the string that controlled the lamp over the table. Three disks of incandescent light fell over the boy's thin, scarred body. She pulled the blanket back over him, out of concern that it would shame him to be found unclothed, and tucked the fabric around him as she gently shook his shoulder.

'Danny? Come on, honey, time to wake up.'

He yawned and smacked his tongue and rolled over. He was getting used to her, thank goodness. The first few days had been one continuous temper tantrum, so exhausting that when Duncan did return her repaired car, Joyce had asked if he wanted to take Danny back in a trade. Duncan had laughed, shook his head, and said, 'Fun, isn't it?' Things had improved, slowly, and now morning no longer meant cries and cowering and having things such as raven's feathers from unwholesome fen and blisters wished upon her. These days he'd only blink and rub at his eyes with balled fists as he did now.

Joyce leaned on the broom. 'What am I going to have to do to keep you in your own bed? I know you miss Duncan, but it's too cold out here.'

He huddled deeper into the cocoon. 'Sir, my liege, do not infest your mind with beating on the strangeness of this business: at picked leisure, which shall be shortly, single I'll resolve you – which to you shall seem probable – of these happened accidents; till when, be cheerful and think of each thing well.' Joyce assumed this was Danny-speak for 'Everything's fine. Leave me alone.' Shakespeare or not, it was typical teenage-boy dismissal.

'All right, but you'd better make sure none of these "happened accidents" happen on Duncan's table. He'll kill us both.' She shooed him to standing, ignoring his grumbles as he crawled off the table and shuffled toward the back; he clutched the blanket around his shoulders and let the bottom drag the floor like a king's robe. 'Get some clothes on. And don't dawdle. Duncan said he was going to be round to get you before seven, and this time you are not leaving without breakfast. Wear something warm!'

161

By the time she'd finished, she was yelling at the closed kitchen door, but damn, it felt good to be yelling at a kid about breakfast, only about breakfast. She smiled and went to finish her rounds, reminding herself, as she approached the rest room, of Ozzie's breakdown on the exact odds of finding a rat backstroking in the toilet two days in a row.

She was dicing potatoes when she heard the deep-throated chug of TJ's Thunderbird pull into the lot, the gravel crunching as the car rolled to a stop. It was six A.M. She hefted another pile of tiny white potato cubes into the steel bowl of ice water where they'd sit until she fried them up on the grill with red peppers and onions for hash browns.

The lock on the back door rattled and clicked. TJ came in and hung up her coat on one of the hooks Joyce had installed. It was New Waitress Day again. The wig was blond and straight; she'd braided a few strands near the front, weaving them with beads and feathers. She wore jeans torn at the knee and a loose peasant blouse that rode the outer edges of her shoulders and was embroidered with rosebuds at the cuffs, neck, and hem. Her wrists jangled with dozens of fine silver bangle bracelets. Every finger had a ring, as did several of the toes poking through the ends of her sandals. She grinned her ever-so-pleased-with-myself TJ grin and raised her fingers in a V. 'Peace.'

'Very nice, Nicolette.'

TJ clucked her tongue and pouted. 'Nicolette? Nobody calls me Nicolette any more.'

'Nobody but the guys at Social Security. I went over your employment papers last night. I know what you're clearing waiting tables at the Hoodoo. There's no way you're living, driving, and going to school on what you make here.'

'So' – her voice tightened, defiant even before accused – 'you want to know where the Tequila Jane comes from?'

'No. But I can guess.'

TJ laughed. 'It was a gift. A souvenir of a particularly good –'

'Just go on out front and open the doors.'

'Why are you so angry? I don't see how my admirers are any of your business.'

'Admirers? Is that word for it these days? And I'm not angry.' She dumped another handful of potato cubes into the bowl of water. 'I'm concerned.'

TJ ambled over and picked up a scrap of red bell pepper. She began to munch on it. 'What are you concerned about, Joyce?'

'You. I thought you wanted out of this town. I thought you were a lawyer.'

'I'm an artist. Law is the third oldest art. Survival is the first.'

'If you want to risk your future –'

'Maybe I do. Anyway it's *my* future. Don't worry. I know what I'm doing.'

'I hope so, sweetie. You're too smart for this.'

'Smart enough not to question the path of least resistance, which, for a woman, always seems to lead right to her –'

'TJ. Please.'

TJ leaned across the worktable and kissed Joyce on the cheek. 'Relax. I'm not what's-her-name.'

'Who? What are you talking about?'

'The girl who took off with your kid. I'm the one who thought Danny should be here with you, remember. I'm not about to spirit him away.'

Joyce put down the knife. 'You think you have us all figured out, don't you?'

'Pretty much.' She grinned, and grabbed another hunk of pepper.

Joyce returned the grin. 'Don't be so sure of that.'

'The gods are complicated. People are easy. Some people are easier than others, if you get my drift.' She winked and then ducked, laughing, as Joyce threw a potato cube at her in punishment for the wordplay. 'I'll go open up now.' TJ left the kitchen, singing something in Spanish.

'Maddie,' said Joyce, feeling the smile drain from her face. 'Her name was Maddie.' She wiped the potato water from her hands with her apron and went back to check on Danny.

The breakfast rush was on. Joyce cracked eggs, flipped pancakes, turned bacon. Her perspiration would occasionally drip and sizzle on the grill. Slices of white and wheat bread rolled through the toasting oven, tortillas warmed in a clay casserole, and water dribbled into the coffeepots. The door swung open and shut as TJ brought in orders and filled her tray with orders completed, plus syrups, ketchup, Tabasco, and salsa from a can. She kept bringing in tidbits of gossip: who was seated with whom this morning, who wasn't speaking to his or her spouse, who was wearing new clothes or jewelry. Countless variations of the same tiny details that elsewhere in the world might prove tiresome at best, but here, in Lágrimas, constituted big news.

Danny, with a napkin at his neck to protect his clean blue sweater, sat at the worktable, finishing off a second helping of pancakes. During the month of his new job at the salt co-op, the boy's hair had lightened, and his face had grown even more tan. In spite of the sunscreen Joyce had taught him to slather over his skin, he had freckled across his cheeks, nose, and forehead. She had, at first, made him leave with a hat, and although she reminded them of it every morning when Duncan came round to give Danny a ride out to the salt company, she wasn't sure if Duncan made him wear it. She'd ordered a few clothes for him through a catalog: the sweater he was wearing now, a couple of flannel shirts, blue jeans, that sort of thing. In sizes that fit him properly. Shakespeare hadn't written a way for Danny to say it, but Joyce was playing the hunch that the kid might be tired of oversized khaki work shirts.

When Duncan had learned of this, they'd argued over the expenditure. Duncan wanted to pay Joyce back, and she would have none of it. Thus began the nightly Danny conferences shouted across the Hoodoo as Duncan shot pool and Joyce tended bar.

'If you're going to be buying him clothes, then let me drive him out to the co-op,' Duncan had said, racking the balls. 'Least I can do.'

'You must really miss him.'

'Of course I miss him. I miss having the help.'

'Oh,' Joyce had said as she put clean glasses back on the shelf, 'you miss the help.'

He'd lit a cigar. 'Yeah. Some days are more of a challenge than others.'

'Must you?' She'd tried to wave the smoke away from the bar with a towel. 'I've known lots of people with back pain. You don't have to suffer. Can't you get Milt Freemont to prescribe something for it?'

'Nothing I can take.'

'That's ridiculous.'

He'd almost laughed. 'I agree.' He put the cigar in the ashtray on the table rail and went back to his game, laying the cue stick across one angle, then the next, to line up the shot.

She'd realized something about him at that moment, something, maybe the one thing, they had in common. 'You hate this, don't you?'

'This?' He glanced up from where he stood poised in what must have been an aching posture, ready to shoot.

She lifted her arms to show him she meant *this*: the situation with Danny, certainly, but also the pool table and the reason for it and the Hoodoo and the salvage yard and Lágrimas and the world itself, not life so much as the terrible onslaught of living, the endless, exhausting, hurting work of it. 'This.'

He had paused as though giving it some thought. 'What's to like?' he said, and went back to his game.

So now, a month later, when Duncan let himself into the kitchen to collect Danny and said a sentence or two between greeting and good-bye, Joyce sensed a growing affinity between them. It wasn't friendship, exactly; she doubted either them was capable of that.

She could barely remember what the word meant. Something about the situation was shifting. It was perhaps no more than the simple arithmetic of survival: Danny needed Duncan, and Danny needed Joyce, and therefore, by extension, Duncan and Joyce needed each other. They still argued over almost every detail of Danny's care, but day by day, they were adjusting toward something like a sense of ease in each other's company.

A horn sounded out in the rear lot. It was Duncan's signal that he was here and Danny should be ready to leave pronto. Joyce hurried Danny along, pointing with the pancake spatula toward the apartment, listing off reminders to brush his teeth and comb his hair, and not to forget his hat.

Duncan knocked on the back door. He always knocked. What did he think he was interrupting? She shouted at him to come on in, as always. He did. She told him to grab some coffee, if he wanted. He did. She offered to cook him some breakfast, if he wanted. He declined. TJ had said that in four short weeks, Duncan and Joyce had become so predictable and contrary in regard to each other that anyone would believe them long married. Joyce replied that one's spouse is anything but predictable and that she herself chalked up their ritual to a shared predisposition for order.

Duncan stood well out of her way on the other side of the kitchen and nursed his mug of coffee. He wore his navy-blue rancher's jacket with the tan corduroy lining – which, no, he wasn't going to take off because he wasn't staying – over his usual pressed khaki work clothes – which, yes, he ironed himself – and today, he also wore a navy knit watch cap. Even under the bulk of the jacket, Joyce could see he'd lost more weight. It worried her that he was one of those men who would rather work than eat and that if left to his own devices, he might not think to stop for Danny's sake. She'd taken to fixing them a bag of sandwiches to take with them. If she came right out and said that it was lunch for Duncan, too, he'd have never accepted it. If she'd said it was lunch for Danny, Duncan would have been insulted by the implication of negligence.

So they left each day with a sack lunch that was for neither of them. Heaven knew what they did with the food.

Joyce put a couple apples and a box of cookies in the lunch sack. 'So, I know how TJ is supplementing her income.'

Duncan sipped his coffee. 'The girl is nothing if not resourceful.'

'I tried to talk to her.' She folded the edge of the lunch sack shut. 'Maybe you could talk to her, too. She might actually listen to you.'

He lowered the mug and stared into the coffee. He was trying to hide his laugh. 'Oh, I have talked to TJ.' He raised his face and regarded her, plainly delighted by her concern. 'And she has listened.'

'I am serious, Dun –' Understanding hit and Joyce clamped her mouth shut.

He fought the laugh with less and less success. 'I swear, if a woman could shoot brimstone through just a look in her eyes, I'd be –'

'I don't care what you do.' She lowered her voice. 'But Danny shouldn't be –'

The swinging door bashed inward, and Eugene bashed in behind it. He was wearing the same jeans, Harley T-shirt, and leather vest he'd been in when he'd stumbled out of the Hoodoo the night before. He stopped short of bashing straight into Joyce, exhaled, shook his head.

'What?' Joyce said, glancing over at Duncan.

Eugene motioned them toward the dining room.

The breakfast stragglers had left their cluttered tables to gather at the bar to watch the television, their upturned faces bathed in blue glow. TJ was behind the bar. She held a white dishrag by its corners, twirling it tight one way, then the other. Joyce pressed her way past Lucas and Charlie to get closer to the screen where she could now see a young man in a blue-gray suit arcing his arm in demonstration across a map of Southern California. He spoke in a melodious baritone perfectly suited to his movie-star looks – angular jaw, dimples, sculpted hair. His teeth were white as bleached chalk.

'. . . as this graphic indicates, these dueling lows set up the sort of unique situation we see maybe every decade or so . . .'

On the map, a vast computer-generated swirl of clouds obscured most of the southern coastline and much of Mexico, while another clouded area pressed down from the Sierras. Trapped between them was a clear high-pressure region that increasingly took on an hourglass shape as the time lapse of the forecast progressed. The crimped midsection where the two low zones would collide lay over the place where Lágrimas would be marked if Lágrimas rated notation on the map.

'. . . which produces our old friend the hot Santa Ana out of the east, but as you can see, tonight the wind won't be able to access its normal corridors, so . . .'

'It's coming through here,' said Charlie from behind Joyce. He answered before she had a chance to ask. 'It's the Owl, darlin'.'

Joyce turned back to the TV. Sure enough, set on its side like that, the hourglass shape did resemble wings. 'It's a storm?'

'I'll tell you what it is,' said TJ as she flipped the towel around so tightly it doubled back on itself in a knot. She took a maraschino from the tray of drink garnishes that Joyce had insisted was essential to any civilized bar. TJ set the cherry on the bar and said, 'This is us.' She set the knotted towel on the cherry, and pressed down on it with both palms, twisting her wrists as she flattened it against the dark granite counter. 'This is *el búho de dios*.' She lifted her hands to hold up the towel and show the broad blotch of red and pieces of smashed cherry flesh. 'That is what it does.' She fixed her eyes on Joyce and smirked. 'I told you so.'

Two

Duncan waited for Eugene to catch up. The ex-biker jogged across the parking lot, the rope of his long ponytail slapping the back of his leather vest with each ungainly stride. 'Looks to be a big one,' he said, searching the sky. 'We got six, maybe seven hours tops. You taking Danny on out to close down the yard?'

Duncan, who had just put Danny in the truck, craned his head toward the heavens. You'd have to have been through one to see the aura of the Owl's approach, the slight cataract sheen of salt dust, a membrane over the blue sealing them shut. 'Do you have enough crew to batten down the co-op? We could stop on by for a while.'

Eugene shrugged. 'I suppose you have enough to do out at the yard. But we could use the extra hand. Or two. Then we could all truck out to your place, see what needs doing.'

Duncan looked at the sky again and nodded. No one around here asked for help easily; when it was requested, no one refused. Minutes later, he and Danny were following fast behind Eugene's pickup – with the Harley, the bike his disabled body would never ride again, strapped up in the truck's bed. A couple of miles from the co-op facility, the rollback hit something in the road – a pebble, a grain of sand, a molecule from the tender center of the goddamned princess-proving pea – something; the truck vibrated one quaver off pitch, and the portal opened. The pain came home in a fury, scraping its way down his spine, blind-drunk on sensory rage. Duncan pulled his foot from the accelerator. His mouth dropped in a silent yowl, and his vision rippled as the rest of his body reacted in a reflexive grasp – skull, shoulders, scrotum, feet clenching down, muscle on muscle on bone – digging in so as not to get sucked into the expanding maw of grinding needle teeth.

Danny, watching, had pushed back against the door truck's door. Duncan's pain, in those moments he couldn't conceal it, frightened the boy for reasons Duncan assumed were based as much in empathy as anything else, and he tried to gesture across the space of the truck cab and the void where language had been, tried to make a shape with his hands that said, *We're all right; we're OK.*

The boy's eyes welled. He whispered, 'Alas, now pray you work not so hard! I would the lightning had burnt up those logs that you are enjoined to pile! Pray set it down and rest you. When this burns, 'twill weep for having wearied you. My father is hard at study: pray now rest yourself. He's safe for these three hours.'

'Fine.' Duncan forced the word through his constricted throat. 'Everything's fine.'

'If you'll sit down, I'll bear your logs the while. Pray give me that: I'll carry it to the pile.'

'Danny, keep yourself calm. I just need to catch my breath.' He got his hands back on the wheel, his foot back on the gas, got forward motion in the truck. 'We need to get ourselves out to the co-op. There's work to do and not much time.'

'You look wearily.'

'Wearily – that's the sum of it, Danny, my man.' *And let's change the subject because talking about it only keeps my mind pierced on the hook of it.* 'We ought to talk about tonight. There's going be a storm . . .'

'. . . but it's a storm unlike anything you've ever seen before,' TJ said as she rinsed a plate in the flow from the faucet before sticking it in the dishwasher rack. The window over the sink had steamed

170

up; she wiped an arc clear with her rubber-gloved palm and studied the sky.

Joyce scraped another plate over the trash before handing it to TJ. 'I've seen a few impressive storms where I come from. Nor'easters, blizzards.'

'Nothing like the Owl.'

'This Owl is the same sort of beast as Neb the snake-eating dog, I take it. An invention to scare the kids.' She dumped syrup-sticky utensils into the sink.

'It's attitudes like yours that get Lágrimas in trouble.' TJ flicked a soapy fork at Joyce and miniscule bubbles took flight from the tines. 'Duncan tells me you're worried about Danny being *contaminated* by me.'

'That is not what I said.'

'That's what you meant.'

'No, it isn't.' Joyce sighed. 'I like you very much. Not at all happy with some of the choices you've made, but it is your life. I'm not trying to judge you; I'm trying to take care of Danny. You cannot hold my desire to do what's right for that boy as a reason for the weather.'

'And you know what's right?'

'When it comes to my children, I certainly think so.'

TJ dropped the fork into the dishwasher's utensil bin. 'Danny isn't *your* child.'

'No. No, that's not what I meant –'

'You think you understand him better than the rest of us, huh?' She leaned her hip against the edge of the sink and crossed her arms, hugging herself with sudsy fingers. 'If you're so good with kids, where the hell is yours?'

Joyce looked past TJ and fixed her eyes on the six bottles with their six steam-wilted flowers. 'I suppose that evens the score.'

'I suppose it does.' She gave Joyce a smirk. Her shoulders relaxed, she released her arms. 'OK. I'll tell you. Neb? Yeah, he's a local creation, the exaggerated ghost left behind by a 1940s

171

missionary whose pet shepherd got bit by a rabid something or other. But the story of *el búho* is very old, old as the valley itself. The native people told it about the Latinos; the Latinos tell it about the whites. We in Lágrimas tell it about strangers. It's always basically the same: a traveler seeking access to holy ground ignores the many signs and warnings not to proceed. Turn back, go away, you don't belong, blah, blah, last chance. He barges onward until the gods have no choice but to protect themselves from trespass –'

'It's a storm, TJ. Not divine retribution. Weather happens everywhere.'

'But the Owl happens only in Lágrimas, only in this valley . . .'

'. . . because of how this valley is situated, its narrow exits and the bowl of the middle.' Duncan had no idea if Danny was following any of this, but the teaching gave him an anchor out there where the pain was not. 'When all the right random events happen at the right time, like what's starting above us right now, the wind is forced into the valley from both directions. The currents collide and try to get around each other, which starts a spin. The spin grows, picking up dirt and salt and sand – the whole valley becomes like a cotton-candy machine. We're going to spend the night at ground zero of a motherfucking monster of a cyclone that has nowhere to go . . .'

'. . . except to soar round and round the valley, whipping up the desert in clouds of dust that bury footpaths and extinguish signal fires until the arrogant traveler is lost beyond hope of finding even his way home.' TJ pulled off the rubber gloves and hung them over the edge of the sink. 'Or *her* way home.'

Joyce wasn't certain if she should laugh at TJ or fire her. 'You're saying *I* brought this storm upon Lágrimas?'

'You. Somebody else.' TJ shrugged. 'You're right, you know, it is just weather. Tonight we're going to get hit by freak weather that turns up – you heard the TV – about every ten years. Yeah, we know what causes it. Yeah, we know what will happen. Big winds. Flooding. Lots of damage. We'll survive, one way or another. We always do.' She began to play with the beads she'd braided into her hair. 'But you know how it is with the stuff you survive. You want your survival to mean something more than wrong place, wrong time. So, here we tell stories about the Owl, try to figure out what brought it down. Not to explain what happened, but to, you know, give it some significance. The Owl teaches humility; some things are bigger than we are. If the lesson applies to you, Joyce, take it now. Spare yourself, spare the rest of us escalation. As the old ones around here say, "Listen as you will, learn as you are able."'

'And the lesson is I shouldn't be taking care of Danny?'

'The lesson of the Owl is that there are places you are simply not allowed to go. The storm is just a storm. *El búho* rides in on the storm, and *el búho* can take many shapes. Never doubt that the gods will act without hesitation to protect their own. They will say no until you hear them.'

'I shall consider myself warned,' said Joyce. 'When do we leave?'

'Leave?'

'Yes. Evacuate? Where do people around here go to ride this out?'

TJ looked around the room. 'You're standing in it, honey. The Hoodoo is the oldest structure in Lágrimas, which means it's made it through every *búho* yet unscathed. In a few hours this place is going to be packed with folks who have nowhere else to go. You haven't figured that out yet? Lágrimas isn't these people's last chance; it's the place they ended up when they blew that last chance. Right now, they're all gearing up for the party at the end of the world.' Her eyes brightened with realization. 'Your son. If he's around, this is where he'll come. Tonight may be the night, Joycie.'

'Maybe.' Joyce pulled the plug on the sink and watched the soapy water circle down the drain. 'And maybe he's the one who brought down the Owl.'

The facilities at Flor de Lágrimas had been shaped for the wind as much as the hillsides beyond them had been shaped by it. Squat and windowless, the bottling plant and business office sat at a diagonal to the lake bed, the corner of the building breaking through the gusts like the prow of a sunken ship cutting deep water currents. Off in the distance, the ovoid depressions of the evaporation pans shimmered ripples as rubber-booted workers slogged through the shallows, dragging their board scrapers in zigzag paths, drunken sailors at the rudder. *Paludiers* was what the co-op hype called them. The evap workers had adopted the middle syllable as the more accurate description: Lewd work, it was called by those who did it. The Franco gentility of the rake's name, the *lousse*, had faired little better. If the co-op lottery had you on evap for the month, you told folks that you were dancing with Lewd Lucy or Lewd Louis, depending on your personal preferences.

Beyond the buildings and the evap pans, the lake bed took a dogleg turn between the hills where it narrowed and blunted to an abrupt end. Situated back in the cul-de-sac was the mining operation known as Blue Clay Bay. The excavation pit was close to twenty feet deep, blue-gray walls veined with semisolid brine. It was into the excavation cavity, below the reach of the wind and buttressed by hills, that they moved the equipment: backhoes and light standards, water barrels, wash screens and boxes of product, labels, file cabinets, anything the Owl might get in its claws and fling. Tarps of sailcloth fitted with gale-duty grommets were lashed with ropes onto hooks bolted into the earth to cover as much of the stored equipment as possible. The tarps snapped and bucked in the already-building gusts, but an hour or two beneath the Owl, and enough soil would have fallen from the sky to settle them down and weight them still.

174

It was nearing one in the afternoon when they finished at the co-op and a caravan of rust-eaten pickups, beetle cars, sedans, and hatchbacks trundled down the dirt road behind Duncan's truck. He felt like a third-rate Pied Piper. Danny was out the window, urging them onward to action, because the ship was, as always, under the wrack of Prospero's tempestuous whims. *Yare! Yare! Shut up, Danny.* As always. Although now Duncan imagined those behind him singing a chorus of the same, in unison with Danny.

He'd noticed it the day he'd had to trek out to the evap pans because the kid had forgotten the cap that Vermont was insisting all sane people would wear in the sun. Danny was working with Eugene and Lucas, dragging a Lucy across the evap floor and dumping the collected sludge of muddy salt onto washing screens. He was chanting his way through the scene in which shipwreck survivors assess the island in puns and politics, tripping through the six different voices as though all six souls resided in his tongue.

'Which, of he or Adrian, for good wager, first begins to crow?'

'The old cock.'

'The cock'rel.'

'Done! The wager?'

'A laughter.'

'A match!'

'Though this island seem to be desert –'

'Ha, ha, ha!'

'So, you're paid.'

'Uninhabitable and almost inaccessible –'

'Yet –'

'Yet –'

Duncan knew it well; Danny was bitching about having to work. The work was boring. He was tired. The day was too hot. *Yeah. Yeah.* Duncan put the cap on the kid's head and Danny, still smarting from the perceived exile from the salvage yard, hadn't looked up.

'What impossible matter will he make easy next?'

'I think he will carry this island home in his pocket and give it his son for an apple.'

'And, sowing the kernels of it in the sea, bring forth more islands.'

'Ay!'

But it wasn't only Danny. Duncan heard other voices. Eugene was reciting along. And Lucas. Duncan laughed. 'The kid does get stuck in a groove, doesn't he?'

Eugene had leaned on the Lucy and shrugged. 'It's kind of a limited playlist, like them classic-rock stations. You learn to go along with him.'

'Or go crazy,' Lucas added as he drained a screen full of salt sludge, letting excess moisture drip back into the evap. His watch started beeping. 'We send him to another pan before that happens.' He stared sadly into the rippling water.

But today, Lucas – the whole crew for that matter – was in high spirits, fueled in equal parts by the anticipatory rush of the impending disaster and the bottles of booze that had begun emerging from brown bags and coolers, shiny toxic seeds slipping from protective husks. Duncan – hurting as though steel-tipped burrs were lodged between his vertebrae – had tried without any pretense to dissuade them from helping, to send them off to ready their own families and homes for God's sake already; but they had insisted on returning the favor of his assistance. It was a waste of precious energy arguing with drunks bent on proving their friendship, so he'd given up and let them follow him home like the pack of numbskull lemmings they were.

They milled beside their vehicles outside the garage, their backs to the accelerating wind. To stand into the blow was to get stinging in your eyes and grit up your nose and in your teeth and down your gullet. Duncan figured that without instruction from him, they would merely idle, drinking and trading trumped-up stories of *búho*'s past as the dust thickened closer to intolerable. That was fine. He wanted only to dump the diesel and pull the spark plugs from the EZ-Crusher, get the crane tied down and double-check the gun safe. The scanner and the computer would be protected enough in the garage. He set Danny to unplugging the electronics and tying them up in plastic garbage bags. As for his other valuables: the replacement for the chair MacGruder had knifed – Duncan thought the childish spite of the act as pointing only to MacGruder – was still being constructed to specs in Chicago. The bank-account numbers were all in his head. He kept no papers or mementos, no telltale souvenir by which he might be tracked. No photographs, no wedding ring, no past except for the pool table, which he kept off-site in a public place on the outside chance that if it were in his possession, someone might remember it and connect him to that night in the bar called Duncan's on Northwest Dupree Street where one Tobias James, the person he used to be, played a game of nine-ball on the world's ugliest table with the understanding that if she lost, Liz Bradley, the world's most magnificent woman, would marry him. He won, and in doing so, lost everything.

It was getting on toward three. A hooked wedge of dense, charcoal-colored cloud cut along the hard blue horizon, its leading edge sparked by lightning like a cold chisel blade scraping metal. Owl's claw, they called it. Duncan and Danny and the rest of the caravan wound its way back to the Hoodoo, tacking with the wind at odd angles to the road in order to make forward progress. The parking lot full with cars crammed up against what was hoped would prove the lee side of the building. When no room remained, ad hoc establishment of secondary parking was determined by wherever it suited the driver to stop. Duncan steered the rollback off the road and bumped along amid the scattered cars. Squalls of miniature dust storms raced among the vehicles, some of which, those with all the windows intact, were packed to their ceilings with clothes and books, lamps and the like, the things you might need to start over, as though their owners anticipated having no other option once this thing had blown over. But part of the logic was simple weight: the heavier the car, the less liable to go flying. In the backseat of one old heap Duncan spotted, someone had piled broken concrete and desert rock, while on the front passenger seat, nested in a towel, a close-to-popping mamma cat licked her tabby paw. Birth nor death had any sense of convenience. He wished her luck in her upcoming travails. He set about finding a place to park the rollback so that it was turned into the wind and away from any smaller thing that might be thrown up against it and crushed in the collision.

The Hoodoo itself looked braced. The turret windows were covered with planks; the satellite dish had been taken from the roof. Lucas and Eugene had stayed behind to lend Joyce a hand with boarding up and taping cracks and shutting down the propane and other storm preparations. Charlie had stayed behind to smoke and supervise. Ozzie had stayed behind to drink and relay probabilities on flash flooding, electrical fires, and the damage that Owl's eggs – hailstones the size of tennis balls – could do.

Eugene was at the back door, unloading five gallon jugs of drinking water. He looked up and saw Duncan and the others fighting the wind to walk across the road; he raised a hand in greeting. Duncan raised his in return and was struck by a raindrop. It felt like he'd been hit by a ball bearing. Apparently Eugene had gotten pinged as well. He rubbed the back of his neck, laughed, and then hollered, 'Damn bird!'

Three

The power went out around six. In the sudden dark, the older kids cheered, and the younger ones cried, and the adults saluted the Owl with the flames of their lighters. Their outbursts of laughter gave way to whoops of appreciation as the wind roared up big enough to shake the Hoodoo's walls. TJ – sans wig and tip-generating persona – moved from table to table, running down bilingual instructions that they were to save their flashlights for emergencies. She passed out candles and salad plates, demonstrating as she went how to let the melting wax drip onto the plate and secure the candle upright. Joyce listened for Owl sounds, screeches or hooting in the air that would justify the name, but she found herself thinking about water. The sound was more like that of a waterfall, as though all of Niagara's fury were smashing down on their heads.

The candlelight threw long shadows about the Hoodoo and put a luster on the skin and hair and eyes of those around them. The romance was illusory. The smell of paraffin and sulfur was not welcome. It was breathlessly hot in the building. What air was available was already rank with the sweat, belch, and fart effluvia of human beings – upward of three hundred, but Joyce had lost count – crowded together in numbers several times past the legal capacity of the room. Ventilation – outside the natural drafts in the old building – was impossible. To open the door an inch was to allow a rain of dirt, stick, and stone, and billows of suffocating dust. As it was, dust was seeping in through undetectable fissures. It put salt in every breath you drew and made for gold halos of refracted light around open flames. Men, women, and children vied to keep the small measures of space they'd managed to carve out in the front room and in the kitchen. Joyce recognized only a couple dozen of their faces. They sat on the tile floor, huddling about the shopping bags and cartons crammed with the absolute essentials of their lives. The rest of their worlds remained in cars and at homes, some of which, like those at the trailer park, would likely be gone by morning. Over in the corner, somebody worked at tuning a guitar, plucking one string again and again. A poodle yapped incessantly. It belonged to an old blind gentleman whose pleas that the dog was his only family had garnered dispensation in Joyce's prohibition on pets. Adults scolded children and pulled apart young lovers trying to make out in the shadows. Only Duncan seemed to have staked out adequate space early on at his pool table, what with Danny shoving onlookers and inadvertent trespassers out of the way. Duncan eventually gave up his game and gave over the surface to a few young mothers so that they might spread quilts on the felt as beds for their infants.

Joyce worked the bar, filling glasses and opening bottles at such speed she had no way to keep track of the sales. She'd set out an empty gallon pickle jar that now spilled forth ones and fives. Someone's child came to the bar and said that the toilet wasn't working again, but before Joyce could turn to answer, she heard Eugene say that the tank hadn't refilled – something to do with the temporary plumbing he'd set up. He said he'd take care of it. Joyce turned to thank him, but he'd already gone. Ozzie was taking wagers on what would be standing come sunup. Charlie, needing a smoke bad, had hunkered down grumpily at the far end of the bar, still pissed at Joyce's general announcement that anyone caught lighting up would be put outside and not allowed to return. Adding to Charlie's discomfort was Lucas's tireless erudition about the pancultural symbol of the Strix, the owl, as a demonic creature that prefigured vampires and witches as the night-borne thief of children. Charlie kept eyeing Lucas as though wishing a night-borne thief of garrulous, fish-obsessed intellectuals might swoop through to save him.

TJ made sandwiches of processed cheese slices on white bread and organized a delivery system that employed Rachel's three older boys: one to hand out the sandwiches; one to write up the one-buck-each bill; one to make sure it got paid. Pretzels and chips were on the house. When their paths crossed, TJ would raise an eyebrow in inquiry and Joyce, playing along, would tense her lips, shake her head, solemn but hopeful. No, she hadn't seen *him* yet.

Milt Freemont and his round, happy wife, Victoria, were back in the comparable quiet of Joyce's apartment running a makeshift clinic for those who were already ill and needed seclusion. Milt had his shortwave radio with him to get updates on the storm. Every thirty minutes or so, Victoria, in her rhinestone-studded cowgirl shirt, would emerge from the kitchen like the pert figurine on a cuckoo clock and tap a spoon to her water glass until the ringing got their attention. When the room quieted, she would fill them in on the latest information as to wind speed and damage reports in the vicinity. She would then withdraw to await the next installment. At last count, the National Weather Service was clocking forty-seven miles per hour for sustained winds, with occasional gusts of sixty plus in the Lágrimas area. More cheers.

The first fight broke out around ten. It was no more than a shouting match over the ownership of a misplaced beer. TJ, with practiced barmaid diplomacy, scoffed at the men's barking as though it were just puppy-dog roughhousing, and told them to sit tight; she'd get them each a brand-new bottle, her treat. She chucked her finger beneath each complainant's chin. She smiled and winked and wiggle-walked her way over to the bar where she took two beers Joyce had opened, and whispered, 'Everybody's hot, cramped, and drunk. We're about an hour away from a full-scale brawl.'

TJ was wrong, but not by much. At about a quarter to midnight, when most of the little ones were snoozing cradled snugly against a loved one and the overall mood of the crowd was that of fuzzy dullness and the wind was a nonstop lowing howl, a woman's cry of rage rose in the center of the room, followed by a string of garbled accusations that ended with the clear pronouncement 'He's my husband.' In quick response, another woman – identical to the first, with the same bleached, teased, sprayed hair – yelled back, and the man, on whose lap she was seated, threw his head back and brayed a *nyee-haw*-sounding laugh. The two women were shouting simultaneously, making it impossible to hear precisely what either one said, but it wasn't difficult to discern the source of the conflict.

The lap-seated woman jumped to her feet and, hand on hip, fringe on her vest shimmying, pointed her finger in her accuser's face and proceeded to holler all manner of insults. It was like watching a person cuss out her own reflection. On she berated until Outraged Wife cocked her fist and sent it into the juncture of jawline and throat on Fringed-Vest. Fringed-Vest went down sideways, falling into the still-braying object of their debate. She dropped with sufficient force to knock him over, and he went down backwards, chair and all. He landed, smack, his head on the tile. Matters no longer struck him as quite so amusing. He pushed his lady friend into the legs of the next table and leapt up, swearing. He grabbed the chair and held it high, readying to bring it down on his wife, who had her arms lifted, her head cowering into her body. And then Duncan had the guy, his right arm hooked around the guy's neck, his left locked on the chair to keep it from dropping on the kids, who, awakened and rubbing their eyes, had hurried over for a better view of the fight. Duncan was hauling him backwards, ordering that his captive should calm down – 'You hear me, Morton? Relax' – when Fringed-Vest lunged upward from the floor, upward at Duncan, the knife she gripped flashing silver in the candlelight.

'Let him go!'

Apparently Duncan saw or sensed her intent and swung Morton and himself out of her trajectory, but not quickly enough to prevent her slashing his left arm about midway to the shoulder. Danny yelled a tangle of syllables and leapt toward Fringed-Vest. Eugene caught the boy by the shirt collar and yanked him back. Duncan threw Morton aside and clasped his right hand over the wound. Fringed-Vest caught sight of the blood spreading through the khaki cloth of the sleeve. She dropped the knife, clutched the hair at her temples, and screamed. Fell to her knees. Screamed some more.

Duncan glared down at her. 'For chrissake, Hillary. Knock it off.' The woman buried her face in her hands and wept.

'You!' – Danny shouted as he thrashed against Eugene's restraint – 'are three men of sin, whom destiny – that hath to instrument this lower world and what is in't – the never-surfeited sea hath cause to belch up you, and on this island, where man doth not inhabit, you 'mongst men being most unfit to live . . .' It was, as Joyce had learned, Danny's stance of righteous indignation; Shakespeare's Ariel holding forth on who screwed up and how they're going to suffer for it. Joyce heard this speech often.

Victoria Freemont pushed into the fray, hands pressed to her heart. 'What on earth is all the commotion – Duncan? Milt! Milt Freemont, get out here! Duncan's hurt.'

'It's nothing,' Duncan said, raising his voice over Danny's ranting, repeating himself when Milt appeared. 'It's nothing.' Milt wove his way with weary care through the onlookers, pulling himself along on folks' shoulders, thereby moving them, gently, out of the way. 'You know, when me and Vic moved out here,' he said, speaking to whoever cared to listen, 'I thought I'd be treating sunburn and skin cancers, not forever stitching you people back together after your romantic spats.'

'Duncan was trying to break it up.' Joyce heard herself defend Duncan before she realized she wanted to.

Milt glanced over at her. 'I don't doubt it.' He looked at Duncan hard. Duncan shook his head. Milt shrugged and then carefully lifted Duncan's hand off the injury.

'It's nothing, Milt.'

'It's a mite more than nothing. Come on back and let's have a look. And Hillary? Charlotte? Either I cut Morton straight down the middle or you two figure out how to clone him, but find a way to settle this, because one of these days one of you is going to get killed, and then what will the other two do for fun?'

Joyce followed them into the apartment, hushing the barrage of questions from those who had not seen what had transpired. TJ wandered over with a candle that she held up to Duncan's arm. She yawned. 'You got off easy. I could tell you Hillary-and-Charlotte stories that would straighten your teeth and put you off sex for the rest of your life. The Cox sisters: identical twins, both evil.' She turned and ambled away from the apartment with the curious in thrall behind her.

Joyce closed the canvas curtain, shutting them off from the kitchen. It was the closest she'd been to peace in hours, and for the first time she felt the leaden fatigue in her legs. She leaned against the doorjamb. The candlelight seemed cleaner, less hazed in here. It was as though she could breathe again. It was cooler, and the air held a freshness due in part to the mentholated cream Milt had been using on the small boy now sleeping on the couch. The child coughed mightily. Bronchitis, Victoria said, but not to worry, if he could sleep through this – she pointed at the ceiling – they weren't going to wake him. The wind was much louder through the walls of the apartment, and it whistled reedily through hairline crevices in the boards over the window.

Duncan was still protesting this concern as unnecessary. Milt had him sit in a straight-backed chair up close to the small round table on which one of the candles burned. Victoria brought Milt's bag over from where he'd left it by the door. 'Good thing you came prepared,' said Joyce, yawning as she watched him unpack what he needed.

'It would help if people knew when to stop drinking – better yet, when to stop serving.' Milt pulled on the second latex glove, snapping it against his wrist. 'But that's not going to happen around here, now is it?' Joyce felt her face flush. The good doctor obviously didn't know drunks. If she cut them off; they'd just climb over the bar and take it. Under candlelight her anger must have registered as remorse or responsibility, because Milt nodded and took up a pair of bandage scissors. He set about cutting the sleeve free from the shirt. 'So, what was that about, Dupree? An old hero compulsion kicking in or just your garden variety suicide impulse?'

Duncan gave him an impatient sneer and went back to working the buttons on his cuff. 'What should I have done? You know how these people get. They'd have watched Morton beat the shit out of Charlotte like it was television – a rerun at that.'

Milt chuckled. 'Joyce, you're going to have to get a better class of programming on the box out there. The Conflict Resolution channel, perhaps. Or Mediation TV.' He put the scissors down and pulled the sleeve off Duncan's arm. 'What can you do? Some folks love their drama. Ah, you don't need sutures. This is nothing.'

'Second time that's been decided.'

'Let's just be sure she didn't nick you anywhere else.' Milt lifted the candle and used the light to examine the rest of Duncan's arm.

Joyce followed the amber radiance as it traveled down the smooth, muscled slope of Duncan's biceps, and, as Milt turned his arm forward, she saw the light break into shadows against the rippled plain of raised scars, a miniature range of nightmare mountains.

Duncan felt her staring, the cold fire of the fright in her eyes, and he looked up to meet it for an instant before Joyce turned and hurried out of the room.

'I miss something?' said Milt.

'No.' The throb in his sliced arm had set up an interesting

syncopation to that in his back. 'Put a Band-Aid on the thing or whatever it is you do.'

When his arm was wrapped to Milt's satisfaction, Duncan left the apartment and went to look for Joyce. She was back at the bar, clearing empty bottles and glasses from the counter, gathering them in loud crashing handfuls into a dishpan, purposefully not seeing him. Morton, an arm around each weeping twin, called out to Duncan, asked if they, he and Duncan, were: 'OK, man, still buds?' Duncan raised a fist that could be read as either solidarity or a threat. Joyce, eyes down, dishpan on her hip, excused herself and tried to get past Duncan. He didn't move. She tucked her hair behind her ear, her body jolting with tiny quivers like a wire stretched to its tensile limit.

He raised his arm more into the light of the stub of melted candle beside her. He positioned himself so she'd have to either look at the scars or his face. 'When you find your boy, if he turns up here, if he's still alive, chances are this is what he's going to look like.'

Her face jerked up. 'What are you talking about?'

'Those pictures, Vermont. I know junkies.'

She sucked on her upper lip, her eyes blinking very fast. 'It wasn't his fault. He had a girlfriend and she, she – and you don't take anything for your back because –'

'An opiate is an opiate.'

'There's other medications.'

'Nothing that works.'

'But it would be different; you're in so much –'

'I won't go there again, medically sanctioned or not. I won't. Worse things in the world than hurting. Trust me.'

She dipped her chin a couple times. 'How long?'

'How long what?'

'How *long*?'

'Clean? Coming up on fourteen years.'

'Danny, is, um, safe?' Her eyes had a sheen of feral fear that dulled the edge of the insult.

'If you mean safe when he's with me, I hope so.'

'That's hardly reassuring.'

'Would you prefer I lie to you?'

She began an agitated shifting from one foot to the other and he saw she was perplexed by the problems in the possible answers. 'I don't know,' she finally said, and understanding how troubled she was by that indecision, he stepped aside to let her pass.

As Joyce lowered the heavy tub of glasses down into the sink, the wet plastic of the tub slipped from her hand and fell the last few inches, landing with a bright crash. Joyce grimaced against the sound of breakage. What else did she expect? She held on to the sink's edge, dropped her head and willed her mind blank. *Work*, she told herself, *just work*. She turned the taps; the faucet only sputtered and dripped, and she remembered the pump had been shut down even before the power went because the storm could flood and thereby contaminate the well and it was best to keep it shut down until things could be disinfected. She realized she had run out of chlorine bleach the day before. For this she started to cry.

Then TJ was standing beside her. She put her arm around Joyce, rested her chin on Joyce's shoulder, and said, 'Yeah I know. Doing dishes has the same effect on me.'

'I'm all right. I'm just very tired.'

'And sad?'

'Maybe a little.'

'And maybe a little freaked out? Milt said you saw Duncan's awful badge of honor.' TJ took her arm away and leaned against the sink. 'I'm thinking maybe it's time for a new theory, maybe Joycie-with-the-lost-kid knows more about this stuff than she's been talking about.'

'It's none of your business. It's none of Duncan's, either.'

'Might be someday. Ozzie's got it at two to one that eventually, you and Duncan, you know' – she crossed her fingers tightly –

'kismet, sweetie – even if it is backasswards: the two of you have a seventeen-year-old son together and you've yet to have your first date –'

'TJ, stop being silly.'

She crossed her arms over her chest. 'He's never given up cigars for any of us.'

'He's given them up?'

'Yeah, around the Hoodoo he has. He never said anything; but anyone could tell how much you hated them. You haven't noticed?'

'Apparently not.'

'I wonder what else you don't see?'

'What I don't see?' *The dimming light of blue dusk, the talc-white powder in the neatly folded bag, the needle, the kitchen table – No.* And after *No* all she could hear was the echo of her own heart and the mournful keening of the wind. It surprised her when TJ started, her head jerking around toward the back door. Joyce realized it wasn't her heart she was hearing but the fierce, deliberate pounding of someone who wanted inside.

'Wait for the gust to die down,' TJ said between breaths. 'OK. Now.' She and Joyce shoved against the door again; this time it budged. A sheet of dust fell over them and set them both to coughing. 'You're going to have to help us!' TJ shouted through choking gasps. Fingers curled over the dimly lit edge of the door and pushing was joined by pulling. The door opened wider. The storm avalanched in, and out of it emerged a woman, who coughing, crying, coughing some more, collapsed in Joyce's arms. The wind slammed the door shut.

TJ, coughing, pounding at her chest, trying to clear it, ran to find Milt. Joyce half-carried the crying, coughing woman to the cooler of drinking water set up on the drain board, turned on the spigot, and used her cupped palm to press water to the woman's face, cleansing away the dirt and mucus from her nostrils and mouth and eyes, the whites of which had been irritated to a beefsteak red. As the dirt came away, Joyce saw that the woman was but a teenage girl. 'What the hell are you doing out in this mess?' Joyce tried to ask, but her own words came up in hacking noises to match those of the girl, who had begun to retch. She pushed away from Joyce and vomited dirt into the sink.

Milt, getting in close, his big head dwarfing hers, used a penlight to examine the girl's eyes, holding them gently open with his fingers. 'What say I give you the "You're goddamned lucky" speech and spare us both the "How could you be so foolish?" lecture?'

She coughed and nodded. 'Thank you,' she said, the first time she'd gotten sound from her damaged throat; her voice sounded very weak, sandblasted thin. When Milt moved back, her eyes squinted up, as though even the candlelight hurt them. She pulled the towel tighter against her shoulders apparently to catch the errant dripping of water from the dark tangle of her wet hair. Joyce had put the girl in the shower stall with a drum of water and a sauce pot to ladle away some of the dirt, resulting in a good-sized delta of desert soil settling over the shower drain. She'd given the girl her long-sleeved dress, a yellow knit which hung shapeless on the girl's twig-slender body. The color was a harsh contrast to the blue undertones in her complexion so that even in the ambient gold of candlelight the girl appeared sickly. She also wore a pair of Joyce's white anklets to keep her feet warm. She kept rubbing the sole of one against the top of the other. Still, even in the overheated close- ness of the Hoodoo, she complained of being cold, and shivered, her teeth chattering. Joyce brought her a sweater and a blanket.

'It's the shock, dear,' said Victoria as she gently worked a comb through the girl's wind-knotted mass of waves. 'She'll warm up soon enough.'

'Yes, I remember,' said Joyce. 'I mean, I know.'

Duncan paced outside the shut apartment curtain. 'Has she said where she left her car?'

Victoria ticked her tongue in disgust. 'The poor dear can hardly speak at all. You'll get the car tomorrow after the storm passes.'

The girl's eyes grew even bigger with concern. 'I don't know where I left it,' she rasped. 'I don't know if I was even on the road. It got so dark. And the wind. I was trying to find a place called Lágrimas.'

'Your luck continues,' said Milt, waving a tongue depressor in her face.

'That can be argued,' said Duncan. The curtain rustled as he passed by it.

'Pay no attention to the man behind the curtain,' said Victoria, patting the girl on the head. 'You found Lágrimas just fine.'

She made a gurgle of disbelief, it was the most she could manage, as Milt was using the tongue depressor as it was intended and looking at the girl's throat with the penlight. She began to gag.

'You'll be all right,' he said, snapping off the light. He tossed the wooden depressor into the waste can. 'For the next few days you're going to feel like you swallowed a hunk of steel wool. Prescription for treatment: hot tea with honey and a shot of scotch. Tea's for you. Scotch is for me.'

'I can't do hot tea until we get the power back.' Joyce stood. 'But scotch is available anytime.'

'Then give the girl a scotch with honey.'

Victoria swatted her husband. 'I thought we frowned on children drinking. Perhaps we can heat a bit of water over one of the candles –'

'I can help,' said the girl. 'I have previous experience in the food-service industry.'

Laughing at the earnestness of the declaration, Joyce said, 'You looking for a job, sweetheart?' She pushed the curtain aside.

'I might be.' The girl sprung to her feet in what must have been intended as a display of enthusiasm. 'I worked for the Pretzel, um, fast food. I've worked fast food.'

Milt scoffed. 'Don't let TJ hear about it. We still haven't found all the pieces of the last innocent job seeker who tried to hone in on her turf.'

Duncan appeared in the doorway. 'Do you remember anything at all – a curve in the road, a Joshua tree, a rock – anything about where you left –'

'If she does recall, you'll be the first to know,' said Joyce, letting her eyes meet his long enough to transmit her displeasure at his hounding the girl. He transmitted displeasure right back at her.

'I'm sorry,' the girl said. 'I found this place by pure accident. The wind blew me right up against the building. I couldn't keep my feet on the ground. It was like I was flying. The car? I hope it won't be too difficult to find. What will you do if we can't find it?'

Duncan cocked his head. 'Lots of things flying around here tonight. You have a name?'

'Aa –' She started to cough again and when the coughing calmed, she said, 'Alice-son. Allison. Allie, for short. You can call me Allie.' Even Joyce caught the awkward attempt at constructing an instant alias.

'Christ, another one,' said Duncan. He walked off toward the dining room. 'Why did you ditch the car, Alice-son? Is it stolen?'

She pushed past Joyce and ran up behind him. 'It was my car. *Is* my car.'

'Uh-huh.' He kept walking.

'I'm telling you the truth,' she said, and grabbed his arm right where the tatters of the cutaway sleeve hit the bandage. She must have seen it, must have known it would hurt. 'Why don't you believe –'

Duncan wheeled about and caught the wrist of the offending hand before it had a chance to drop. 'You get one. That was it.'

'You're hurting me.'

'My intent.' He released her, shoving her the slightest bit away from him, just as Danny sauntered into the kitchen. Danny halted, staring. A strangled whimper escaped his throat. He clutched at his heart and said, 'Most sure, the goddess on whom these airs attend! Vouchsafe my prayer may know if you remain upon this island, and that you will some good instruction give how I may bear me here. My prime request, which I do last pronounce, is – O you wonder! – if you be maid or no?'

Alice-son, furrowing the whole of her face in confusion, turned first to Duncan and then to Joyce. When they didn't respond, she shrugged and answered him: 'No wonder, sir, but certainly a maid.'

Danny took a step forward: 'My language? Heavens! I am the best of them that speak this speech, were I but where 'tis spoken.'

'*Tempest*.' The girl giggled and applauded. 'Weird. My school did *The Tempest* this year. It was right before I, before – I played Miranda. Not exactly. I was her understudy. I never got onstage, but I know her part.' She tilted her head, squinting at Danny through the gloom. 'I *was* Miranda.'

Danny ventured a couple steps closer and began again: 'Most sure, the goddess on whom these airs attend! Vouchsafe my prayer may know if you remain upon this island, and that you will some good instruction give how I may bear me here. My prime request, which I do last pronounce, is – O you wonder! – if you be maid or no?'

This time, Alice-son stepped up to meet him. She ducked her chin and curtsied, demurring, 'No wonder, sir, but certainly a maid.'

Danny, barely above a whisper: 'My language? Heavens! I am the best of them that speak this speech, were I but where 'tis spoken.'

She took Danny's hands, pulling them gently from his chest, but she spoke to Duncan: 'What is't? a spirit? Lord, how it looks about! Believe me, sir, it carries a brave form. But 'tis a spirit.'

Danny, boisterous, condescending: 'No, wench: it eats, and sleeps, and hath such senses as we have –'

'Oh,' said the girl, as Danny continued. She nodded in understanding of what no one had yet explained. When he finished, she touched her fingers to his face, and said, 'I might call him a thing divine; for nothing natural I ever saw so noble.' She giggled. 'Cool.'

The wind pitched a lonely, questioning cry, sounding at last like the creature it was named for. *Who?* the wind asked. *Who?* Duncan was looking at Joyce, and she at him, and his face told her they both heard, saw, feared the same monsters. Joyce, however, knew the monster's name. Maddie. Different form, different drug. Same ending. Same ending. No escaping it. *And I let her in.*

She was moving before she realized it, walking out of the kitchen on the numb sticks that were her legs and heading straight to the bar and grabbing the first bottle her fingers brushed and without second sight or second thought she was swallowing the storm into the hollow inside her.

III. Unmasking

One

Once, on the shipping platform, one of the drivers dropped a carton of ten thousand ball bearings. The carton split on impact, and the ball bearings careened off the lip of the dock and fell to the metal grating in a shiny steel tumble of thunderous clanging sound. It was that sound Joyce now heard, endless between her ears. A light stabbed at her eyes, sharp, like oncoming high beams. It made her eyes squint shut involuntarily. Squinting made the ball bearings fall faster. She put her fingers to her face, trying to bar the light, and realized her head was against something flat, hard, and cold. She forced her eyes to slit open and saw sunlight glaring between her fingers. Her head was against a wooden tabletop, and not far away was the sunny rectangle of an open door.

She pushed herself upright; the ball bearings slammed into reverse and crashed into the back wall of her skull. She called out his name, clipping the last syllable when she remembered where she was. She raised her voice a few decibels to cover the mistake and yelled, dry-voiced, 'Danny!' Except for a few sleeping drunks slumped about the room, the Hoodoo had been abandoned and was in such a disarray of overturned chairs and trampled brown bags and broken bottles that Joyce thought for a minute that the Owl had gotten inside and torn the place apart. She stood, very slowly, in deference to the nausea seesawing in her belly. 'Danny!'

No one answered. She checked her wristwatch and held it to her ear to make certain it was working. Two-thirty? *Well, of course they're gone,* she scolded herself. The storm was over and they'd all gone home to assess damage and tally losses. Danny was safe with Duncan, and – the girl? *Yes, there had been a girl and she had known part of Danny's play and then I came in here.* She touched her fingers to her lips. *Oh no. Please no.* The gin bottle was right there on the table, less than an inch left. The cap was missing. No glass. So she'd been swigging it straight, and they'd seen her, all of them. She could not remember the first swallow, let alone what came after, but the whole of Lágrimas had seen her guzzling like the lush she used to be.

'It wasn't as though I was the only one.' She said this aloud to those passed out alongside her. 'And given the circumstances . . .' Joyce patted at her hair, flattening out the muss. 'Well, these things happen.' She shielded her eyes against the sun's dazzle, and, steadying herself on tables and the Hoodoo's walls, she went out to begin an assessment and tallying of her own.

Neither Danny nor the girl had the faintest notion what they were dealing with; Duncan knew he had to get them separated. They'd still been going at it well after dawn when the Owl blew itself out. They sat cross-legged on the bar counter, knee to knee, hands occasionally touching, as they ran through lines from the play while around them the storm refugees dozed. *O brave new world.*

Around eleven the doors had been opened and the inhabitants of Lágrimas ventured out bleary-eyed and hungover to see what had been left for them. In the parking lot, where vehicles had been wind-shifted, some overturned, Eugene volunteered to head up reconnaissance out to the co-op, if only to prolong having to deal with what might be waiting for him back at the trailer park. Others said they'd join him or be out shortly. Duncan changed into one of the fresh shirts he kept in the truck and felt better once the wounds, old and new, were covered. He piled Danny and the girl into the cab, under the pretense they were all setting out to find the girl's car, but he took Danny straight out to the co-op, saying they needed the boy's help shoveling out the evap pans. Danny, unhappy with the loss of his playmate, had run after the truck until Lucas and a couple of the others chased him down and hauled him back.

Duncan ignored her questions about Danny as they drove up and down the debris-strewn main roads and all the dust-erased tangents where she might have ended up. The girl who was calling herself Allie sat school-rule straight in the passenger seat. Although Duncan had bottomed out of patience for her performance of 'Girl Trying to Remember Location of Automobile,' her posture was a sight to envy. If only to underscore his sense of deficiency, he repositioned his hands on the steering wheel so that the pain would reposition along his spine.

'I'm sorry,' she said, her voice still rasping.

'You can quit saying that.'

'But I am, really. About the car. About your arm. Everything.' She dropped her head, defeated, and slouched back against the seat, tugging at the sleeves of Vermont's yellow sack of a dress. Her voice went soft. 'I don't think we're going to find it.'

'Whatever you did with it, you did it good.'

'I didn't do anything. We went through this over and over last night. I got lost in the storm, and I tried to find help.'

'Uh-huh. Why are you faking your name?'

'Excuse me?' The whites of her watery eyes were still very pink.

'"Alice-son?" Royalty doesn't work that hard naming their firstborn. You want to tell me what's what, or are we going to wait for your picture to be the lead-in on one of those "most wanted" shows?'

She didn't answer, only stared at her reflection in the side-view mirror. In this fine afternoon sun, her complexion was a papery pale overlaid with the lacy red webbing of irritation from the storm-driven dust. She looked sick, the victim of some wasting agent. *Parasite* was the word that came to Duncan's mind. More the reason to get her the hell out of Lágrimas.

'I'm waiting.'

Her head stayed turned away. 'I, um, ran away from home.'

'Yes, well, that I figured. Somebody hurt you?'

She shook her head, shrugged.

'But you don't want to be found?'

Another feeble head shake. 'It's for the best, really. I'm seventeen, after all, not some twelve-year-old child. I can work. I have some money.'

'Then where's your car?'

She studied her fingernails. 'OK, OK, OK, already. I sold it. When I was almost here, I started to get paranoid about being followed or somebody calling in my plates. So I sold it at this roadside used-car sort of place. It was called MacGunder's? No, Mac –'

'MacGruder's?' The unavoidable implications made the heavy word even heavier on his tongue.

'That's it. MacGruder. He gave me a ride almost all the way into Lágrimas. By then the weather was so bad, he said I had to get out or go back with him. I was so scared. He was really creepy. I wanted to get away from him, so I got out and walked the rest of the way. I wandered around in town for a long time trying to get into one of the buildings, but everything was shut up tight. It was so dark; I started walking where the wind would let me go. I found the Hoodoo, pure blind luck.' She sounded genuinely astounded. 'Do you think Mr MacGruder called in to check the license plates or anything?'

'Not unless there's a benefit to him. Is there?'

'I took less money for the car so that he'd promise not to say anything to the police or anybody.'

'Police? You're expecting the police to come looking for you?'

She chewed at her lip. 'That's who comes when they report you missing, right?'

'Seventeen-year-old girl, unhappy at home, takes off in her own car – it was your own?'

'Yes.'

'Did you leave a note?'

'I wrote not to worry and that I loved them.'

'Nobody's coming to look for you, Alice-son.'

'I should have kept my car.'

'Probably. It would simplify getting back to those who are worried out of their heads today and wondering how, if you loved them, you could be this heartless. That's what you need to be doing, getting yourself home.'

'What I need to be doing is getting myself a job. I'd ask again at the Hoodoo, but the owner hates me.'

He wasn't about to offer her reassurance on that point, but Vermont's reaction to the girl had been troubling at the very least. The woman had curled into that hooch like she'd been reunited with a particularly fond lover. He should have figured her for a drunk; it made her purchase of the Hoodoo less an act of madness – that was one junkie interpreting the actions of another, of course, but still it had a logic he could appreciate. It was her problem, and she was welcome to it; the big concern here was Danny. Duncan wasn't about to leave him in Vermont's care another day.

'Do you think I should ask again?' Allie smiled. 'Maybe if you spoke to her, you know, explained.'

'The only person I'm speaking to on your behalf is you: Go home.'

'Maybe I am home.'

She may not have been right, but she was close. Duncan fought the certainty of it, but he could not deny the increasingly solid sense that the previous month had been invisible maneuvering for position, as though God were setting them up for a geometric grand slam that would clear the table in one spectacular, behind-the-back, blindfolded jump shot. What else could it be? This one slip of a girl blows in on *el búho*, riding MacGruder's grubby wings, and inside minutes she has Danny befuddled into believing he's met his Miranda, Vermont diving into cheap-gin oblivion, and Duncan worrying about future events he had no words to describe.

She was watching him with quick, sidelong glances as though about to test the limits of her luck. *Test away, baby. Give me something I can use.*

'I couldn't tell you this without telling you more than I wanted, but Mr MacGruder had a message for you. Delivering it was part of the payment for the lift into town.'

'What was the other part of the payment?' *Even MacGruder, that walking mass of rat shit, wouldn't –*

'I'd rather talk about the message.' She turned her head so far away, it seemed she was looking behind her.

Or maybe he would. 'All right. Was it something about horse thieves?'

She whipped her head back and let go one of those sheltered-little-girl gasps of surprise as she stared at him. 'How did you know?'

Duncan braked the truck and breathed and girded himself for the joys of getting through a three-point turn. 'We're going back. I'm going to leave you with Rachel. Maybe she has work enough around the Hotel to clean that dust out of your brain and get you thinking straight again.'

He drove her back past the Hoodoo where the more recently sobered were comparing damage to their vehicles, and farther on down the road into storm-scoured Lágrimas. The Owl left clean, that was for sure. The town had a wire-brush-and-borax sting to it. Painted surfaces on buildings and cars had been stripped to their bare hides of wood, masonry, or steel. The water tower got through this one with no additional dents; it needed a new paint job anyway. The buildings, proven stable in *búho*'s past, appeared starkly triumphant as the boards over windows and doors were being taken down. Uprooted Joshua trees were caught up in door-ways, stacked about and atop one another like bizarre acrobats. The delicately spined casings of old birdcage primrose plants had piled up in the crooks of corners. The two automatic doors at the grocery were propped open, and the storekeeper – skeletal and mean-tempered old Margaret – was sweeping dirt in poof-ball clouds out one door, and the slight breeze of the afternoon sent it right back in the other. Something big had rammed into the stand of mailboxes, hard enough to bend the framing and break open the front, setting uncollected mail to the wind. Envelopes and magazines and brochures hurried breeze-blown about the street as though looking for their owners.

It looked as though much of the debris had lodged itself on the Hotel's verandah where Rachel leaned wearily on a push broom, watching her kids untangle tumbleweeds and trash and catalogs from the verandah railing. After Duncan shouted his request from the truck, Rachel waved the girl to come along. Alice-son apologized one last time before leaping delicately to the pavement and banging the door shut.

He continued out past the trailer park. The Owl had tossed and tramped around there good. One of the trailers had been cleaved right down the length like a loaf of bread. Paper and clothing, toys and linens, couches, tables, plaster lawn ornaments and shattered gewgaws, mattresses and television sets lay in heaps around toppled homes. Owners hugged and held each other upright as their little ones splashed in the few remaining puddles. Rain had been through here, although you would not know it to look at the desert, which had sucked up what it could before the sun sucked up the rest.

The repaired Lágrimas Salvage sign had stood firm through the storm but had been sandblasted down to the wood. Great, knotted rounds of thumbleweed had hooked in midtumble on the posts and now provided rough shelter to a trio of ravens tearing at a rabbit carcass. *Not too bad, if that's the worst of it* – 'Yeah, because I am that lucky,' he said to the sign as he made the turn.

Up ahead, in front of the garage bays, a pack of starving coyotes were lapping water from a rain puddle. Good sign. Must mean his house was intact, or they'd be down there feasting. Duncan hit the horn a couple of times, and they scattered. He pulled closer and heard the incongruous growl of the engine on the EZ-Crusher. He shut down the truck and listened harder. That can't be. He checked the glove box. The plugs he'd taken out of the machine yesterday were gone.

The EZ wasn't like the coffeepot or the iron, you didn't just use it and forget to turn it off. Realization fell over him in all three dimensions of trouble: who, what, and why. He started up the rollback once more and eased past the garage as close to the machine as he could get. From where he sat, he could smell the diesel smoke, see the humping throb of the crushing plates as each attempted to complete its task. Whatever it was, it was still in there. He waited until he almost forgot why he was waiting, and then he killed the engine on the truck and eased himself out of the cab.

He backed himself, with slow, quiet steps, running his hand along the cab until his fingers found the latch on the tool compartment. He fiddled and finagled with it until it came open, and he reached for the shotgun just as he remembered everything was in the gun safe down at the house. Makeshift weaponry. *What do we have?* A massive socket wrench, a heavy-headed Mag light, a pry bar with a blade on one end and a toothed notch on the other. The pry bar made the best sense, but he couldn't do it, just could not. The Mag light would have to do. His hands were shaking, so he had to force them to close around it. And once he had, he realized his palms were so slick with sweat, he was uncertain he'd be able to hold on to it should the need arise to swing it at somebody's head.

Lousy excuse for not moving. He gripped the Mag light as best he could and made his way toward the EZ's control console. His balance felt unsteady, as though each step he took was setting off individual earthquakes to rumble the junkers, but it was only his legs trembling along the fault line of his escalating anxiety. He watched for movement to his left and to his right, his torso, neck, head turning smoothly. If he had to fight, he could; in the rock-paper-scissors of Duncan's world, fear stoked anger, anger smothered pain.

It took several centuries, end to end, but he eventually reached the switch panel and shut down the engine, which died out with a whining sigh that descended into an exhausted groan. The crushing plates were only partially down and the pistons half-extended. He stood there sweaty, shaky, breathing great chestfuls of diesel fumes as he checked around him again. Again. He was just about certain he was alone. Of course, he'd been just about certain of that another time. And he was back in the warehouse, cornered before he knew it. They were coming at him, iron bars banging on the concrete floor. No way out of this one.

Duncan shook his head hard, made himself think. No, he was alone. If they were coming after him, they'd just do it and be done. This was a message. He powered up the EZ again. The engine coughed and grunted resentfully at being kicked back into action. Whoever had been using the machine had set it to Manual so that each of the crushing plates had been operated independently. Independently he released them. He threw the switches; the hydraulics heaved and sighed as each successively bigger plate withdrew, slid away, lifted.

The old tow truck, large and heavy as it was, had not crushed cleanly. The boom and rear end were only crumpled, although the cab had complied fully. Even so, the yellow lettering on the door was still evident, as was MacGruder's clean, flattened palm held fast between two pleats of metal, as though he had been trying to hold back the piston-driven wall.

Joyce, dry-mouthed and dull-headed, was walking toward Lágrimas, heel-toe, straight, or straight enough, a self-imposed test of her sobriety down the faded line of paint that marked the shoulder of the road, when two black cruisers from Larkin Sheriff's Department flashed past, lights ablaze and sirens blaring. Dirt roiled up behind the cars as they sped straight through town and on out toward the salvage yard. Seconds later, an ambulance came through. Joyce felt a sobering ice bolt of dread. *Duncan?* She picked up her pace and hurried toward town.

A few minutes later, a steady beeping sounded behind her. Lucas's old yellow VW Beetle rattled to a stop beside her. Ozzie was with him. Lucas was shouting at her before Ozzie got the window rolled down.

'Gus MacGruder is dead.'

'Dead,' said Ozzie. 'Murdered. Out at Duncan's.'

'Is Duncan all right?'

'He's OK,' said Lucas. 'He's the one who called. You want to ride out with us?'

'Ride out with us, Joyce.' Ozzie wrenched the door open. 'Duncan needs us right away. We're his alibi.' He leaned forward to release the seat so that she could climb in the back.

'The whole freakin' town has an alibi.' TJ was seated on the hood of her Thunderbird; she gave a two-fingered wave as Joyce passed by. 'We spent the night at the Hoodoo together. Besides, you know MacGruder was the one with the grudge here – if motive still counts for anything.'

The officer taking down notes gave a conceding nod. 'We have to work through all possibilities. Can't very well put this one down to the ever-loving Owl, now can we?'

Joyce saw Duncan over by the crusher. He was speaking to a pair of detectives: a big redheaded woman and a man whose skin was almost as dark as Duncan's. The female officer walked away shaking her head. Once she'd gone, Joyce saw how Duncan's stance altered. He braced himself against the crusher's control box. The officer indicated Duncan should move away from the machine. He complied, but his pain was obvious, as was his anger. Joyce couldn't hear what he was saying, but she'd known him long enough to read that hunch in his shoulders and the way he kept pointing about in the air as he spoke.

Camera flashes went off around the men and the machine as the photographers took picture evidence of the weapon and its victim. Joyce edged over toward the ambulance, where the paramedics and the redhead and a pair of uniformed officers were engaged in a laugh-riot debate about how best to transfer the body because no way was the tow truck going to fit on the gurney. It was decided that they'd have Duncan haul the whole nightmare into Larkin on his rollback under police escort – thereby solving two transportation problems in that they were going to have to bring Dupree in for questioning anyway. 'What do you know, Dupree,' one of the officers shouted across the yard, 'looks like you're finally getting a call!'

Lucas offered to bring the rollback around, back it up into better position. Duncan told him to stay the fuck out of it. Lucas withdrew into the crowd of locals where Joyce stood with TJ, Ozzie, and some others who had arrived before the entrance to the yard had been roadblocked. They watched as Duncan got the rollback lined up with the crusher trough. He jumped down from the cab, slammed the door shut, and worked the levers on the side of the deck, releasing it to slide back and incline, stopping it just as the back edge of the incline dropped beneath the point where the front end of MacGruder's tow truck bent upward, away from the ground. Duncan ran his hand over the surface of the rollback's deck, swore, and went back to the cab and ripped open the tool compartment. He pulled out a full jug of emerald-green dish soap. This he dumped – the entire contents – onto the bed and then set to spreading it along the surface with a squeegee/brush tool like the one Joyce kept in her car for snow. He released the cable on the winch; it slid and skipped down the soap-slicked deck. With the cops shouting at him to be careful and photographers getting in his way to document the process in case of damage to the evidence, Duncan hooked up the undercarriage of the truck. He threw the winch into Reverse, and with a groan, the engine began to rewind the cable and pull MacGruder's bad luck, squealing misery in spite of the soap, up onto the deck. Duncan raised the rollback to level and began to secure the vehicle with chains that locked into the deck frame. He was limping badly. His face, running with perspiration, was set in grim lines of determination.

'Why doesn't anyone help him?' Joyce had to look away.

'Why doesn't anyone help him?' said Ozzie, echoing Joyce's despair. 'He doesn't want help. He doesn't want ours, and he certainly doesn't want theirs.'

'It's a guy thing,' said Lucas, pushing his glasses hard into his forehead.

'It's a Duncan thing,' said TJ. 'They're going to impound the crusher as evidence, and that will be the end of business out here. Don't you see? MacGruder gets whacked and he still wins. Duncan would rather his heart explode than admit he's beaten.'

'That's just bullheaded stupidity,' said Joyce, starting off toward the truck in spite of the insistent pleas behind her. Duncan was securing a tarp over the macabre cargo, so she went around the front of the cab and climbed into the passenger seat. Through the windshield she could see TJ, Lucas, and Ozzie. They were all moving their heads, back and forth. *No.*

Duncan wrenched open the driver's door, saw Joyce, and pursed his lips for a second. He wiped the sweat from his forehead. 'Vermont. Out.'

'It's not a good idea for you to drive up to Larkin alone.'

'Get out. Now.'

All right, perhaps this wasn't her best-thought-out plan. 'I just wanted to, you know, be of some sort of help.'

'You want to be helpful? Keep the hell away from Danny.'

'You can't mean that. If it's about last night, I had a slip, it happens –'

'Vermont, booze is the least of your problems. I won't have you doing to Danny what you did to your kid.'

'What are you talking . . .'

Duncan's expression went frigid, as cold and hard and unpredictable as pond ice. Before he even spoke, Joyce realized she hadn't tested him well enough. Her mind filled with the terrible noise of inevitable disaster. 'How old was he when he started, Joyce?'

'I only wanted –'

'Eleven, twelve?'

'Duncan, please.' She tried to find the latch that would open the door.

'How old? Twelve? Twelve, Joyce? What the hell could possibly be so bad in a twelve-year-old boy's life that he has to self-medicate to get through it?'

Where was that door handle? 'Look. I'm getting out. You can stop now.'

'What was he trying to get away from? Huh, Mommy? Did you ever figure out that maybe what he was trying to escape from was you?'

She waited for his face to tell her he knew he'd gone too far. When the fearsome set of his expression did not soften, Joyce swallowed back her tears. 'I only wanted to help.' She found the door handle, yanked it, and slid out of the cab. Duncan heaved himself behind the wheel and shouted at TJ. 'Nicolette Cortez, I'm expecting you to look after Danny until I get back!' He started up the engine. Hands gripping the wheel, he didn't look at her. 'Close the door, Joyce.'

Two

It was the world's sorriest parade. They rolled through Lágrimas, Duncan driving the mystery float. Police cruisers flashed lights fore and aft. Behind them came the tagalongs that had gathered at the entrance to the yard. You would have thought the storm would have been thrill enough, but no. Kids from the trailer park ran out toward the roadside yelling. Rachel and her brood lined the verandah. The kids waved; Rachel, obviously having heard what the procession was about, blew him a kiss. The Alice-son girl was on her knees near the roadside where she had collected a stack of pale green paper. She was smoothing the pages with her hands. On seeing Duncan, she leapt to her feet and ran alongside the truck, trying to show him the pages. He was too tired to pretend interest.

Larkin was a fifty-five-mile trek on unmarked back roads, a shortcut that the locals held as a close-kept secret to prevent truckers and tourists from overwhelming it in an effort to shave thirty miles off the highway drive. By the time Duncan and his escorts made the third turn, the last of the Lágrimas contingent had turned back. The crimson rim of the sun was but seconds from slipping beneath the dark of the horizon. Night was coming, and these folks had drinking to get done back at home. Duncan opened the heat vents in the cab; it was cold and he'd forgotten to grab a jacket. Not that he'd taken time to consider such necessities. The drive, however, was giving him plenty of time to contemplate the lay of the table, and as the world went black beneath the star-crazed sky, he settled into the strobing of red, blue, and amber lights of his police escort and tried to calculate the angles and potential outcomes from this new set of events.

He was worried, but not about the law. They'd question him, just as the big redheaded cop, who had stayed behind in Lágrimas, was questioning others now. It wasn't a problem, only procedural formality. *El búho* did not allow for running around carrying out bizarre murder schemes. Even if time of death was placed after the storm cleared – the most probable scenario – Duncan had spent the morning with Alice-son. He had alibis by the dozen, besides which, MacGruder was a cockroach of a man. No one was going to come straight out and say it, but the world felt a whole lot cleaner with him gone. They'd explain it away as the sort of finale a man has to expect if he goes around selling out associates to save his own cowardly skin.

And that's what the killer had counted on. MacGruder's death was a means to an altogether different end, of that Duncan was certain. He was starting to get a basic hold on the geometries at work here. Whoever had crushed MacGruder had orchestrated the past month's reign of petty terrors, playing MacGruder's potent hate for Duncan toward larger goals. They'd probably even sent MacGruder to grab the spark plugs from the rollback and hightail out to the yard, where they slapped his back and congratulated his cunning as they watched him power up his own extermination. No, this wasn't about framing Duncan before the law; it was about putting him out of business and forcing him toward secondary sources of income, because even after all these years, they still believed he had *it*. Duncan didn't even know what *it* was, and he'd explained, screamed, wept that fact at one or another of his accusers as they had set about – iron on concrete – splintering his shinbone before fracturing his back. Fact makes frail defense against a crowbar. They didn't believe him. Or maybe they did, but having searched for and not found *it* themselves, they'd come back round to Duncan to begin again.

212

That's what worried him, worried him so much his palms left sweat prints on the vinyl of the steering wheel. He made himself breathe, long, slow ins and outs. He tried to empty his mind, but empty was the desert, and the desert brought him back round to why he'd chosen Lágrimas. It was flat and open, nothing to hide behind. You could see things coming at you from miles away. Ambush was next to impossible. Except at night, of course, like now, when it was dark.

Larkin, a bedroom community of about twenty thousand, had bloomed around a glut of restaurants, hotels, and outlet shopping centers. It was high-energy, major metropolitan living by Lágrimas standards. He followed the cruiser along the side streets through rows of ranch-style houses. They'd been hit pretty fiercely by last night's wind. Some telephone poles were down. The streetlights and traffic signals were out. Palm fronds and yucca spikes littered the curbside and scattered about the yards. Through the cab's vents, he was picking up the scent of wood fires burning in the hearths of homes without heat. He could see into candlelit kitchens and dining rooms, young families, older couples, singles settled down to dinner. The same event, house after house. As Duncan's procession passed, the diners would pause midbite or midconversation and gaze out at the flashing lights moving down the street. Two mysterious worlds passing close enough for mutual observation.

The procession reached its objective. Larkin General Hospital had been notified of the impending delivery of the MacGruder puzzle box, and they were waiting in the main parking lot with generator-powered lights and a jaws-of-life for peeling the metal away from the body. A couple of reporters from one of the local television outlets were shining spots and shoving microphones into the face of any viable bystander for reactions as the wreckage was offloaded. A guy in a white lab coat meandered about chatting with the officers. He'd have to be the doctor rooked into coming out and pronouncing MacGruder snuffed. Because it was the sort of situation that called for an educated opinion.

Duncan dropped the deck and slowly winched out the cable so that the truck slid gently to the floodlit pavement. The cops said that that was good enough, so he shut down the winch and limped away from the ceremonies, finding a place to sit beneath a stand of squat palms on a low retaining wall at the side of the lot, out of range of interest, theirs, his, anyone's. He ran his hands over his face and regretted it as his eyes began to sting with the mix of grease, dirt, and soap still griming his palms.

The engines on the jaws-of-life roared, and curlicues of blue exhaust rose into the work lights as the EZ-Crusher's work was undone. The shearing cries of metal separating from metal were short-lived. The engines cut out and human voices took over with shouted orders to turn cameras aside and for onlookers to get out of the way. MacGruder's removal was met with the inevitable exclamations of distress and disgust. One of the reporters strode away from her cameraman, past Duncan, her hand over her mouth, no doubt willing herself not to give in to the physical response of her own horror. Weak stomachs did not get the big stories; or maybe they did. Duncan wouldn't have a clue.

The young detective, Something Carlisle, who'd ridden back into Larkin with the escort, was up on his toes, craning his neck, more than a bit of panic in his face as he searched the scene.

'Over here,' Duncan called, loud enough to see the detective ease back down to his heels. He started to trot over; his designer trench coat – no doubt a second from the outlet mall – floated dramatically out behind him. He stopped about middistance as though he expected Duncan to meet him halfway. When Duncan didn't budge, he continued his trot over to the wall. His aftershave, a cheap imitation of the expensive scent Duncan himself used to wear, arrived before he did.

'Looks like they cuffed him to the wheel so he couldn't get out.

It's quite a mess.' Carlisle took a handkerchief from his coat pocket and blew his nose loudly. 'You don't want to see?'

'I can imagine it well enough. So, you holding me or what?'

Carlisle rubbed his scruffy-for-the-effect beard and made a pensive, humming sound that went on long enough to tell Duncan they had nothing, yet this young detective dude intended to impart an aura of threat. Normally, Duncan would have left the kid to meditate on the bleak future of his dead-end career and gone about his business, but he was willing to bet Carlisle was the only black guy in the Larkin detective bureau, and he was willing to indulge the kid an expression of authority he wouldn't have to fight for. He waited.

At last, Carlisle broke off humming. 'I've been on the cell to my partner – she's on her way in from Lágrimas. I should wait until she gets back, but she says your story checks out. So, I'm going to say you're good to go.'

'I appreciate that.'

'But you need to stay where we can find you. You heading back to Lágrimas?'

'No place else to be.'

'I hear that.' He rose up on his toes and then lowered. 'You eaten yet?'

'Nope. You?'

'Nah. I won't be hungry for a few days, not after this. There's a Mexican place in Old Larkin that's good, if you like the spicy stuff. Old Town got its power back this afternoon. The fast-food places out at the interstate are still shut tight, waiting for the juice to come back up. Just a thought. It's been a long day.'

'A long day. Yes, it has.' Duncan understood the duality of the concern here. 'I know the Cantina. I think I will get a bite before hitting the road. Probably be there an hour –'

'Or two.'

'Or two. In case you need me after your partner gets back.'

'Thanks for letting me know.' Carlisle made to go back to what was left of MacGruder.

'You return the favor,' Duncan said after him. 'One way or the other.'

Carlise checked back over his shoulder. 'I'll be in touch.'

Duncan left the rollback in the parking lot of the Old City branch of Larkin Savings and Loan, ignoring the posted prohibitions against doing so. Let them go ahead and ticket him. He'd been more than cooperative, and once this episode was settled he was going to bill the city for mileage on the transport. Both ways.

The Cantina was across the street from the Orpheus Theater, at one time the closest movie house to Lágrimas. He'd come up here a lot in the first couple of years, just to get the hell away from the drunks and the sea-heavy taste of salt in every breath of Lágrimas air. The Orpheus was one of those gilt-and-velvet houses where golden cherubs played among the stars painted on the vaulted ceiling. The seats were broad-backed and deeply cushioned; one of the few places he could sit at length and remain comfortable. The movies, good or atrocious, had proven a wonderful distraction. The theater had gone broke after the multiplex opened at the outlet mall. After the better part of a decade of emptiness and disrepair, the city had adopted the Orpheus and now kept it running as a stage for traveling companies of third-rate performers of puppetry and dance and Shakespeare. They advertised events as far afield as Lágrimas. Duncan received the occasional brochure in his mail, which went immediately unopened into the trash.

But tonight he asked the Cantina's hostess if he might sit at one of the window tables up front, simply so he could ponder the significance of the Orpheus's marquee. He ordered his usual *pollo con queso*, rice, flan, and tea. While he waited, he imagined all the big plastic letters in red and black jumbled together in a case and the volunteer, because it would be a volunteer, laying out the words on the sidewalk to make sure the letters were all there before using the telescoping pole to place them in proper order, sliding them along the supports on the white lighted board:

The Nouvelle Monde Players
present
William Shakespeare's
The Tempest

He managed to get down less than a third of his meal as he lingered there by the window, sipping cool tea and bantering with the hostess to elicit details about this Nouvelle Monde outfit. Did they ever come into the Cantina? Did they ever mention misplacing one of their players? He ended up giving Carlisle far more than the two hours lead time he'd requested. It was close to ten when he decided to head for home. The whole of the drive back to the yard, he was thinking about Danny and how stupid he, Duncan, had been not to realize exactly what the boy had come out of – *one of these roaming theater troupes, you idiot* – and how damn close he might be to losing his last tie to a purposeful life outside servitude to his pain and wondering how many times a man can lose his purpose without losing his goddamn mind. He let himself into his still power-deprived house, exhausted, barely aware of the flickering of candlelight, so completely distracted that when she spoke, he was startled into reaching for the gun he didn't have.

'How does this work?'

'Vermont?' He had to shake the illusion of the gun from his hand. 'Have you any idea what I could have – Where is Danny?'

'With TJ.' She was in the kitchen. He couldn't see her but picked up her movements in the multiple planes of shadow on the wall. 'Danny's at the Hotel. I'm not supposed to get near him, remember.'

'You're drunk.'

'Not very. How does this work? What is it exactly you're supposed to do?'

'Do with what?' He went to where she was sitting. 'What are you talking . . .' The sight of the syringe jammed the words in his throat. Still in the jeans and work-stained shirt of the previous day, she was seated in the chair closest to the wall, rocking it on its rear legs, as she poked the needle against the tip of her finger. She'd been doing it for a while; he could see the points of bleeding where she'd punctured herself. A bottle of gin was on the table, and the wooden box she'd rescued from her car that first day was open before her. Beside it lay a spoon tarnished by time and soot and the crumpled strip of photographs. She was wearing a large silver locket. She cleared her throat, on the brink of or at the end of crying. 'I want to know how you do this.'

'You know how it works.' He yanked the thing away from her. 'You just want to rub my nose in your mess.'

'I don't get it.' Her voice was soft with authentic mystery. She let the chair legs fall back to the floor. 'Why are you always such a bastard?'

'Necessity.' He dropped the syringe to the floor and crushed it with the heel of his boot. She was still questioning him, but he lost her sound in other, more demanding sensations. In coming down on the syringe he had landed on the edge of his heel, hitting too hard, setting off a chain reaction in his overworked nerves that felt like a string of daisy-chained cherry bombs going off from his ankle to the base of his neck. Duncan grabbed for anything and caught himself between the table and the counter. He stared at the floor, and in that insane way his brain managed the extremely bad times, he locked on to a realization, as far away his body shook and dripped sweat and his belly clenched in preparation of vomiting, that this flooring was cursed by perhaps the ugliest pattern – gold and blue and brown flowers – ever dreamed up by humankind. Vermont was, Christ almighty, still here and jabbering questions as to whether he was all right. All right? How can a man be all right when he is forced to endure atrocities such as the vile, electrified razor wire and shit garden of this goddamn awful flooring?

She was trying to help him to stand or sit or something, all of which were impossible. He couldn't use language to explain this to her, so he elbowed her off of him, probably too hard. He saw her land on the floor, which was a terrible fate for anyone, given that it was this terrible floor. He turned, somehow, so that he was facing the stainless steel sink, elbows locked in pillars of support, he let the counter take his weight. He felt air flood into his lungs. *Breathe,* they'd chant in rehab, *breathe through it.* So, breathing. He glanced up at the man in the window glass, who shook and sweated as much as Duncan did, the window man's nostrils flared with each dragging inhale and his mouth was set so taut his lips had gone pale and twitched with the effort and tears were streaming down his cheeks. This guy looked scared. Duncan was glad he wasn't this guy. Nothing to be scared of. It was, after all, just pain.

And then Vermont was there with the window man, asking if she should call someone, Milt maybe? And window man shook his head. *No.* Milt would feel horrible and do something horrible if only to make himself feel better. *No.* 'Can I get you something?' *No.* 'Let me see.' *No.* But being Vermont, she didn't listen to the window man and began, gently, to pull his shirt and then his undershirt from the waist of his pants and, gently, rolled the cloth upward. Window-Vermont's face changed as she saw what was there to see; she bit her lip and swallowed, at first hiding her revulsion and then surrendering to it. 'Oh, my God,' she said, and he could smell the alcohol on the invocation, and then he felt her fingers tracing downward. And then the press of her palms. And then the heat of her face as she leaned against him weeping.

'Most of that is left over from what they had to do to fix it,' he said, despairing of her pity more than the pain, but then came a kiss and then another along the knots, and her palms ran around under the shirt to his chest, and her arms closed, pulling herself into him, and God, it hurt, but he let go of the counter and turned into the embrace and saw in her eyes not pity but comprehension. She closed her eyes and he bent to kiss her pain. Favor given; favor returned. Broken is broken. They set about trying to fix it.

Entr'acte: Duncan

Got out of town on a boat
Going to southern islands
Sailing a reach
Before a followin' sea

That song again. They were playing the hell out of that song around the time Liz left me. Every radio I turned on, every elevator I stepped into, every jukebox I plugged a quarter into. I couldn't escape it.

She was makin' for the trades
On the outside
And the downhill run
To Papeete

I mentioned it to Liz the way the song was driving me batty. Liz said they weren't playing it any more than any other song, but I was hearing it more because God or the Devil or Something In-Between was trying to get through to me.

In a noisy bar in Avalon
I tried to call you

If I wasn't going to listen to Liz, I certainly wasn't going to listen for messages in an overplayed pop song.

But on the midnight watch I realized
Why twice you ran away
Think about . . .

Toward the end, when Liz's desire to save me was giving over to the realization she was going to have to save herself, she sent me a card she'd found in a bookstore that specialized in the paraphernalia of spiritual reinvention. The card's a simple thing; it lists, under the title 'The Universality of the Golden Rule,' variations on the Christian rule of thumb. The script is gold gilt on night-colored stock. The quotes feature major players such as Confucius: *What you do not like when done to yourself, do not do to others;* and Aristotle: *We should conduct ourselves toward others as we would have them act toward us;* as well as up-and-comers such as Aristippus of Cyrene: *Cherish reciprocal benevolence, which will make you as anxious for another's welfare as your own.* I remember reading down the card and laughing, imagining Big Daddy upstairs smacking himself in the forehead and deciding that before He could redeem our immortal souls, he was going to have to come down here and teach us something about the economies of a great tag line. Laughter was probably not the response Liz hoped for.

I have since learned an older rule lay hidden under the gold leaf of my religious education. When you get down to the bottom of things, where the struts and buttresses of human doings meet the bedrock of this small, lonely world, we all, from our most sacred to our most profane extremes, are governed by only one shared absolute: You don't take what isn't yours. Heist an old lady's handbag, slur a man's history, bruise a child's ribs, invade a neighbor's land or a woman's body, it's all the same transgression. It's theft. Not of temporary possessions but of permanence, of safety. The punishment, elegance that proves its divinity, comes built into the crime; destroy another's security and lose your own. Until that gets understood, your crimes continue until you have nothing

222

but emptiness trying to fill up on emptiness. This is addiction. Chocolate, caffeine, nicotine, crack: Choice of substance doesn't matter. Only, the addict believes it does, like the thief believes that the nature of what he steals defines the severity of his crime.

I am a thief.

> *. . . how many times I have fallen*
> *Spirits are using me*
> *Larger voices callin'*
> *What heaven brought you and me*

If you want reasons, the back story I believe they call it, I can't give you any. Don't have reasons to give. I gave up the reasons when I gave up the drugs. I had to. Reason is the way it gets into your head; reason is the primary addiction. All I can do is list my crimes and regret them.

Cannot be forgotten

Liz is first on the list, of course. High-minded, scary smart, beautiful in a way that changed sex from recreation into revelation, her body made my body want what it never had before, something beyond my own pleasure. I don't know if that qualifies as love, but it was an appetite almost powerful enough to silence the other hungers I was prey to. Almost. I saw us with kids and dogs in a big house with a garden – Liz, happy; me, somebody else altogether. What I didn't see is how we were going to get from here-and-now to there-and-then. I figured Liz would know the way. I married her and took her for nearly everything she had – spirit, stamina, hope – cursing her, punishing her for not being able to lead me away from myself. But she was more resilient than my need to break her faith. She left with nothing more than the knowledge that she was, at least, strong enough to leave.

I saw her a week or so before the warehouse. She was on the

sidewalk, looking in the window of an antique store. It was snowing, and she had on her blue wool coat with a large tasseled scarf of cream thrown over her shoulders. She was wearing her hair straight again. And she had a child with her, a baby, no more than a year old, who sat on her hip and looked about as Liz pointed to things in the window. The baby was a girl child in a shiny pink parka, and she wore a pink headband to warm her ears. Liz was wearing mittens, so I couldn't see a ring. It may have been one of her siblings' kids; Liz had seemingly thousands of nieces and nephews. But the girl looked to be no more than a year of age, and her little face radiated the same open joy I had almost obliterated from the woman who held her. I stood there, doing the math, counting months backwards until it came to me that either way, my heart was broken. I walked on past without saying anything. If she saw me, she didn't react, although I do imagine her pulling the shawl closer, suddenly more aware of the cold.

I planned to go back to that store and try to figure out what had charmed them so. I was going to buy it and have it delivered anonymously. The fantasy was a comfort, but as I played it over and over in my mind it mutated, and I saw Liz recognizing me in the gesture and smashing whatever trinket I might choose and scrubbing the girl's hands for having touched it and . . . I had all the reason I needed for that night and the one after and the one after.

> *When you see the Southern Cross*
> *For the first time*
> *You understand now*
> *Why you came this way*

I worked for a private security firm. I'd started doing part-time temp gigs for them my second year in college. Low-level bouncer-type positions at low-level clubs. It was great, quick cash but lots of late nights that ate into my studies and sleep. Final-exam week, I was in the library, slapping my own face to stay awake when this matchstick-thin freshman flicks a couple tabs of speed across the table, saying that it would keep me awake. I needed to be awake. I took them. No fanfare for the damned, no wailing of angels. I put the pills on my tongue and swallowed them back with a hit of vending-machine coffee. That was it. The first step in your basic journey of a thousand miles straight down.

Since I could now study and work endless hours, they pushed me up to the longer gigs at the better clubs and concert security. Before long, I was bodyguarding minor musicians and actors, some of whom were so obnoxious that if they had been assaulted, I would be facing a major moral dilemma as to whose back I was going to get. After I graduated, I signed on full-time. I was twenty-five. They sent me to train in small-arms tactics and defensive driving and other urban-warrior techniques. After that I was promoted to bigger-named musicians and actors, some of whom were so obnoxious that I thought I'd have to take them out myself.

The drugs were everywhere. I believed that that was the real problem. I told myself that I had an environmentally based habit. If I could just get away from these infantile idiots with their bowls full of pills, if I could get away from the sound of fifteen-year-old children promising assorted obscenities in return for just another hit, if I could get away from the limo orgies and the migraine throb of nonmusic and the smells of stale smoke and vomit and sex, if I could just get away from these zombified ghouls who kept handing me packets and vials and bags of horrors they didn't want to be alone with, if I could just get away, I could stop. I would stop.

I turned thirty. I met Liz. I wanted to be a different man, an improved man, for her. I thought wanting it was enough. I put in for a position as a courier. The money wasn't as good, but it was a quieter life. Better perks. I got to travel to places like Paris and Madrid, first class with attaché cases handcuffed to my wrist. Liz sometimes came with me, and we played spy as I delivered documents and coin collections and art and jewels. Occasionally, I rated bodyguards of my own; all right, my delivery rated the protection. It was work to which I was suited. I was happy – a man unshakably in love with a good woman, a man with a good job and only a minor problem involving needles. I was careful, and I was certain I could keep each universe spinning in its own separate box. Never was sure if that was pride or stupidity. Anyway, Liz found out about the smack and said I'd have to quit or she would. I said I would do it. I didn't. Sometimes, I think she married me in order to up the ante: *See what I'm willing to lay on the table for you? What are you willing to lay down for me?* She was fierce-willed that way, willing to play poker with both our lives. We both thought that controlling the drugs was the solution. Addiction is a two-stroke engine, however, control in and control out; upping the controls only ups the horsepower on the engine driving you straight into ruin. Even today, I don't know if she kept on loving me or was simply unwilling to accept the limitations of her love, but eventually she did what I couldn't; she surrendered to reality. The marriage lasted nineteen months. Not once did I even try to quit.

> *'Cause the truth you might be runnin' from*
> *Is so small*
> *But it's as big as the promise,*
> *The promise of a coming day*

When I finally rolled in, after medicating myself to euphoric indifference for Liz and the child, I found an assignment on my voice mail, a crosstown job that would take a couple of hours at most but was time-sensitive in the actual commission. I was to pick up a satchel and take it out to the airport where I was to deliver it to a contact who had a thirty-minute layover here before flying on to Europe. Insurance on the contents had been set at about one million eight, so the agency was sending me in one of their cars.

I think back now and wonder if I had been clean, would I have tuned in to a dissonance in the details. I also wonder if I'd been clean, would they have chosen someone else.

So I'm sailing for tomorrow
My dreams are a-dyin'

I met the car at the curb the next day as planned. My head felt as though solid-lead dominoes the size of skyscrapers were tumbling slow motion, one against the other, slamming to the ground with a thunder that reverberated down my bones to tremble out the ends of my fingers. I'd worn my heavy black turtleneck, and under the camel-hair coat, I still couldn't seem to get warm. The driver was wearing a suit, of course. We didn't know each other, and after a few feeble attempts at conversation, we rode in silence to the pickup point.

We ended up in an alley behind an upscale office building, a vertical warren of import brokerages. An elderly man in a gray silk suit let me into his ground-floor offices. He spoke with a thick Dutch accent, agitated with concern that I was going to miss the connection and his European colleague. I tried to reassure him that we had plenty of time. He raked me over, head to foot, with an appraising gaze and asked if I needed to check the contents before he signed the manifest and how much time that would take and could we afford to take that time.

I asked if he packed the case himself. Yes. Had he left the case alone for any length of time? Only to let me into the building. Was there anyone else in the office? Except for me, he was alone. No, I said. Sign the manifest and we'll be on our way. I initialed beneath his signature where he had waived itemization. Most of our clients did that; they didn't want their possessions written down publicly, especially when they might not be legal in the strictest definition of the term. He locked up the case and handed it over. I asked him if he wanted to ride along. He said no, no, that wasn't necessary.

He'd talk to his colleague by phone later. Besides, if he were going to go himself, what was the point of hiring me? *Me,* he said. Not the firm, mind you. *Me.*

We got to the airport in plenty of time, as I knew we would. I met the handoff, another Netherlander, this one a strapping young woman in thigh-high boots, an ankle-length sweater coat, and a snakeskin cowboy hat. She signed the receipt voucher without opening the case. She said she trusted me. I should have insisted. The trust line should have tipped me; trust was not the foundation of my firm's business. Instead, we flirted for the rest of her short layover.

> *And my love is an anchor tied to you,*
> *Tied with a silver chain*
> *I have my ship*
> *And all her flags are a-flyin'*

You don't need me to tell it, do you? At five-thirty the next morning, my phone rang. The Dutchman was dead, and although the case made it safely to its destination, the contents that were supposed to be inside it were nowhere to be found. I sat in my boss's office that afternoon, going over the job minute by minute, and when we reached the minute where I signed off on the manifest, I saw my job going into the acid bath with the rest of my life, and so, I lied. I said that I did most certainly verify the contents and that that other name on the manifest, the Amazon at the airport, must be responsible for the disappearance. If I was being set up, I was more than willing to pass that setup right on down the line. He asked if I had counted the diamonds. Made certain the coins were in their cases. Validated the seals on the papers. Yes and yes and yes. But, he revealed, neither diamonds nor coins nor papers were in the case. How could I have verified the contents and not know what they were? *Ka-boom* goes the last domino and the vibrations run along root stems into the bowels of my being and awaken all

manner of demons, summoning them to the surface as spikes on
the polygraph readout my boss insisted I provide. Proving truth to a
machine at his discretion; this was, he reminded me, in my contract
of employment. Were you on time? Were you following established
procedures? Were you, upon physical inspection, satisfied with the
client's description of the satchel's contents? Were you sober?

She is all that I have left

He fired me for the lie. He'd known about the drugs for a long
time. He said he could have forgiven the fudged paperwork; time
constraints and client demand would have worked in my favor.
I asked him what had been in the satchel, what exactly had
gone missing? He said that that was information for authorized
employees only. He called security to have me escorted from the
building. He said he was sorry but this betrayal of his faith was
a *debilitating blow*. In five days' time, five days being my best
estimate, that phrase would come back to me: debilitating blow.
In five days, I would, when conscious, chant it to the fever rats –
DEBILITATING BLOW – investing the words with all manner
of portents and curses. The fever rats chanted along with me; that's
how I could tell them from the real ones.

And music is her name

So I hit the street, a man with an irresistible reason. I went
through everything I had on me back at my place, and then I
called friends to see what they might have lying about, what they'd
be willing to share or sell. Time got to be iffy. It was dark and then
light and then dark, but I can't tell you if those were days passing
or me moving from one room to another. I was on the phone a
lot. I can't remember who I talked to, but I'm damn sure what the
subject was. I have a flash of a memory, like the bright crack of an
electric whip in my brain. I remember agreeing to meet someone

at a peculiar address. It was a familiar voice on the line and we were joking – or something said struck me as funny. I remember I was laughing when I hung up.

Think about

Time passes. Light. Dark. Light. I'm standing on a corner – somewhere. Full sunlight like needles in my eyes. Fine swirls of glittery snow blow off the rooftops. It's freezing. How can the sun be out and not work? *Come on, come on.* Suddenly the light was just gone. I don't remember getting jumped. I don't know what they hit me with – the doctors would later speculate that whatever the weapon, it was used with sufficient force to cause my memory problems. Why I am so foggy on the befores and so fucking clear on the afters. Reasons. See, everyone's a junkie.

Time passes, but how much, I'm not sure, several hours at least because when I come to, I am looking into the stars through a broken window. It takes a few minutes – hours? – to triangulate from the window and the stars and my aching skull that I am lying down on my side. Cold and hard surface, gritty with debris. The floor of somewhere cold and hard. My head hurts so bad that if I'd had a mirror I would not have been the least bit surprised to see an ax buried in my skull. I'm thirsty. My tongue feels swollen and I taste blood. *You got mugged,* I tell myself. *Happens. Get up and get out of here,* I say.

how many times I have fallen
Spirits

I manage to get up to all fours. I stay there, vision swimming with slow-motion stars as I gather my strength for the rest of the trip to standing, which I undertake with a distinct foreboding that if I get all the way upright, I won't have anything left to maintain the position. Turns out that's not going to be a problem. My right shinbone, five inches below my knee, snaps like a handful of dry spaghetti. The broken edges of it shoot through my flesh, snag on my trousers, and I go down again. I am sitting, bent forward, grappling with the exposed bone – stupid instinct – trying to push it back where it belongs. My hands soaking with blood, my mind flooding with the sort of pain you can't believe is possible, so you don't experience it as real. It's only the idea of something you can't survive. I'm yelling for help. That's when I hear them coming, shoes shuffling on the concrete. I see the flashlight beams scouring the floor. *Hey,* I say, and *thank God,* I say, grateful, just plain undone, weeping with gratitude because I think they've come as salvation.

are using me
Larger voices

I can't tell how many they are. I see nothing but the glare of the pain and the lights they shine in my eyes. One of them says, 'Careful.' His voice is gentle, instructive. I think he's warning me to take it easy. 'You won't need to go as hard as I did for the leg.' I get the first blow on my back. Crowbar, the curved end. We know that from the pattern of the bruises. Another one. My brain is so overwhelmed with sensation and trying to make sense of it, that thankfully, the whole system shuts down, and it's just me grunting with the sudden downpour of blows and pleading for explanations in-between. *Why? Why?* The doctors would later show me the X rays of the fractures, pointing out the inflicted injuries, and they would speculate that the heavy camel-hair coat over the heavy sweater had buffered the blows enough to prevent more severe damage. It could have been worse, the doctors would tell me. If it makes the doctors feel better . . .

It doesn't take long. Less than a minute. And they throw the bars to the ground and run. I lay there in a quiet broken only by my torn-up breathing and sobs. I can think a bit, and what I think is that they had been waiting there in the shadows, waiting for me to wake up. It was important to someone that I be alert, capable of comprehending. I comprehend, as my attackers do, that my back is broken, in several places. I felt the bones split. And I comprehend, as my attackers do, that with a back injury, I have to keep very, very still or I'll make matters worse. But that isn't my primary worry. What I comprehend most clearly, as I am rock-solid certain my attackers do, is that I am already in the first stages of withdrawal.

callin'
What heaven brought you and me
Cannot be . . .

Thinking goes dark. My brain becomes like a room where some hyperactive fourth-grader is flipping the switches off and on as fast as his fingers can twitch. I remember rats and sick and shit and screaming and trying to curl up against it only to have rivets of my own bones pop out of place. I am bleeding where my shinbones are trying to escape my body. I am hoping I bleed all the way out, that my life can escape what my skeleton can't. I need death more than I've ever needed anything or anyone. I will throw Liz and the child who might be my daughter into the pit ahead of me if that is the price of admission just please god let me die please please please please please and i am trying to smile as i beg because my mom always says that god smiles back on happy boys please i am smiling please . . .

I have been around

I don't know who found me.

the world
Looking

232

I only remember waking up in a hospital with a brace screwed viselike against my skull. A halo they call it, an idea inspired, no doubt, by the angels in hell. I couldn't move my head. I had no idea where the rest of my body might be. I must have made some sort of noise because a face appeared over mine. 'You awake?' All I could see were the eyes, clear dark eyes so full of pity and fear that my first questions were automatically answered, leaving only more horrible ones in their wake.

. . . we never failed to fail

I think I started to cry because the face disappeared in a blur, and the voice, which I can only assume belonged to the owner of that face, said, 'Holy shit, dude. You are one lucky SOB.' I'd hear that many more times in the months to come.

You will survive . . .

That was fourteen years ago.

Somebody fine
Will come along

Fourteen years is a god-awful long time.

Make me forget . . .

You think they'd stop playing that damn song.

233

IV. Ordinary Monsters

One

The hurt returned. He had slid, Joyce's weight with his, down to the floor, using the lower cupboard door as support as buttons gave and fingers flew and mouths consumed and they'd come together, mutually defeated by anger and exhaustion and that strange shared agony that neither one of them knew how to talk about. And now she leaned against him, her gin-soured breath ragged and her heart beating so hard in her underfed frame that he felt it against his own sternum. She pushed away suddenly, pulling her bra down over her breasts. She got up in one quick, furious motion and began yanking her legs back into her jeans.

'I'm sorry.' She said it over and over. 'I'm sorry. I don't know why I did that.' Her hands shook as she tried to redo the buttons on her shirt. The locket rattled as she moved. 'I'm sorry.'

'Vermont?'

'I'm so sorry.' She wouldn't look at him. She was fumbling with the wooden box and her car keys. 'Forgive me.'

'Joyce.'

'I have to go get ready for breakfast. You know, the Hoodoo. Work?' She turned to face him, shoving her hair behind her ears. 'Are you all right?'

'Worse things have happened to me.'

'But you were so – and I went and –' The phone began to ring. She looked off toward it. 'Do you want –'

'No.' That would probably be the silent caller, phoning in a silent gloat for the day's activities. 'Let it ring.' He tucked himself into place and began zipping and snapping himself back into the larger realities. The phone rang on. And now another piece of the bastard truth. 'Look Vermont, I'm at a less than advantageous angle here.'

She glanced from him to the phone to him. 'Do you need –'

'No.' He gave her a glare that made it clear he didn't wish to use that word. He raised his hand toward her as far as he could lift it without betraying the pain with a grimace. She put down her things and gripped his extended forearm in both hands as he locked on to her forearm and between the two of them, the phone ringing on and on, they wrestled him back to standing. By the time he was leaning once more against the counter, they were as sweaty and winded as they'd been after the trip down.

The phone kept ringing. She gathered up her belongings once more and gestured with her keys in the direction of the phone. 'You could get an answering machine, you know.'

'Had a bad experience with voice mail. Phones and I have a generally negative history.'

She furrowed her forehead and then risked a glimpse at his arms, knowing what was under the fabric of the sleeves. Her face went from questioning to sad. She didn't ask, didn't have to. And then she left. Without further questions, without lectures or pleas for his understanding, without lobbying for Danny's return, Vermont just left. It was only after he heard her Saturn revving in the drive that he realized she'd left without her bottle. It meant nothing in the long haul, he instructed himself as he dumped the rest of the gin down the drain, but his mind, which, goddamn it all, knew better, was entertaining notions involving the most dangerous word Duncan knew: *future*.

The phone kept ringing.

'Where the hell are you, TJ?' Joyce shouted again to the empty kitchen as she shoveled eggs and potatoes onto plates, often missing the plate and dumping them on the tray. Joyce was in that gray space between drunk and hungover where she knew she was being miserable but didn't quite care. She ached in unfamiliar places and remembered why and then yelled once more at the absent TJ. The tray was heavy and awkward. When she hefted it to her shoulder, a glass of milk tipped over and spilled over the edge onto her neck, but she was already out into the dining room, swearing as the cold liquid rolled down her spine, between her breasts.

The clientele were on their best behavior, all pleases and thank-yous as Joyce slammed their orders down in front of them. She heard the occasional giggle behind her for which she sent dagger glares over her shoulder. She reached Charlie and Ozzie at the bar. Charlie ducked as though expecting a fist.

'Have you seen TJ?' Joyce dropped the tray to the counter with a bang.

'Not since the last time you asked, darlin'.'

Ozzie shook his head. 'Not since the last time you asked. And neither Eugene nor Lucas has shown this morning.'

'Tuition must be going up again,' said one of the guys farther down the bar. He and his buddies high-fived each other. The guffaws melted into a whimper. Joyce turned to see *what the hell now?* only to find TJ had the one concerned for her tuition costs by the little finger and was bending it back toward his wrist.

'Sorry, Teej.'

'You will be.' She let him go. She was still wearing her peasant blouse and the neckline slipped off her shoulder when her posture relaxed. Dark circles of ruined mascara rimmed her eyes. 'Joyce. Kitchen.'

'Don't you think you owe me an explanation?'

'Please.' She didn't wait for a response but rather headed on out through the swinging door.

Joyce followed, ready to deliver the brimstone-studded speech on responsibility she'd been rehearsing all morning, but the sight of Eugene and Lucas fizzled out the fire. Joyce didn't have to ask. She already knew.

He lit the cigar, the second of this cold, bright morning, and went back to solving the problem at hand: how to get at the EZ. Dew slicked the crime-scene tape they'd wrapped about the crusher like a bad gag gift. They'd done it up several times around and over as though in anticipation of Duncan's careful consideration of how to unwrap it, crush a few dozen junkers, and then rewrap it, like an impatient child a couple of days before Christmas. He'd just about devised a means of doing it when he heard the cars in the drive. He knew most of them by the engine: the purr of Eugene's truck; Lucas's putt-putt Beetle; Ozzie's hiccuping Skylark; Vermont's Saturn. This was trouble.

He crossed the yard to meet them. TJ was out of Eugene's truck, on the ground, and running before Eugene had the pickup braked to a complete stop. Duncan surveyed the cars, their drivers and passengers, coming up quick with just what and who was missing. He had one question he didn't want to ask, but the answer was already on her face. He was going to make her say it; it was clear she'd screwed up and he wasn't about to let her off easy. Making her put the words out there, hard and real in the world, would be punishment enough.

She squared her shoulders and pushed her wind-tousled hair out of her face. She pursed her mouth, her eyes searching for something safe to alight on.

'Where's your T-bird, TJ?'

Inhale. 'That Allie *chiquita* took off in it.'

'You sure about that?'

'Car's gone. She's gone.'

'You call the cops?'

'Not yet.'

'Why not?'

She toed the ground. Inhaled again. 'I can't find Danny. Eugene and I have looked everywhere. We think Allie may have taken him when she skipped. They have that, you know, *play* connection. I don't care about the damn car. I didn't want to call the CHP or anyone because I was afraid of what would happen to Danny if they got stopped. You know? They'd put him in the system; they'd have no choice.'

He glanced at the assembled cars. 'So you've put together this posse to track them down?'

'I'm sorry, Duncan. I didn't know what else to do.' She met his eyes; her expression said she was prepared now to accept his fury.

He reached in his jacket pocket for the folded green flier he'd dug through the office waste basket to find and handed it to TJ. 'I'll get the truck.' Lucas cranked down his window as Duncan passed. 'We're going to Larkin.' Lucas nodded and shoved his glasses into place. Joyce was standing, one foot out of the Saturn, and pushing her hair behind her ears, over and over again. Duncan could feel the panic rippling off her like heat off asphalt. Even at a distance she looked unsteady on quite a few levels. He dropped the cigar and killed it, twisting carefully into the dirt with his boot. 'Come on, Vermont. You're riding with me.'

'It's happening all over again.' She clenched and unclenched her fingers. She'd been going on like this since they'd left Lágrimas. 'I don't believe it. It's happening all over again.'

He tried once more to calm her. 'I know where they are, Vermont. That Alice-son girl was trying to show me the Orpheus fliers yesterday.'

'Why would she take him away like that?'

'Who we talking about? Danny or your kid?'

She jolted as though he'd struck her. 'Well, we know what you think about my kid. Maybe Danny is trying to escape me, too. Is that what you're saying?'

'I'm not saying anything.' Duncan focused his mind back on the road. The straightaway simplicity of getting from here to there in the desert was its great blessing. A journey could get complicated in one's perspective or dangerous in the going, but the path was always clear, direction inevitable.

Joyce locked her hands over her knees and watched the broken white bars of the center lane flash past like the hash marks on a clock. She was traveling in circles. It *was* all happening again. Unless she could stop it. *Do what you should have done; say what you should have said the first time. Say it now.* 'Duncan, when my son and Maddie – it was because –'

'Look, what I said yesterday, well, I was really out of line.'

She bowed her head. 'Out of line, maybe, but not altogether wrong.' She could feel him staring at her, but she couldn't find any more words. This was going to be harder than she imagined.

Duncan and Joyce found the others already gathered outside the theater, where TJ had pressed herself against the hood of the Thunderbird. 'OK, so I lied.' She laughed. 'I love my car.' She kissed the metal and slid back to the sidewalk. 'Now, I want to kick me some Valley Girl ass.'

Joyce walked over to the ticket booth to get some distance between herself and the others. She was irritated by the young woman's lack of seriousness and what's more, perplexed by her own irritation. TJ was relieved, happy even, to have found Danny, to know he was all right. Happy made sense, but happy wasn't what Joyce felt. Scared. She was scared. She gazed up at the CLOSED sign on the booth window; she was trying to get on top of her nerves, trying not to think about how good a drink would feel. She heard Duncan close by and looked over to see him at the front entrance, speaking over a swath of velvet rope, explaining the situation to the theater manager, a tiny, tiny blue-haired woman in a red blazer and plaid slacks. Duncan cleared his throat and waved them onward. The tiny blue-haired woman unhooked the rope to let them through.

'She said they've been here awhile,' Duncan said as he waited for Joyce to go in before him. 'Danny and the girl are watching rehearsals.'

'Oh,' said Joyce, but she wanted to ask him what it felt like to know, just *know,* where to look. How had he learned to do that?

They followed the manager to a set of double doors. She raised a finger to the scarlet pucker of her lipsticked mouth to indicate they should be very quiet. She pulled open the door.

The stage was brightly lit and set with pastel drapery; softly shifting sheers hung at intervals that provided alcoves for the actors to enter and exit from without actually leaving the stage. Only one person was out front, standing near center: Danny, clunky and disheveled in his work clothes and boots. His head tilted up toward the spotlights, his eyes shielded as though he were staring into the sun.

'Danny!' Joyce started down the aisle, only to have her path blocked by Allie, who had stepped in front of her and was frantically shushing her.

'Excuse me.' Joyce forced the words through her teeth as she tried to force her way past the girl.

'Let me handle this.' TJ's voice hissed past Joyce's ear. The hiss became a squeak. 'Eugene, get your freakin' claws off me; I'm only going to kill her a tiny bit.'

'You're angry, I know, OK,' Allie whispered, 'but wait for a minute and watch; you are not going to believe this.' She gestured Joyce, TJ, and the others toward the seats. 'Watch,' Allie pleaded, pointing at the stage.

One of the actors strode onto the stage, a man in robes sewn from alternating lengths of pastel and ivory satin. He had dark skin and a kingly bearing. The spotlight gleamed off his skull. On his arm was a slight girl in a draping dress of yellow. The girl drifted off to the side as the man approached Danny and spoke in big bell tones:

> *If I have too austerely punished you*
> *Your compensation makes amends; for I*
> *Have given you here a third of mine own life*
> *Or that for which I live . . .*

'They're almost to the end. Danny's playing Ferdinand – or being Ferdinand or whatever it is he does,' said Allie, but Joyce only half heard her because she was, as were the others, looking from the stage to Duncan and back. Duncan's own face was skewed against what his eyes were taking in. Allie, giggling, turned back to the stage. 'Just wait. It gets weirder.'

> *. . . O Ferdinand,*
> *Do not smile at me that I boast her off,*
> *For thou shalt find she will outstrip all praise*
> *And make it halt behind her.*

Danny said, 'I do believe it, against an oracle.' Joyce found herself moving into the row of seats after the others, feeling for the cushion behind her, sitting. Duncan came down slow and disbelieving next to her as Prospero lectured Danny on the boundaries of his daughter's chastity:

> *. . . But*
> *If thou dost break her virgin-knot before*
> *All sanctimonious ceremonies may*
> *With full and holy rite be ministered,*
> *No sweet aspersion shall the heavens let fall*
> *To make this contract grow; but barren hate,*
> *Sour-eyed disdain, and discord shall bestrew*
> *The union of your bed with weeds so loathly*
> *That you shall hate it both.*

'Christ, he even sounds like you,' TJ whispered through an

awestruck laugh as she sat down behind them. 'Good thing you never had daughters, Dupree. You'd be just as much a killjoy as this dude.'

'Yeah,' he said. 'Good thing I didn't have daughters.'

Danny was foreswearing premarital relations with the sort of eloquent enthusiasm that would tell most parents the deed was already done. '. . . shall never melt mine honor into lust, to take away the edge of that day's celebration when I shall think or Phoebus' steeds are foundered or Night kept chained below.'

Still, Prospero seemed satisfied:

> *Fairly spoke.*
> *Sit then and talk with her; she is thine own.*

As Prospero spoke, Danny's lips moved with the words. They might have given him a specific part, but his mind was marking the order of passage and phrase. His demeanor, however, the drop of his jaw, the shine in his eyes said he had transcended earthly bonds and believed himself speaking with angels. Prospero winked at Danny and called out to the sky:

> *What, Ariel! My industrious servant, Ariel!*

Ariel fluttered in from behind one of the drapery panels. The spirit was portrayed by a young woman in a wig of rainbow strands that hung to her waist. She wore a white leotard and tutu and red high-top tennis shoes.

> *What would my potent master? Here I am.*

From the end of the aisle came muffled laughter and the soft, united voices of Lucas, Ozzie, and Eugene: 'TJ!' Duncan growled at them all to shut up, and Joyce realized that he was taking in more than the easy marvel of the coincidences. His mouth was set hard, and his eyes were narrowed; it was his pool-playing face, as though he were lining up a shot that was going to hurt like hell on the follow-through. He had his hands rolled tight over the ends of the armrest. *I know what you're thinking;* she laid her hand over his and squeezed, exerting definite pressure; *you can't be serious.* She expected to be shrugged off as an annoyance. He let her stay, but Joyce wasn't sure he was even conscious of her presence any longer.

The play continued. Prospero ordered Ariel to fetch the spirits for he had promised Danny and Miranda a display of his art. He then commanded the lovers' attention:

No tongue! All eyes! Be silent.

'I take it back.' TJ laughed, her head bobbing over Duncan's shoulder. 'He doesn't sound like you; he is you.'

The lights went down, and three swirling spots followed a trio of dancers – two men and a girl in multilayered skirts of chiffon and high-tops. The dancers wore masks, elaborately painted and decorated with ribbons, as they performed a stylized ballet and called out to one another words of love and abundance in a theatrical blessing of the lovers' coming nuptials. When they'd finished, they bent to the stage in dying-swan poses before Danny, who threw open his arms and said, 'This is a most majestic vision, and harmonious charmingly. May I be bold to think these spirits?'

Prospero shook his head, chuckling with a delight that could not wholly be pinned to the character.

Spirits, which by mine art
I have from their confines called to enact
My present fancies.

Danny looked about, from the dancers to Miranda watching

246

from the periphery, again to Prospero, and sighed. 'Let me live here!' Nearing tears, his voice broke. 'So rare a wondered father and a wise makes this place Paradise.'

Beneath her palm Joyce felt Duncan's grip grow even tighter on the armrest, and then, she felt the tension in his fist relax. She made to sneak a glance at his expression but found he was already studying her. He nodded as though to tell her it was already decided, and she shook her head. He nodded again. She felt his hand turning and closing over hers. She tried to pull it away, but he held on tight as though he expected her to bolt for the stage. He knew what she was thinking, too: It was happening again.

Prospero had returned to his senses and was remembering the plots against him. Danny was unnerved. 'This is strange. Your father's in some passion that works him strongly.'

Miranda ran across the stage to his side, and Allie, still standing in the aisle, spoke with her.

> *Never till this day*
> *Saw I him touched with anger so distempered.*

Prospero came round and put his arm about Danny, giving him a hearty shake of reassurance.

> *You do look, my son, in a moved sort,*
> *As if you were dismayed: be cheerful, sir.*
> *Our revels are now ended. These our actors,*
> *As I foretold you, were all spirits and*
> *Are melted into air, into thin air;*

Danny's mouth was moving with the words. Allie was still speaking along. Joyce then heard Duncan's voice. He too was reciting the lines, just above a whisper. TJ, behind her, had joined in.

247

> *And, like the baseless fabric of this vision,*
> *The cloud-capped tow'rs, the gorgeous palaces*

Joyce looked down the row of seats. Eugene, Ozzie, Charlie, and Lucas were all mouthing the words, heads nodding. They caught one another's eye. Eugene, grinning, fisted his hand – devil's horn symbol of allegiance with the gods of rock and roll – and his voice grew louder.

> *The solemn temples, the great globe itself,*
> *Yea, all which it inherit, shall dissolve*

Eugene was standing. Next, Lucas was on his feet, followed by Ozzie who pulled Charlie, looking mortally embarrassed, up with him, and they were shouting the lines along with TJ, who jumped up, both fists pumping in the air:

> *And, like this insubstantial pageant faded,*
> *Leave not a rack behind. We are such stuff*
> *As dreams are made on, and our little life*
> *Is rounded with a sleep . . .*

By this point, the action onstage had ceased and that seemed to have an instant dampening effect on the rock-concert ribaldry of the audience; they fell quickly quiet, one by one, back into their seats. Prospero peered out into the audience and spoke, in measured syllables.

> *. . . Sir, I am vexed.*
> *Bear with my weakness, my old brain is troubled.*
> *Be not disturbed with my infirmity.*
> *If you be pleased, retire into my cell*
> *And there repose. A turn or two I'll walk*
> *To still my beating mind.*

Miranda and Danny wished Prospero peace, an out-of-sync attempt at unison. Miranda made to leave the stage. When Danny didn't follow, the girl grabbed his hand and dragged him along after her. Prospero came to the foot of the stage, where he crossed his arms and sighed, gazing out over them, his expression perplexed. 'OK, so what's the story with that kid?'

Two

Vermont wouldn't come backstage with the rest of them. She sat out there, alone in the audience, her face a freeze-frame of disapproval. He couldn't allow this reopening of her newly knitted wounds to prevent him from doing what was best for Danny. He had to take the shot that was available. No use in griping about how difficult it might be. The events of the past twenty-four hours had made it clear that if the monsters were indeed on their way to Lágrimas, he had to get Danny as far away as possible. And after Danny, himself.

He looked at the photocopied schedule of dates the director of Nouvelle Monde had given him. He had interrupted her lunch, which he insisted she continue as he presented his case. The director's name was Sarah, a statuesque woman of maybe sixty who wore her hair in a single long braid that started as silver at her scalp and darkened to jet at its end. Her skin, creased by sun and good humor, was the rosy-brown of freshly picked lentils. In a floor-length dress of white, she exuded a languid elegance, a grace that conveyed warmth and welcome, but her eyes betrayed her as a keen analyst of situations. He would have bet Ozzie a week's pay that the woman played pool.

She listened to him without comment as she scraped the bottom of a yogurt container. Then she took an orange from her paper lunch bag. After peeling it, she broke it in two and offered Duncan half. He declined. She suggested they walk.

They walked amid the crates and suitcases, ropes and pulleys behind the stage set, as she explained the dramatic philosophies of the company, that each actor learned every part and that they drew lots to see who would play what for that particular performance. Today's Prospero might be tomorrow's Caliban or Miranda or the Boatswain. The result was a play, that although identical in every other aspect of presentation, was forever subverting itself. 'Like life,' she said, her voice accented by a Middle-Eastern influence he couldn't quite identify. He responded with 'Ah' and 'Uh-huh' at appropriate intervals. And even though she was obviously enamored of explaining what Nouvelle Monde was about, Duncan read every aspect of her body language as saying she was suspicious of his motives. She was already putting herself between Danny and her intuitions of potential harm. He took that as a favorable sign.

'I can send you money, wherever you are, for his upkeep. Whatever he needs I want him to have.' He folded the schedule and put it in his pocket. 'He likes helping out. So, put him to work.'

'Oh, he'll work.' She laughed. 'I'm putting him onstage. It will be great to give somebody a night off every once and a while. *Tempest* is the only one he knows?'

'As far as any of us can tell. I don't think he understands that it's a play.'

The sharpness in her eyes softened. 'He lives on the island?'

'Yeah, but I can't say it's by choice. He was exiled or he exiled himself there. That's what I think. All I can say for sure is that he's already come up against the worst of the world. He's just a boy, and I'm counting on someone keeping him safe.'

'He's not safe with you?'

'Not as safe as he needs to be.' Duncan said this in such a way as to indicate he wasn't doling out further explanations.

She dipped her chin as if to acknowledge she wasn't seeking any more. 'If things should change, you let us know. We'll send him home.' She offered her hand and he took it, catching the fragrance of orange zest and minted tea. 'Perhaps by the time we return here, he'll have learned another play.'

'Just keep him out of Denmark.'

'Only the comedies, I promise.'

'I'd appreciate that.' *You got it lined up, man, now steady your hand and sink this bastard.* 'I'd better go tell him.' *Yes, but how?* 'Ah, in the play, I forget, does Prospero or whoever say – I want him to understand we won't be seeing each other for a while.'

'I can show you the book, if that helps.' She lifted her hand, three fingers extended. 'Prospero makes three farewells. One to the spirit Ariel when Prospero releases the island.' She folded her index finger. 'One to his power when he releases his magic.' She folded the second finger. 'And one to his exile when he releases the need for revenge.' Her third finger went down.

'The first farewell will do fine. I said good-bye to magic a long time ago.'

'But don't you see?' Her eyes grew sharp again as she opened her palm flat and empty before him. 'For Prospero, it's all the same thing.'

Duncan, book in hand, went looking for Danny. He threaded his way through the starstruck Lágrimas folks as they pestered the actors backstage. TJ was going through a costume catalog with Ariel, comparing price and construction in wigs. One of the dancers who had performed the masked ballet was teaching Eugene basic sword-fighting techniques, each of them brandishing a real-enough rapier albeit with differing levels of grace. The actor, still in his chiffon skirts, demonstrated offense and defense, calling out the French names for stances as Eugene tried to keep up like a gawky adolescent at his first cotillion. Ozzie repeated the French words and called out encouragement and preliminary odds on 'the dude in the skirt slicing you six ways to Sunday.' Charlie, who'd been taking this in, waved his arms in disgust. 'Just stop,' he said. He grabbed the sword from Eugene's hand, and said 'like this' as he swung the blade up to bar the downward stroke of the actor's weapon. The duel was on. The blades clattering, they parried back and forth. The actor who had played Prospero shouted compliments as the two men swashbuckled past, and asked where Charlie studied. Charlie halted the fight and dropped his hands to his thighs, sucking down wind and nodding in acceptance of the praise. He wheezed out something about Douglas Fairbanks. Miranda, Lucas, and Alice-son applauded Charlie, and then they went back to poring through boxes of props and trying on hats for one another's amusement. No Danny. No Vermont, either. His heart knocked a double beat. *She wouldn't.*

He hurried to find his way out front, got confused by the curtaining, and ended up on the stage itself. But he could let himself exhale. Danny was there, still on the island, in the center of the stage, looking up into the lights. Vermont wasn't in the seat where he'd left her. He surveyed the rows, the balcony. She wasn't anywhere, and it occurred to him that up until this moment, the decision had been bearable because he'd known, as furious as she was about it, Vermont's presence meant he would not be alone in the grieving. But the time had come for doing it, and there he was, alone.

He let his mind sink anchors deep into the hurt of his body, mooring itself against the ache that was coming. Nature had imposed limits on all manner of indifferent forces – the speed of light, the length of a day, boiling points, absolute zero – you would think there'd be an upper limit to what we were able to feel. Pain or not, this had to get done. It was for the best and that was fact. But fact was, as always, a frail defense.

'So here we are, Danny, my man.' He walked across the stage, but Danny didn't break his gaze from the spotlights. Duncan put his arm about the boy's shoulder and stroked his upturned head, ruffling the fine wisps of his sun-bleached hair. 'I wager someone around here is better with the scissors than me. Couldn't be worse, huh?' Danny blinked. 'It will be good here, I think. You will be happy with these people – happier. And I expect you to be good to them in return. Understand?'

Danny lowered his head, his face all earnest determination. 'I will be correspondent to command and shall do my spiriting lightly.' He began his forward sweep of a bow, but Duncan caught him by the shoulders, forcing him upright.

'No bowing.' He tapped Danny's forehead. 'No more Ariel. No more Caliban. Now you're Prospero. No more bowing.' Duncan willed his own spine to straighten in spite of the onslaught of complaints such a movement brought. He was hoping the example might work should the words fail. He opened the book to the place Sarah had shown him, and read. 'I'll deliver all; and promise you calm seas, auspicious gales, and sail so expeditious that shall catch your royal fleet far off – My Ari –' Couldn't use that name; Shakespeare would just have to forgive him. 'My – son, that is thy charge. Then to the elements be free, and fare thou well.' He closed the book and placed it in Danny's hand, made the boy's fingers fold over it. 'We'll see you when you come back around.' He clasped the boy's shoulder once more, held it an instant longer before turning away to go round up the crew and head for home.

Joyce wandered about the lobby for a few more minutes dabbing her eyes with napkins from the refreshment stand. She wasn't certain what she ought to do. Part, maybe most, of her was ready go to back in to argue or shout or hit or do whatever was necessary to make Duncan Dupree own up to the insanity of leaving Danny in the care of these strangers. The other part wanted to see if she might join up with the troupe somehow, as a scheduler or bookkeeper or something. To be with Danny, yes, but also for the comfort of a life based on pretend where one's horrible mistakes and the aftermath were washed away with that evening's makeup. Was that why Danny refused to leave the play? Because he needed more than anything to know exactly what happened next?

She pushed back into the theater, just as Duncan came out onto the stage. He put his arm about the boy and tousled his hair. Danny made to bow, and Duncan stopped him. She was about to call to them both when Duncan began to read from the book he was carrying. Joyce didn't know this scene, had not heard Danny use it, but understood it was the end of the story. Duncan was saying good-bye. How could he do that? How could he not? Good-bye was what needing saying.

Duncan handed Danny the book. He gave the boy the briefest of embraces and walked away, his posture deflating as he went. Neither he nor Danny looked back.

Danny went rigid in the spotlight. His head fell back as his arms raised from his sides and up, reaching for the theater's rafters. Then He snapped himself straight to attention, arms at his sides, eyes set on the distance. 'Please you draw near,' he called out. Joyce, not wanting to miss what he might want to tell her, broke into a run. 'Now all my charms are all o'erthrown, and what strength I have's my own, which is most faint . . .'

'Danny. Danny, sweetheart –'

'Now 'tis true I must be here confined by you, or sent to Naples. Let me not, since I have my dukedom got, and pardoned the deceiver, dwell in this bare island by your spell . . .'

'Danny. We can learn it. All of us. We'll get a copy of the play, and we'll learn it. We can do it with you, back in Lágrimas.' She heard the absurdity in the promise. For Danny there was no Lágrimas, no Nouvelle Monde; there was only the island. He hadn't reached the end of play; she had.

'But release me from my bands with the help of your good hands. Gentle breath of yours my sails must fill, or else my project fails, which was to please. Now I want spirits to enforce, art to enchant; and my ending is despair unless . . .'

'Danny. I –'

'I be relieved by prayer, which pierces so that it assaults mercy itself and frees all faults.'

256

'Danny?'

'As you from crimes would pardoned be, let your indulgence set me free.' He opened his arms before him and bowed deeply to the nonexistent audience.

The response was applause, one person clapping as she came onstage from between the drapery. It was a woman in a long white dress. She was smiling at Danny. 'You will make a grand Prospero.' The woman smiled down at Joyce; she pulled the ropelike braid of her hair over her shoulder. 'May I help you?'

Joyce heard the question as though it came from many miles away. She was watching the dark end of the braid pendulum swing to rest. 'Maddie?' She searched the woman's face.

The woman started a bit, then leaned forward, her hands crossed over her chest. 'Who?'

Joyce shook her head. 'No one. Nothing.'

The woman put her arm around Danny. She nodded at Joyce. 'Your friends are waiting for you outside,' she said, then she steered Danny away from the spotlight, leading him off toward the wings, leaving Joyce alone.

'Good-bye,' she said to the empty stage.

She got in the rollback without invitation and locked her door. He anticipated a verbal barrage, almost hoped for it, as he was in the mood to yell himself, but as he drove, Vermont sat quietly, eyes focused forward, her hands folded one against the other in her lap. Her nose was red from crying, and her mouth had the downturned set of someone who wasn't planning on smiling again for a long time. He figured she wasn't paying much attention to anything other than counting down the minutes and miles between being here and hooking up to her first drink. She didn't have enough of the story and was torturing herself on a misunderstanding.

Then disarm the woman. 'It wasn't to get Danny away from you, Vermont.'

'I understand that.'

'You do? OK. What you don't understand is that I needed to get him away from me. My situation is complicated. There's a lot of stuff you don't know.'

'Yes, well, people are dying.'

'Even if we allowed Gus MacGruder some sort of honorary status as a human being, he still wouldn't be missed.'

'That's an awful thing to say.'

'That's fact.' He watched the desert roll by his window, the scrubby green-grays of scraggly plants hanging onto almost nothing for no other reason than the wretched inability to do anything else. Life here was beautiful because of its tragic, single-minded determination to continue at any cost, sinking roots and suckers into sand and rock where it expected to find water; if no water were in this place where the seed of yourself landed, then why be burdened with the need to root or suckle? How could your survival depend on something that had never even existed in the place you were put down and told to survive? The probable solution to this puzzle spoke of a creation so unforgiving, so broken and lonely that instead of pursuing the paradox to its cold, logical core, you simply took what you got and called it destiny.

'I want to go with you.' She cleared her throat, said it louder. 'When you leave Lágrimas, I want to go with you.'

Now here was a surprise. 'Who says I'm leaving?'

'Those phone calls you don't answer, for one. Your sending Danny away, for another. Something is coming –'

'Vermont, you need to be here when your kid shows up, right?' She didn't say anything. 'You want to be here, right?' Still nothing. *Ah*. 'He's not coming to Lágrimas, is he?'

Nothing. 'Is he?'

'No.' She studied her hands as though just now discovering they were a matched set. 'He's not going to show up here. I knew on the first day. Jake, that poor kid, he was trying to be helpful, I guess; he mistook Danny and TJ for – That's why I bought the Hoodoo. I knew they wouldn't ever be coming here.'

258

'And you could go back to drinking.'

'No. I don't know. Maybe.' She exhaled hard. 'There's a lot of stuff you don't know about me, either.'

It was the way she said it, her echoing of his own words. *There's a lot of stuff you don't know. Yes, well, people are dying.* 'Joyce –' *Something is coming.* He held the question on his tongue, hearing in the quiet of her anticipation the pulse of his own heart beating deep in his own ear. She wanted him to ask; she'd been trying to get the question out of him, out of someone from the beginning. 'He's dead, isn't he?'

'Oh,' she said, as though she'd been punched in the gut because hearing it out loud was harder than anything she'd ever done. 'Yes.' The sound sputtered out of her like she knew she had to talk or she'd never breathe again. 'He's dead. Maddie's dead. They're both gone.'

'Overdose?'

'I don't know. I'm not sure what you call it when it's not an accident. I mean I know what it's called, but he left me no way to be sure.' Her head fell forward, but she wasn't crying. She tucked her hair, her hands shaking. 'We'd had another fight about Maddie; this one was bad; things went a little out of control. I did something, I think I may have . . . I'm not sure what, but it was something terrible. Anyway, Paul was working late again, and by the time I got home from my job, it was dark. He was at the kitchen table. I yelled at him for not starting dinner. I thought he was sleeping. But then I saw . . . well, I pulled the needle out of his arm and took everything, the spoon and the pictures, and I hid them in my jewelry box, so his father wouldn't see and be angry. I couldn't take any more fighting. I put what was left of the drug down the disposal with that morning's coffee grounds. I had a few drinks. I remember that, and I don't remember anything after, until Paul's shaking me awake and saying, "Brian is dead." Over and over. "Brian is dead."' Her voice shut off as though the words themselves had severed the cords in her throat.

Duncan drove. He had nothing to offer her except the truth. 'He was gone before you got there.'

She shook her head with one mighty jerk. 'Paul told me the doctors said that if I'd called right away, they probably could have saved him. The time of death. They had a good idea of the exact time of – They found Maddie the next day.' Her breath caught and she held it, and finally she exhaled again, her shoulders sloped over in surrender. She dropped her hands back to her lap, her hair fell forward so that he couldn't see her face as she sat beside him, awaiting sentence.

There it is, he thought, *end of the game.* No matter how you played it, you couldn't win. He and Joyce were proof of that, sitting here together, the leaver and the left, both pinioned beneath the exact same suffering with no way of digging themselves out. His back vetoed the notion with a deep groan of the same-old same-old, but he ignored the opposition; he reached over and laid his hand over hers. 'It'll be soon. I have to wait for them to close up this MacGruder deal; but it will be soon. You'd have to be ready to go with no notice. I can't stick around and wait for you to sell the Hoodoo, understand?'

She nodded. Her mouth went tight. She nodded again.

'It's not rescue, Vermont. I know nothing about rescue. We leave Lágrimas, and our real troubles are going to start.'

'I don't want to cause any trouble, any more trouble.'

He pulled his hand away, straightening his posture. 'Life is always trouble, of one sort or another.'

'Thank you for –'

'Don't – I'm not doing you any favor –'

'Yes. Yes, you are –'

'Vermont.'

'Sorry. I'm –'

'Let's just say we're square, okay?' he said, holding up his hand to indicate he was done discussing the matter. And as usual she ignored him.

'How can we possibly be –'

'Christ, Vermont. Do I have to come straight out and –'

'I'm putting you in such a –'

'Damn it, Joyce. Listen. Danny's gone, all right? Danny's gone and that's for the best, but I don't think I can go back to – You understand? I don't, I can't.'

'It's all right.' She turned her head enough to meet his eyes. 'I know.' He held up his palm again, this time forestalling not only her words but the recognition so plain on her weary face. 'Me neither,' she said, and looked back at her hands.

Three

They arrived back in Lágrimas around four-thirty and found that they had to park off the road at the Hoodoo. The place was as packed as it had been the night before. Duncan and Joyce sat in the truck for a long time. Joyce did not believe a person could be as tired as she was and still get obedient movement from her limbs. It seemed as though they'd rebel and upon receiving orders to walk, reach, lift, they'd simply hang limp and restful until the brain got the message that the body proper was not going to put up with any more of its ivory-tower tyranny. At which point, the brain would haul out the guilt guns to remind everyone who was in charge and why.

The guilt guns always worked. 'I'd better get in there. TJ'll be overwhelmed.' Besides, 'in there' was the bottles, the glasses, the ice. She opened the truck door. 'You hungry?'

'I could eat.' They both knew he was lying.

They crossed the road and pushed through the drunken and bandaged smokers clustered in the parking lot. Post-Owl Happy Hour apparently began shortly after breakfast. With the co-op down for probably another day or two, the population of Lágrimas had nothing to occupy itself with but glasses of beer and comparison of injuries received during cleanup – many of which were due to less-than-sober operation of saws and hammers. Questions greeted them, questions about what TJ had said, about Danny's not coming back. Duncan responded with a few low grunts and nods. Before they reached the front door, Joyce heard the music.

'Not again,' Duncan muttered.

Inside, the jukebox was blaring an old song about sailing. The pinball machine was flashing, the bells pinged and zipped. Morton pounded the flipper buttons, thrusting himself against the table as Hillary and Charlotte cheered him on. Tables had been pushed aside and in the open area, couples – including Milt and Victoria Freemont – were two-stepping, while around the dancers eddies of young girls bopped and chatted and swigged at long-necked bottles. Allie stood off to the side by herself, hugging her shoulders as though cold. She saw Joyce and Duncan; she started toward them, shouting something Joyce couldn't make out until the girl was close enough to be yelling almost in Joyce's ear.

'My fault,' she said, waving her hand in the direction of the noise. 'The machines. They weren't broken. Just unplugged.'

'And you plugged them in?' said Duncan.

'I didn't realize it would be so loud.'

'Well, I should have cut the goddamn cords right off.'

'I'll go find some scissors.' She turned on her heels and charged off as though on a mission.

Duncan leaned into Joyce, and shouted, 'Hire that girl.'

Joyce pointed at the bar. 'What about TJ?'

TJ, appearing tonight as herself, was behind the crowded bar, mixing something in a shaker. She grinned at Joyce and then downshifted the smile into an icy sneer for Duncan. He made a face back at her and headed off for the pool table. Joyce headed for the gin.

She got to the bar to see TJ pouring frothy chocolate milk from the shaker into the row of glasses lined up before Rachel's children who were seated at the bar. Rachel was on the end stool, downing her milk straight. She drained the glass, wiped her mouth with the back of her hand. 'Pregnant again,' she shouted at Joyce as she pushed the glass back for a refill. Joyce grabbed the milk jug from the bar fridge and handed it to TJ.

'Who is the father of all those kids?' she asked as quietly as she could.

TJ shrugged. 'Never stopped to think about it – Yes, Ozzie, I see your glass is empty. Just a sec. You working tonight or what, Joycie?'

'I'm working.' She headed down to the other end of the bar where the regulars were semi-watching an all-news channel, waiting for sports coverage to roll round again. A commercial came on, and Charlie went back to teaching swordplay to Eugene, using the Hoodoo's plastic-sword swizzle sticks. Lucas had managed to leave the theater with a hat shaped like a goldfish. It was made of orange felt with quilted scales and gills; it had yellow glass eyes. He had it shoved down tight over his forehead, his face alight with a goofy grin. A billboard for happiness.

Joyce filled their mugs and glasses. She grabbed the gin bottle for herself. She took a tall glass from under the bar and was unscrewing the cap from the bottle when a cry of betrayal spiraled up from the center of the room. It was Allie. She raced toward the bar, pointing at the television. 'Turn it up! Turn it up!'

Ozzie finished peeling the wrapper from a candy bar before obliging the request and cranking the volume loud enough to hear the TV over the din of music. Still, they had to lean over the bar to hear it clearly: An arrest had been made in connection with fires set in the L.A. area earlier that fall. Based on an anonymous tip called into a talk radio show the night before, authorities had tracked down an individual who had been overheard bragging about his responsibility not only for a series of small arson incidents, but for October's devastating blaze that had ravaged Madera Canyon and the mountains beyond. Film of the arrest showed maps, plans for fires yet to be started, and stockpiles of incendiary devices. The film also showed the accused, a bland, middle-aged man in a rumpled sport shirt, being led away in handcuffs. Under the caption CAREFUL ARSONIST CAUGHT, the commentator explained that the man's claims aside, investigators still believed the Madera Canyon fire to have been the result of natural conditions.

Allie said, 'No.' She said it again and again, her voice growing in pitch as she backed away from the set. 'No. No. No.' She stomped her foot. 'They're my fires. Mine.' She stared at the television and then turned from one person to another, pleading, as they stared back at her. 'I lit them.' She turned to Duncan, who was more intent on aligning the diamond-shaped rack full of billiard balls. Allie marched over and slapped her hand against the felt. 'I'm the one they want. They're my fires.'

'I'm not sure that that's the sort of accomplishment you want to be claiming as yours, Alice-son,' he said without looking up at her. He lifted the rack away. 'If you will kindly remove your hand from my table, I want to shoot some nine-ball.' She didn't move. Duncan straightened. 'Now, Alice-son.'

'Abby. My name is Abby.' She pulled her hand away and bit on her knuckle. 'You were right, OK? I lied about my name because I thought – I thought they were coming after me.'

Duncan laughed. 'We can hope.'

'You don't believe me.'

He hefted the pool cue and pointed it at her. 'You ought to go home.'

'I can't.'

'I can call the guys at the CHP; you should be able to get your car back, no problem. And keep MacGruder's money.'

'If I go home, I'm going to jail.'

'But you'll have your car.'

Abby clawed her fingers and shook them in frustration. 'Why don't any of you believe me?'

Lucas raised his hand. TJ pushed a beer at him. 'What, Lucas?'

'I believe you, Abby.' He pulled his fish hat lower over his eyes. 'Why would you lie about doing something terrible? Lies are for getting out of trouble. Nobody believes me, either. If that makes you feel better.'

'Why?' Abby squinted at him. 'What did you do?'

'What I did?' He pushed his glasses up hard against his forehead. 'I – Did you realize that some of the stars over Lágrimas are moving faster than the others? Gravity is breaking up, like the continents; time is starting to drift. Soon it will be impossible to be both here and now simultaneously.'

'OK buddy' – Eugene clamped him on the shoulder – 'reel it in.'

Joyce poured herself a healthy two, make it three, fingers of gin, straight up. 'Allie – Abby, whoever you are, let the rest of us have our fair share of bad judgment. Trust me, there's plenty to go around.'

Charlie raised his glass to the girl. 'Listen to the good woman, darlin'. Look at you. You're a sweet little girl with no cause to be torching any old thing. At least that arson idiot might have something of a reason –'

'I had a reason.' She stepped closer to Charlie, glaring at him when he started to chuckle. 'It wasn't a good reason, not a save-the-world sort of reason, but it made sense to me. At the time, at least. I was trying to make things right for this stupid, loser, geekazoid magician.'

'Magician?' said Charlie. He turned to Ozzie who had paused mid-candy-bar bite. TJ cocked her head; her jaw worked for a second before she made any sound. 'Magician?'

'I'm not lying.' The girl's face screwed into a confused pout. 'OK. Maybe he wasn't a magician, not really, not yet. Maybe never. I mean, he was getting his butt kicked out of Academy Arcana. You flunk out of magician school, I guess you're not really –'

Joyce halted the glass, inches from her lips. 'You're kidding.'

'No way,' said TJ, pushing herself between Ozzie and Charlie, almost climbing over the bar to get closer to Abby. 'No way. No fucking way. Was his name Jake?'

'Jake.' Ozzie put the candy bar down.

Eugene laughed. 'It couldn't be. We wouldn't know where to start figuring the odds on that one. How could you bet on that?'

'Jake? Who is Jake? I don't know what his name is.' Abby caught up the skirt of her dress, twisting it as she backed away from the bar. 'I felt sorry for him. I wanted him to feel better.'

'So did I,' said Joyce, hearing her own amazement as she lowered the glass from her lips before she could take the first swallow.

'Me too,' said TJ, her face radiating delight.

'What are you talking about?' Abby's expression wavered between confusion and fear. 'All I wanted was to burn down the school, so he'd feel, I don't know, lucky maybe. I wanted that fire. I really did.'

Joyce looked over at Duncan, who was poised, head down, about to break a new game. 'Wanting a thing to happen isn't the same as making it happen.' She swirled the glass's flat bottom against the bar and considered the vortex forming in the gin. 'Not the same thing, no matter how hard you want it.'

Abby studied her nails. 'But if I want something really awful to happen, and it does –'

'Do you think the Hoodoo would burn?' Joyce stopped the glass and looked up.

'What? This place?'

'Well, you're the expert, right?'

'Are you crazy?'

'Yes, she is – I'm coming, already,' said TJ, waving to the customers calling for her at the other end of the bar.

'What do you think? Would it burn?'

Abby surveyed the room with its wooden tables and paper-covered walls and open glasses of flammable beverages set carelessly about. She allowed a smile to curl the corners of her mouth. 'I've never done a building, so I can't really say.'

'That's a shame,' said Joyce. 'It would be good to know about these things, you understand, with some degree of certainty. In the meantime, do you still want a job?'

'I can stay? I can work here?'

'Hey!' said TJ as she gathered beer mugs to be refilled. 'I heard that.'

'Relax, Nicolette. You can never tell when you'll need extra help.'

'I don't need any help.' TJ set the mugs beneath the tap, began filling the first one, her head bobbing in thought. She apparently hit the core implication of Joyce's reasoning because she turned with a jolt, her eyes narrowed with suspicion. 'Should I be getting out the FOR SALE sign again?'

Joyce shook her head, leaned backward to pluck a book of matches from the bowl by the cash register. She righted herself and tossed the matches, clumsily, over the bar. The girl caught them, almost losing her balance in the effort. Abby looked at the cardboard book. 'You're giving *me* matches?'

'I guess I am,' said Joyce.

'Why?'

'I'm not sure.' She went back to considering the gin, the ways she could make it move in the glass. Duncan shot the break, the balls clacked, colliding noisily in thrall to those age-old and unpredictable gravities that forced shape and significance into everything. Joyce looked back into Abby's young, mystified face. The girl was waiting, but Joyce had no answers, no ideas, no plans left for anyone. She thought she ought to explain at least that, but found she could not. Her own words failed her. She scoured her heart for something. 'Brave new world,' she said, at last. 'Brave new world.'

269

Afterpiece: Jake

I pulled into town late in the afternoon. It was hard to tell which was more worn out, me or the car. Between fixing the breakdowns, losing my way on bad shortcut directions, and having to wait three hours at an urgent-care clinic when my hand got infected, it had taken four and a half days to drive from Pennsylvania to Maine. Four and a half days. My head ached from too much coffee and not enough sleep. My arm ached from the tetanus shot I told them I needed because of that lady who gave me the ride. She didn't tell me it was going to hurt so much. I should have let her just go on and hoped someone else came along. Anyway, since I was tired and sore and basically miserable, I saw no point in waiting to face him down.

I called his service and they gave me the address of where he was working. A birthday party for a bunch of nine-year-olds. He'd put his signboard out on their snow-dusted front lawn. It's his advertising schitck – signboards like painters and vinyl-siding firms have. MAGIC BY MERLINO THE MYSTERIOUS. Shiny silver paint on matte black. I stood there in the lazily circling flurries, staring at the silver owl's silhouette that perched atop the final *s* in *Mysterious*. The owl's eyes, the spaces where the owl's eyes would be, were circles of golden glitter. I'd glued that there for him when I was a kid. Over the years, a lot of it had flaked away, and again I wondered why he hadn't yet repaired it. He was probably waiting for me to do it for him. That was going to be it for my magic career. A bottle of glue and a school kid's tube of glitter. I couldn't go in and face him. It was too humiliating. I'd failed my own dreams. I'd failed his.

I was about to walk away when the front door opened and the hostess emerged – the woman who, when she was a teenager, used to baby-sit me and my sister. She let fly one of those joyous high-pitched screams of surprise. 'Jake! Jake Matthews! Come in! Come in!' And she was across the lawn, hugging me to her softly fleshed maternal body with the same force she employed when, skinny and mean-tempered, she used to wrestle me to the dinner table, the same force with which she was now corralling me into her home. 'Come in. Your dad's almost through. So how's our big-time L.A. magic man? And what about that fire? It's like you got out of there just in time. Scary, huh?'

'What fire?'

She didn't answer but chatted on about her daughter's party and how much the children were enjoying Dad, and then we were in her living room. The kids, about twenty of them, were seated on the carpet and Dad had the birthday girl up by his magic table with the glitter-eyed owls painted around its skirt. Behind them, the asthmatic bubble machine was going, the blower wheezing out occasional clouds of iridescent soap bubbles that he waved out of his face toward Myrtle the dove, causing her to sidle unsteadily, annoyed, along the perch he'd placed behind him. Dad had the birthday girl holding a cone of newspaper into which he was about to pour a pitcher of milk. She was standing as far away as she could get from the expected spill. He was teasing her, threatening to miss and pour the milk on her party shoes.

It was the same performance he always gave. Same fraying top hat on his gray head, cape tossed over his shoulder so that the worn satin lining shone silver in what was left of the snowy daylight, belly straining at the silver satin cummerbund; he was intoning the same lousy jokes that I had tired of when I was nine. The little girl laughed like she'd never heard any of them before, or maybe because she was embarrassed to be up there and the center of attention, but she laughed all the same, so hard her pigtails swayed. She looked just like her mother back when her mother had used pinching, hair-pulling, and ear-piercing shouts in her baby-sitting reign of terror.

He happened to glance up at that instant. He saw me. He didn't finish the trick. He handed the milk pitcher to the little girl and came across the room, hiking his steps to climb over his pointy hat-wearing audience. He grabbed me in his arms and held on tight. I had to push him back. I couldn't breathe.

'You came home,' he said. His eyes got shiny and he wiped them, briskly, laughing. Now he was the one embarrassed. 'Boys and girls' – he started hauling me up to the front of the room – 'boys and girls, this is my son, Jake.' The kids gave a half-hearted attempt at a unified 'Hi, Jake.' Dad slapped me hard on the back. 'He's studying to be a magician at college in California.'

'Not anymore,' I said quietly, trying to keep it right in his ear. If I did it here, he wasn't going to kill me. Not in front of the kids. That would be bad for business. 'I left the school.'

'You what?' He pulled me closer, his face went stern. 'You didn't quit, did you?'

'No. I flunked out.' I couldn't look at him; I looked instead at the birthday girl. She handed me the pitcher of milk. 'It's heavy,' she said. It was; I tried not to drop it. Props are expensive.

'You flunked out? You did the work?'

'Yes, Dad. I worked my –' The birthday girl smiled like she knew where I was going with that one. 'Yes, I did the work.' This was worse than the worst I'd let myself imagine. The twenty kids in their party hats blinked up at me. 'Can't we talk about this later?'

'You're the one who brought it up now. I don't understand. Why'd they flunk you?'

I tried to whisper. 'I'm not adroit.' He narrowed his eyes the way he did when he was studying a trick that didn't impress him. 'That's what they said, Dad. I'm too clumsy.'

He concentrated harder. Then he threw his head back and laughed. 'Of course you're clumsy. That's not a failing. That's genetics.' He took the pitcher from my hands and turned to set it on the table. In doing so, he caught the hem of his cape on the table's corner, he turned and the table turned with him, toppling over to the carpet, but not before knocking over Myrtle's perch, sending the poor, clipped-winged bird into a frenzied attempt at flight. She hit the floor on the same beat as the table. The force of the impact triggered the release hidden behind the owls and the secret door in the tabletop popped open. Out tumbled Karrots, the elderly lop-eared rabbit. I'd named him when Dad brought him home from the pet store, back when I still thought the bunny angle worked. Now, the ancient rabbit scanned the room and appeared to be contemplating exactly what he'd done in a previous life to rate reincarnation as the fuzzy brown-and-white finale of this rickety bit of theater. Myrtle, in her panicked running around trying to attain altitude, ran headlong into Karrots. They bounced apart, shaking themselves. They shared a moment of meaningful eye contact and then made a break for it – the best they could. Myrtle cooed and made thrumming sounds deep in her chest that I bet you anything would translate into bird-talk obscenities as she, flapping her wings, waddled in hopelessly earthbound circles. The rabbit, his nose wriggling in fury, tried to escape recapture by hopping away from the table into the squealing crowd of delighted, bunny-grabbing children.

'What'd I tell you?' Dad sighed, shaking his head and lifting his arms – milk pitcher aloft, he said, 'Merlino the Mysterious thanks you.' He tipped his hat and bowed. The kids, chasing the rabbit, clapped and yelled, but not necessarily for Dad. 'The real trick,' he said, trying to contain his laughter, 'is making the screwups look like part of the act.'

With that, he turned the pitcher of milk over my head. I didn't flinch; I knew how the trick worked. The milk was only a thin sheet of liquid trapped between two planes of glass. When poured, the liquid disappeared into an inner recess. An illusion of empty. The kids saw this and forgot the rabbit. They broke into wild applause. The rabbit took advantage of the distraction and burrowed under the sofa. Myrtle kept running in circles. Dad was laughing big belly laughs. He gave the trick pitcher back to the birthday girl, who immediately turned it upright and watched the thing refill. Her face went pouty with disappointment, but only for a second. Her expression began to change; toward what new understanding I couldn't say, because at that moment Dad put his arm over my shoulder, straight-jacketing me in his cape. He thanked his audience and made me take the final bow with him. The kids cheered. I felt ridiculous. My life was as stupid Myrtle's pointless running, failed as Karrots's attempt at escape. Yet, the kids clapped on for the entertainment of it. Life was ridiculous. That was the truth. I started laughing then, laughing until my sight went watery with tears and my sides hurt so that I had to lean on Dad to keep from dropping to my knees.

I was laughing for these damn dove and bunny tricks, laughing for all this clumsy, inadequate magic. It's all ridiculous, but what can we do? It's the only magic we've got.

A NOTE ON THE AUTHOR

Karen Novak is the author of *Five Mile House*.
She lives in Mason, Ohio.

A NOTE ON THE TYPE

The text of this book is set in Linotype Sabon, named after
the type founder, Jacques Sabon. It was designed by Jan
Tschichold and jointly developed by Linotype, Monotype
and Stempel, in response to a need for a typeface to
be available in identical form for mechanical hot metal
composition and hand composition using foundry type.

Tschichold based his design for Sabon roman on a fount
engraved by Garamond, and Sabon italic on a fount by
Granjon. It was first used in 1966 and has proved an
enduring modern classic.